I0685666

AMELIA (AMI) JANE GRAY
THE DRAGON AND THE PHOENIX

DARLA A STONE

Edited by
KAREN LAMANNA

AMELIA (AMI) JANE GRAY:

DECEIVER

Jack Cranston stood before Sloane and me. He was a painful ghost of Sloane's past, and he, along with four wolves, trapped us between our new home in Pack Lingwir and what I would've considered one hell of a fight. My mates, Brevan and Mathias, along with Emmer and Cash, two other members of the pack, just came through the trees. All four of the men were in wolf form, and they were doing their best to be utterly menacing as they growled at the intruders. They'd seen Sloane's distress fireballs, while I was confident Brevan and Mathias felt my panic through our unbreakable bond.

Slowly, I turned to Jack and informed him of his new situation. "Jack, you are so screwed."

Jack let out an ear-piercing cry of frustration. Once again, I'd completely messed up his plans. I also wondered if whomever he answered to would be as patient and understanding as Newton was. Poor Newton Peabody met his end in a very unseemly way. Newton was unceremoniously decapitated. His head was thrown defiantly into the celebration at the packhouse as we celebrated our mating ceremony.

As Jack cried out, Brevan and Mathias moved to stand in front of

1

me. Emmer and Cash took a position in front of Sloane, and we were all in a virtual stalemate. Jack quickly realized he was going to lose this fight. In true coward fashion, Jack turned and ran in the opposite direction. To my surprise, Sloane leapt over Cash and Emmer in pursuit of Jack. It appeared Sloane was out to put an end to the psychopath's reign of terror. There was no way I could allow Sloane to go after him alone. Sloane was my brother, and I would always have his back no matter what.

The wolves circled each other, and when the wolf in front of Emmer lunged, the fight began. My concern, how was I going to get through the large mass of flying fur and to my brother, who already held an enormous lead on me as he pursued Jack. Suddenly, an idea struck me! If I could summon enough energy to conceal myself, I would be able to maneuver around the fighting wolves and follow my brother. Quickly I cast, "dolth gwathren" and melted into the shadows. As I skirted around the wolves, my spell dropped, but not before I was clear of the melee. Adrenaline filled my body and I took off after Sloane. As I ran, from somewhere behind me, I heard the pained cry of a wolf and prayed no one from our pack was harmed.

We were on pack lands, and I knew them fairly well at this point. I managed to track the pair of men with their footprints in the soft earth and quickly caught up to them. As I loosened my swords from their sheaths, I approached the two men cautiously as they were fully engaged in battle. I watched while Sloane fought well against Jack, but Jack was slightly more skilled, which was another surprise. When did Jack learn to use a sword? I needed to cause a distraction to help Sloane and give him the upper hand. There was only one surefire way to grab Jack's attention-- my radiant wit. I tucked my swords under my arm and spoke.

"Jack, well done for an old man," I laughed out as I applauded. "What did you do, study *Swordplay for Dummies?*" As I hoped, Jack snarled in my direction. Sloane took advantage of the opportunity and knocked the sword clear from Jack's hands.

When I thought we held the advantage, a new figure emerged. She was a tall, blond woman with all too familiar features and a harsh glare. Even though I registered who she was on some level, my dread kept me in denial. There was just no way she was who I thought. Brevan told me she passed away, which was why her daughter ran Pack Lumen. A pack that was initially run by the very ghost of the woman who was standing behind Jack.

"Jakkel, it is time for us to leave. We will not be successful this evening." The woman called Jack, 'Jakkel.'

"Lycandra, we can't leave these two whelps here. They've now seen you and know too much." Jack responded, and in doing so, confirmed my worst fears.

Lycandra, the original leader of Pack Lumen and mother to both Brevan and Aerin, stood there alive and in Technicolor. The main deceiver and master manipulator of everyone around her. She looked every bit the part that Brevan described to me. What I didn't understand was why she faked her death. What was the point? She had everything, power, money, and, most importantly, her pack. What else did she want? And how did she get the Queen of the Alfar to aid her in her quest? Lastly, what did Sloane and I have to do with it all?

As these questions flew through my mind, Brevan ran up behind me in his wolf form. At the sight of his mother, he pulled up short, and I could see even his wolf, was stunned at her appearance—no one expected to see the mother of my mate alive and well. I gathered my senses, grabbed the back of Sloane, and pulled him towards the direction of the packhouse. Not one of us was prepared to confront the likes of Lycandra. If I learned anything about the woman in question, she would already have plans A, B, and C in place to cover her ass.

"Sloane, we aren't ready for this fight. Jack's one thing, but this witch is Brevan and Aerin's mother," I warned my brother. As I spoke the words, the warning registered, and the witch cackled.

"You see, Jakkel, she can be taught respect," Lycandra cooed to Jack in a sick sort of way.

"Lycandra, don't mistake caution for respect. Respect is earned, and that isn't something you have done. After all, you wouldn't approach a poisonous snake on a whim. You, in this scenario, are the poisonous snake just in case you didn't get the hint." I felt the analogy fitting since it was a poison that she used to kill Lady Lylaine and ruin poor Marta's life.

As Sloane and I backed away, Brevan took point in front of the two of us. While his eyes were still full of the realization his mother was indeed alive, he was also aware of his commitment to protect Sloane and me. Brevan's gaze didn't waver from the spot his mother stood. He was determined Sloane and I would make it out of this in one piece.

We still lacked critical information in this game of move and counter move. Lycandra was the one who'd been pulling the puppets' strings all along, and I held onto several questions which needed answers. The physical distance between our two parties grew larger. That was when the other members of our pack caught up to us. Mathias was the only one who didn't stop when he reached Sloane and me. He, in wolf form, chased after Lycandra and Jack.

"Mathias, NO!" I yelled, but it was too late.

Mathias was so fast that in one breath, he tackled Jack and forced him to the ground. Lycandra screamed, and the fury she unleashed was like nothing I'd ever seen before. In swifter movements, then I'd ever witnessed even from Brevan, she pulled out a dagger and ran it through Mathias' shoulder. Sloane managed to cast one last fireball and threw it at Lycandra, which caused her to run off, leaving Jack behind. Brevan ran to Mathias' side and crouched down as he snarled at Jack. Jack wasn't going anywhere. We acquired a prisoner from the opposition. Perhaps we could finally get some information.

My real concern was the dagger in Mathias' shoulder. If Aerin learned her poison trick from her mother, he was in a great deal of danger, and we didn't have a vampyr on hand who could suck the poison out. It wouldn't take long for the poison to seep into his system, and by my calculations, the clock was running out extremely fast.

A gut-wrenching dread flooded me at the thought of Mathias dying from the dagger lodged in his shoulder. I couldn't lose my heart. He was the ocean upon my shore, and I couldn't picture him coming to an end at the hands of yet another deranged and diabolical woman.

Aerin was a ball of non-compos mentis, but her mother was the original queen of evil.

Miraculously, like angels descending from heaven, General Pax and four of his men descended upon our location. They weren't a full squadron, but enough of them came to our aid to manage what needed to be done. I moved swiftly over to the General.

"General Pax, I'm so glad to see you! We have a situation we greatly need your help with," I began in the way of an explanation.

"Mathias and I need to be taken to Lord Oren or Lady Nova right away. He was stabbed with a blade belonging to Lycandra, and I fear it might've been laced with poison. We also have a prisoner that Brevan is guarding. Lycandra called him Jakkel, but I know him as Jack Cranston. He needs to be locked up until we can question him." I finished my explanation as quickly as I could. There was no time to waste hanging around.

"Did I hear you correctly? Did you say Lycandra?" The General was dumbfounded.

"Yes, General. Lycandra stabbed Mathias, and we need to move, like now! The longer we wait, the more danger Mathias will be in..." desperation filled my voice.

General Pax rushed over to Mathias and scooped him into his arms. Pax also ordered two of his men to stay behind and help Brevan. I went to the remaining guard and wrapped my arms around him as tightly as I could. I hadn't flown by Gargoyle since the night on the beach after we washed up on the shore of the island, but it was a feeling I'd never forget. The take-off was rough, but when a Gargoyle glided on the breeze, it was unlike any other sensation that I experienced. While we soared high above the land as the trees and ground passed, there was a feeling of freedom. At least this time, I wasn't headed to the prison at the council hall. As we flew, my only wish was to get my mate the help I knew he desperately needed.

AMELIA (AMI) JANE GRAY:

MATHIAS

The guard and General Pax flew directly to Lord Oren's estate. We entered the home of Oren and immediately came across Lyros. Lyros hurried to meet us as we walked right into the lounge where Oren received Brevan and me for our previous private get together. My heart broke a little more for every moment the dagger remained in Mathias' body. Tears started to form in my eyes as I saw Mathias become weaker with every passing second. Mathias was carefully placed onto one of the couches in the lounge. General Pax, along with his guard, stepped back and excused themselves from the scene. They were headed over to the council prison to ensure Jack was safely secured. Pax assured me, should we need it, he would send help as soon as he could.

I held Mathias' head in my hands as I breathed out my instructions and my plea. "Mathias, I'm going to pull out the dagger. Please shift back for me."

Mathias blinked his eyes in recognition, which was my signal to move to his shoulder. I steadied myself and grasped the dagger firmly in my hand. With a quick yank, I removed the blade and tossed it to the floor. Mathias let out a whimper and shifted back from wolf to human. At that moment, Drew came running into the room with vampyr speed.

Drew, stunned at the sight before him, inquired, "Ami, what happened?"

I couldn't hold back any longer as the tears cascaded down my cheeks. The sight of my friend flooded me with too many emotions. As I let the tears fall, I looked at Drew and told him what happened. "Drew, Mathias was stabbed with a poison dagger. Please, I need your help. I can't lose him." I was an emotional mess, and all thoughts of anything else flew directly out of my head.

Drew moved so swiftly he was a blur. He told Lyros he needed water and a bucket. Without another moment's hesitation, Drew extended his fangs and bit into Mathias' flesh. Lyros was back a moment later with the bucket and water Drew requested, placing them as close as possible so Drew didn't have to move himself from his current position.

Drew didn't stop to rinse until the third mouthful was spat into the bucket. That was when Oren blazed into the lounge. General Pax made it back to the council prison and informed Oren of the situation with Mathias.

"Andrew, take a break. I will continue." Oren said to Drew, and they traded positions.

"Oren, there is a subtle licorice smell and taste to the wound. I think it's the poison." Drew explained after he rinsed his mouth clear of blood.

When they switched back, and Oren cleaned his mouth out, he continued the analysis. "Andrew, you are correct. I suspect it is derived from the Moonflower. Even though the Moonflower is incredibly beautiful to look at, it can be a deadly poison in the wrong hands. Lyros, please get a healer. We are going to need to drain him dangerously close to the limit."

"Lyros, please find Neemah. Please..." I desperately pleaded through my tears but couldn't finish. Thank goodness I didn't need to because Lyros rapidly strode over to me, kissed my forehead, and left a second later.

I watched as Oren and Drew continued to switch off, draining more and more blood out of Mathias. The more blood that came out of him, the paler Mathias became. When his head began to loll and droop, I moved over to him and held his hand.

"Mathias, don't you dare leave me. Do you hear me? Don't you dare!" I demanded as though my will power alone could keep him alive.

"Do not cry, my Amelia. Gods, you are beautiful." Mathias weakly cooed as he closed his eyes.

"NOO! Mathias, you wake up right this instant! Mathias!" The devastation I felt came through in my voice.

My sweet Mathias lost consciousness, and I was losing hope of being able to save him. How would I be able to exist losing someone else I loved? It took Drew and Jackie years to put me back together again after my parents died. But to lose someone else who was so vitally important to my existence would be impossible. Yes, I also had Brevan, and he too was my mate whom I loved, but the loss of Mathias would shatter me beyond repair.

Mathias was the one who made me laugh when I was frustrated. He was the one who curled up with me when I just needed a cuddle. Where Brevan was my rock, safety, and passion, Mathias was my touchstone, heart, and home. I loved them both fiercely and couldn't even fathom life without either of them.

Lyros used his vampyr speed to find and retrieve Neemah. Sooner than I'd hoped, as he raced into the lounge with the healer in his arms.

"Put me down, you banana brain. Do I look like someone who enjoys being carted around like a damsel in distress? For the love of the Gods, I am over seven hundred years old and still have my wits," Neemah ranted at Lyros, who very patiently stood there and took it.

Neemah carried her usual carpetbag full of medical supplies she always used and placed it down on the table to examine Mathias.

"Step aside, Oren. Let me see him." Oren rose from his place after one last long pull of blood.

"I believe we were able to extract most of the poison; however, it came at a cost. The boy has lost a great deal of blood." Oren explained to Neemah, who nodded her acknowledgment.

She leaned over Mathias, sniffed his wound, and then the bucket they'd been using to deposit the dirty blood.

Neemah then felt his pulse and lifted his eyelids. It almost appeared as though she wasn't going to stop moving for a moment doing her healer thing. When Neemah finally came to a halt, she spoke.

"Oren, the two of you did well in extracting the poison. It was absolutely Moonflower extract. The trouble is Mathias has lost too much blood to fight off what is left in his system." Neemah's words were not hopeful. She was the best healer around, and even with all her years of experience, she was at a loss for what to do.

We all listened to what Neemah said, and as I dared a glance at Drew, I saw an encouraging look come across his face. It was an expression I'd seen a thousand times before when he would come up with one of those ideas he thought would fix everything.

"Excuse me, Neemah, but why don't you just give him blood?" Drew asked as if we all missed the obvious solution.

"Young man, do I look like I can just stick blood back into a body? It is one thing to extract it, but putting it back is entirely different altogether." Neemah replied with her usual grandmotherly sass.

Drew, however, was right, and it was enough of a shock to my system for me to bottle up my tears and think for a moment. A blood transfusion might allow Mathias the opportunity he needed to heal. If it came from me, then perhaps some of my healing ability would go with it. I knew my blood type, thanks to the donation drive our junior year in college. I was O negative, which meant I was a universal donor, and anyone could receive my blood.

"Neemah, we need a couple of needles, some tubing, and a bottle with a cork. I'm going to give Mathias my blood, but we don't have time to waste," I commanded with far less confidence than I wished.

We needed to put together a makeshift blood bottle and set up an intravenous system to extract my blood and put it into Mathias. At least that was my theory, and we needed to put the idea into practice.

Neemah searched through her carpetbag, pulled out two old glass syringes with cork plungers, and set them aside. She then pulled out a third syringe and placed it down. Oren quickly left the room and returned with a clean empty wine bottle and some small sausage casing. I tried very hard not to think of where the casing came from because sterilization was not high on their priority list.

Drew and I explained to Neemah how an I.V. worked and what needed to happen. With experienced hands, as though she'd done this sort of thing a million times, Neemah put together the makeshift I.V. and tied off my arm.

"Dear girl, if this works, I am going to have to give you medical credit. Are you sure you do not want to become my apprentice?" Neemah asked, and I shook my head.

"You saw how much of a wreck I've been. Could you imagine me having to treat someone? Besides, this was mostly Drew's idea anyway," I answered while Neemah used our conversation as a distraction. As soon as I finished speaking, Neemah jabbed the massive needle into my arm. My blood began to flow through the tubing and into the bottle.

The blood didn't move fast enough, so I began making a fist and releasing it. I'd managed to fill half the bottle when Brevan walked into the room. His face was fifty shades of furious. He stopped short at the sight of the medical equipment, which was rigged up around Mathias and me. When Brevan noticed I was also hooked into some of what was going on, his fifty shades went to fifty-one.

Oren sidestepped the setup, grabbed Brevan, and dragged him out into the hallway. All I could say was thank God for telepaths, because the last thing we needed in here was Brevan losing his shit while we attempted to save Mathias. I could barely hear Brevan out in the hall, even with his raised voice. He was extremely pissed off, but from what I was able to make out, it wasn't at me, and again, I heard Jakkel and something about "my uncle".

Neemah and Drew brought my attention back to the room. She was instructing Drew on what kinds of high sugar foods he needed to go find because of the amount of blood I donated.

"Search for oranges, melons, baked goods, anything along those lines. She needs it to help with the blood loss." Neemah advised Drew.

"What about juice? If I can find some, wouldn't that be better?" Drew asked.

"Yes, Juice would help also," Neemah agreed.

I attempted to stand from my seat on the opposite sofa from Mathias. That was when my legs and head decided standing wasn't a good idea. My butt landed right back down on the couch, so I waited for Drew to return with the food items Neemah listed.

Drew managed to find some orange juice and watermelon, which I ate greedily. As the sugar hit my bloodstream, I began to feel better. When I finished with the food, I crawled my way over to Mathias. I took a seat on the floor in front of him and held Mathias' hand, while I rested my head on the sofa cushion. Slowly, I took some deep breaths and calmed myself as the last of my tears rolled down my cheeks. "I love you, Mathias. More than you know."

My eyes grew heavy, and I slipped into sleep.

SLOANE IVAN CRANSTON:

JACK

As soon as Amelia, General Pax and his guard took off with Mathias, Brevan and I followed the remaining two gargoyles who'd taken custody of Jack. We behaved as escorts as they did the old cuff and stuff and brought Jack to the dungeon of the council chamber.

When we arrived at the dungeon's entrance, Brevan shifted back to human and immediately dressed in some spare clothing left there for the wolves in case of an emergency. As I followed suit, I could barely keep up with the Alpha as he stormed through the hallways. Anger was riding him harder than any other emotion, and I feared he would tear Jack into pieces. Not that I wouldn't have liked to do the same myself, but we needed answers. It was the only thing keeping Jack from being skinned alive.

Brevan entered the dungeon and approached the cell in which Jack was locked up in. He took the key off the wall and opened the lock. Once the door was opened, he tossed the key to me and locked himself inside. Brevan then grabbed ahold of Jack and began his own form of interrogation.

"Jakkel, for every question you fail to answer, I am going to break a bone in your face. First question, where is she hiding?" Brevan's question and the warning were a mere courtesy.

"Ah, my dearest nephew, you wouldn't hurt your old uncle, Jakkel?" Jack replied, and I was terribly confused. Why did he refer to himself as Jakkel?

"Wrong answer," Brevan growled and, with a closed fist, punched Jack in the jaw hard enough to snap his head backwards. I heard a distinct popping sound and knew Brevan made good on his warning.

"That is one bone down. Now, I shall ask you again; where is she hiding?" Brevan demanded again.

"I don't know! Why don't you go find her yourself?" Jack snidely responded. I knew he was lying, and so did Bevan because, after his last response, the other half of Jack's jaw was hit.

"Let us see if the third time is the charm, shall we? Where is my mother hiding?" Brevan gritted out between clenched teeth.

"Fuck You!" Jack spat out.

Brevan lost his shit at Jack's response. He began beating the crap out of Jack as I fumbled with the keys to the cell. I needed to get in there to stop him, or he would wind up killing our only definite source of information. While I realized Jack could and would provoke all kinds of responses, including the immense urge to want to kill him, I couldn't let it happen.

Finally, I managed to open the door and bounded into the cell. As I grabbed ahold of Brevan's arm, I was thrown forward by the sheer force of strength he possessed.

"Brevan, STOP! You'll kill him, and we need to make sure it doesn't happen." I looked over at a bloody Jack, "Yet!"

Honestly, I wasn't a hundred percent sure Brevan was going to stop. The pent-up anger he was riding on was almost too much, even for me, and I wasn't too fond of Jack. Yet, somehow, I managed to get through to him. Brevan backed out of the cell, and reigned in his temper. I followed directly behind and made damn sure Jack was locked up tight in his cage and escorted Brevan out of the dungeon.

"Brevan, man, oh man, you certainly did a number on Jack's face. Would you care to explain the total and complete loss of your sanity?"

I wondered, and a part of me already guessed the details. However, I still needed confirmation.

"Sloane, you keep calling him Jack. Why?" Brevan questioned me and I could see the barely contained rage that burned in his stare.

"Brevan, he's the asshole who raised me. You know the guy who broke my arm because I was upset my dog died. Care to answer my question now?" My nerves were already paper-thin as I pushed for an explanation.

"Sloane, the man in there is my treacherous Uncle Jakkel. He is the only wolf other than my mother, who tried to take over Pack Lingwir while my father was alive. Jakkel disappeared approximately twenty-four years ago without a trace. Now, you tell me he is the man who raised you... How is that even possible?" Brevan was just as confused as I was at this point. At least I was beginning to put some of the puzzle pieces together.

"Brevan, somehow, he must've followed Ami and me through to the land where she and I were raised. I would need to confirm with Jackie about when Jack and my mother were married, but the timeline fits. The other question I need an answer to is; how did he find me? I was supposed to have been magically hidden as a safety precaution. Still, as far back as I can remember, Jack was always known to me as my father." I paced back and forth in an attempt to help my brain put more of the pieces together.

What I needed to do was speak with Jackie. She was the only other family member I could potentially get answers from. Jackie was living with and betrothed to Lady Nova. Their vampyr coven wouldn't rise until nightfall, so I would have to wait until then before I could see her.

"Sloane, I need to get to Amelia and Mathias. Something is terribly wrong. I can feel sorrow coming from Amelia, unlike anything I have ever felt before in my life. I fear Mathias might be dying." I didn't have a clue how a man wore two emotions simultaneously, but Brevan was showcasing both anger and pain on his face.

"Brevan, get out of here. My sister needs you, and if what you fear is true... well, I don't even want to think about it." I practically pushed the Alpha out the door.

There was no way we would be getting any answers from Jack, and Brevan was needed elsewhere. As for me, I needed to head back to the packhouse. Undoubtedly, Aisling was there worried out of her mind, and I didn't need another wolf consoling my girl. Aisling and Ami were two of the best things I had in my life, and I would do anything to protect either one of them. Unfortunately, they were both tied to Mathias, whose life now hung in the balance if Brevan's empathic connections were accurate.

At this point, there was only one thing left to do. I needed to find General Pax and ask him to put additional guards on Jack. While Jack might be hated, loathed, and despised, we needed to also make sure that he remained alive. At least for no other reason, then perhaps we could use him as a bargaining chip.

Finally, having been able to convey the information to General Pax, I left the council hall and headed home. Home... what a funny word. I wasn't sure when I started thinking of the packhouse as home, but I surmised I woke up one morning and realized I'd found my place in this world in some way. A place I needed to make sure I didn't let get ripped apart by the likes of Jack Cranston, a.k.a. Jakkel.

BREVAN:

RAGE

I left Uncle Jakkel in the council prison but not before I took a few liberties with his face. However, he was a wolf and would heal quickly. If it were not for Sloane stopping me, I might have beaten Jakkel to death. As it turned out, poor Sloane was raised by that bastard. Jakkel somehow made it to Amelia's world and changed his name to Jack Cranston. It was Sloane who convinced me to let him live only because we all needed answers.

Swiftly, I stormed into Oren's home when I arrived. My mate and my brother were both in here somewhere. Mathias might not be my brother by birth, but Amelia brought us together as a family. It was a family I did not expect to have, but now that I did, I would kill anyone who tried to take them from me. As I marched down the hallway, I heard the commotion coming from Oren's private lounge. I did not need the audio clue because I could feel Amelia's heartbreak from the council prison.

I burst through the doors to the lounge, and my eyes nearly jumped out of my head. They had set up some strange contraption and it appeared as though they were siphoning blood out of Amelia into a bottle. My anger morphed into pure rage at the sight. Neemah had come up with some strange medical solutions over the years, but

16

this was beyond anything she ever did before. The life's blood, which flowed in my mate's body, was now leaking into a bottle. Was she insane? Why, in the name of the Gods, would she ever think of doing such a thing?

Just as I was about to say something, Oren stepped in front of me and forcefully dragged me from the room. One of my oldest friends was yanking me away from my family, and it took everything within me not to rip him limb from limb him as he held me back. I could barely contain the rage which surged within me, much like a wild animal trying to protect its own.

"Oren, I will say this only once. MOVE! NOW! I demand you let me pass," I growled at him.

"Brevan, my old friend, you are not in the right mind to be in there. Amelia is trying to save Mathias' life, and there is more you need to understand, but I cannot tell you while you are in such an agitated state," Oren spoke his objections.

"Oren, I do not wish to harm you, but you are standing between my family and me. The last man who tried to do the same thing is now in the council jail with a broken face. Now, GET OUT OF MY WAY!" I started to shake as I held back the urge to shift into my wolf. It was extremely difficult holding my human form with this much rage flooding my veins even with being an Alpha.

"Brevan, you would not be able to harm me any more than I could stop having sex with men. Now, calm yourself and explain to me what is going on," Oren quipped and was not going to move regardless of what I threatened.

I took a few breaths in an attempt to calm myself and told Oren about what happened on my pack lands. As I recounted the story to him, the small amount of calm I managed to grasp onto began to slip away. "THAT BASTARD JAKKEL... He is alive... MY UNCLE..." It was all I could get out as a conclusion because my rage consumed me once again.

"Brevan, Lycandra used Moonflower extract to poison her blade. The blade was sunk deep into Mathias, and we had no choice but to drain his blood to the point he was near death," Oren began and inhaled a deep breath before he continued with the explanation. "Andrew and Amelia came up with the idea of using her blood to replenish Mathias' tainted blood. It has something to do with her being a *universal blood donor,* whatever that means. When your healer agreed to the idea, I allowed it to happen because I know how much you have already lost. If there was any chance to save your family, I was going to approve it. If you are angry with me for this, you have my deepest apologies." Oren's explanation calmed me somewhat, but I still needed to get to my family.

"Oren, thank you for looking out for my loved ones. It means a great deal to me you care enough to protect them. However, I cannot calm myself completely until I can hold my mate in my arms and know she is alright." I steadied myself and continued. "So, please, let me pass." It was the last time I was going to ask him to move aside. He must have seen the resolve in my eyes because he stepped out of the way, and I immediately passed through the door.

Neemah was the next one to stand between myself and my family. I always gave the pack elders a great deal of respect, but with everything going on around me, my patience was being stretched to its breaking point.

"Neemah, please move aside," I requested with as much calm as I could muster.

Neemah scolded in a firm hushed tone. "Lord Brevan, you listen to me, young man. If you are here to upset my great-granddaughter, I will tell you, right now, it will not be a pleasant experience when you have to answer to me. DO I MAKE MYSELF CLEAR?" Neemah scolded me like I was a young pup, but then her words sunk into my muddled brain.

"Neemah, did you just say Amelia is your great-granddaughter?" I needed to make sure I heard her correctly.

"I did, and I will tell you I have my eyes on you, young man. If you think for one second I will allow you to upset that smart, brave, big-hearted young woman, you will have another thing coming. I was going to wait for a more appropriate time to tell everyone, but with the reemergence of your mother and uncle, it seems the right time will never present itself. As it is, I have already lost her childhood. I do not wish to lose any more time with her." Neemah was adamant and resolved.

"Neemah, I swear to you, on my honor, I would never intentionally harm Amelia in any way. I just need to be with her. She is the only person right now who can calm me, even if she is asleep. We can discuss everything else when we are all home." My rage began to vanish as I pleaded with Neemah. How could I be angry with her for protecting the last of her family?

"Fine, but I am still watching you," Neemah scoffed and moved aside.

Carefully, I lifted my mate off the floor. As I did, Amelia stirred and opened her eyes. "Brevan, I can't leave him. Please don't make me go."

"Do not worry, my little wolf. We will stay here for as long as it takes Mathias to heal enough to bring him home. I am just going to put you in my arms and hold you for a while." I softly explained to the woman who turned my world upside down and brought my heart back to life.

She patted my arm, and sleepily spoke to me again. "Thank you, Brevan. I love you."

"I love you too. Now, close your eyes and sleep. I will watch over you both." It was a promise and a vow.

My world spun around so many times today. The loss of my friend Liam, the fear when I discovered Mathias, Amelia, and Sloane were all gone to parts unknown, then when Mathias returned to the pack with a potential spy. The sheer terror I felt from Amelia as she and Sloane were surrounded by wolves from the old Pack Lumen nearly ended me. Then last, but not least, the realization my Uncle Jakkel and my mother Lycandra were both alive. It was the pair of them behind all of the trouble brought down on the city of Tenebris. All I knew was I just needed everything to stop for just a moment while I spent time with and held my family. I sent a prayer up to the Gods, "I swear with my last breath to protect them, but please, could you send me a little help in keeping them safe. I could not go on without them, either of them."

When I arrived at Oren's, I was full of rage and wanted nothing more than to rip into my loved ones for scaring me beyond anything I have ever felt before. I could feel my anger was starting to subside as I held my mate in my arms. As promised, we were not going to move from there until we could bring our entire family home.

MATHIAS:

WAKING UP

When I opened my eyes, for a moment, I did not recognize the room I was in. As I tried to move to get a better look around, a tremendous pain in my shoulder brought my movement to an end. The pain was my reminder of what happened and where I was. It was unbelievable I managed to survive, but then again, with Amelia in my life, the improbable often became probable.

The flood of feelings and memories came back to me as I remembered the events from earlier that day. It was the look of desperation and heartbreak on Amelia's face; it was the nightmare I woke up to. I could not get the sight of constant tears as they fell from her eyes, which stained her cheeks with the overwhelming sadness she felt, out of my mind. My poor sweet Amelia, how was I ever going to be able to make this up to her?

I was not done loving this amazing woman, nor did I believe for one moment I ever would be. Amelia was a drink of cold water on a hot day and the moon which shined through the clouds in a night sky. The moment I laid my eyes on her, I knew beyond a shadow of a doubt, I would lay down my life to keep her safe. Shortly thereafter, I realized Amelia was not the only member of my family who would have been concerned about my welfare.

Gods, what must Aisling be going through. She surely was out of her mind with worry by now. Indeed, by this time, she would have heard the news of what happened to me. Our mother passed away in childbirth, and our father died while on a peace mission to the north. So, ever since Aisling was a baby, it was just the two of us. Sure, there was Marta, who was a surrogate mother to us both, but Aisling and I learned to rely on each other.

I unexpectedly felt something stir and peered down.

Amelia's head rested upon the couch cushion while she practically held my hand in a death grip. She was also wrapped up in Brevan's arms, who appeared as though he just drifted off to sleep. Lightly, I ran my free hand over her hair. I did not wish to wake her, but more than that, I needed to make sure she was real and I was not dreaming. She looked so peaceful asleep there. Amelia owned my heart in a way no one else ever came close to. She made the three of us a family, and it was a family I never expected but always thanked the Gods for the blessing of them both.

Suddenly, Brevan jolted awake and snapped his eyes open. I placed my finger to my lips to tell him to keep quiet, but he was the Alpha of our pack and was going to do what he wanted.

"Mathias, you are alive! Thank the Gods!" Brevan announced none too quietly, and as soon as the words were out of his mouth, Amelia roused.

She lifted her head, with her eyes half-open. "What's going on? Do we need to get Neemah?" she mumbled sleepily.

"No, my love. Neemah is not required right now," I whispered to her.

As soon as my voice registered in her mind, she rapidly scrambled out of Brevan's lap and climbed on top of me.

"Mathias, you stupid, crazy, son of a sea hag. Do you have any idea how insanely worried I've been? Do you?" She yelled at me while she slapped my chest. I just laid there and let her get her emotions out. Honestly, if the roles were reversed, I would probably be saying and doing the same as her—just less hitting.

"Mathias, you nearly died." She declared as her anger deflated, and she began to cry again.

"Shh, come here, my love. I am alright." I pulled Amelia down and held her in my arms. Softly, I spoke with comforting words to calm her tears. I could feel how worried she was and how much she loved me. A lesser man would have run from the overwhelming depth of feelings she held for me, but nothing on Earth would take me from her.

"Mathias, my brother, I concur with Amelia's assessment. You are a crazy son of a sea hag, and I could not be more grateful you are alive. As your family and your Alpha, you are under strict orders never to do that again. Neither Amelia nor I could take it if we lost you." Amelia's emotional outpouring I was prepared for, but Brevan's words rendered me speechless. All I could do was nod my response.

"I am going to go find Neemah. I want her to examine you to see if it is alright to move you. Oren's generosity has been exceptional, but I do not wish to overstay our welcome. I will be back momentarily." Brevan stood and walked out of the room, leaving Amelia and me alone for a moment.

I rubbed at Amelia's back. Her tears were slowing, but I needed to get them to stop. She was utterly breaking my heart. "Come on now, sweetheart, dry those tears. I need to see your beautiful smile, which lights up my world," I softly cooed to Amelia.

"Mathias, both you and Brevan are so essential to my existence. I wouldn't survive it if I lost either of you," Amelia whimpered out, and I could not argue.

"I love you too, Amelia! From the moment I saw you, my heart was yours, and it always will be. You shook my world, literally knocked me on my ass, and turned everything inside out and sideways. I would never change one second of it, though. Because to do so would mean I would not be able to hold you in my arms, right here and right now." I was never very good with words, but I hoped she understood what I was trying to say.

Amelia lifted her head from my chest, and I cupped her face in my hands. I placed my lips to hers, and with all the love I felt in my heart for this amazing woman, I kissed her tears away. I kissed her as though if I stopped, the world would end. It was the kiss of a thousand wishes and the hopes of a man who never believed he would ever have someone like her in his life.

"Young lady, would you mind getting off my patient? Somehow I doubt he needs you to help him breathe." Neemah interrupted our kiss all too soon. I could kiss the woman in my arms all day because of all the love I felt for her.

"Sorry, Neemah." We both remarked and then chuckled. Gods, it was good to see the smile on Amelia's face even if it did not quite reach her eyes yet.

As Amelia was in the process of climbing off me, I mumbled, "You are wrong, Neemah. I do need her to help me breathe." Amelia's face brightened even more as she began to get a little flush on her cheeks.

"Alright, young man, sit up so I can take a gander at your wound," Neemah instructed, and I complied.

"You are one lucky young pup. Moonflower extract is deadly, and you received a substantial dose. If it were not for my great-grand-daughter's fast thinking and her blood now running in your veins, I have no doubt you would be in the grave." My brain nearly exploded at what Neemah just disclosed.

First of all, Amelia's blood now ran through my veins. How in the name of all the heavens was it possible? I clearly remembered Oren and Amelia's friend Andrew trying to get the poison out of me, but I remember nothing of them putting her blood into me.

Secondly, she just called Amelia her great-granddaughter. I lifted my head and stared at the old healer. I needed to make sure she had not lost a few of her mental processes. Was it possible she was mistaken about Amelia being her family? Fortunately, I did not need to ask Neemah what she meant because Amelia did.

"Crazy healer says what?" Amelia's question was quite comical and made her sound just like Neemah.

"Crazy, you say? Well, the apple does not fall far from the tree, dear." Neemah laughed.

Neemah only took a moment or two longer to examine me before she continued. "Mathias, you have my approval to move back to the packhouse, but you are to head straight to your apartment and not emerge for one week. I do not wish to see you reopen your wound, and the muscles are still knitting themselves back together. As for the question, great-granddaughter, you will just have to wait until later." Neemah rebandaged my shoulder and packed her things back up.

"I will check in on you in about a week. Make sure you stick with only moderate movement until then. Well, as moderate as you can, at any rate." She waggled her eyebrows and left the room.

What in the name of all that was good and pure did I miss? I did not think I was unconscious for all that long. Before I could even ask the question on my mind, Brevan spoke up.

"Amelia, please help Mathias to the carriage out front. I am going to find Oren and extend our gratitude for his hospitality and assistance. I will meet you out there shortly." Brevan gave Amelia a kiss on the cheek and left the room.

"Amelia, you did hear what I heard, right?" I asked her, still a little bemused.

"Yup! Sure did, and the way Brevan didn't blink an eye at it tells me he already knew." Her eyes squinted together as she spoke.

It was obvious both Amelia and I wanted answers, but we were in no way going to receive them at this moment. Amelia helped me up off the couch, and we headed out the door with my uninjured arm around her shoulder. She got into the carriage first then extended her hand to help pull me in. I struggled a bit with still being weak. Thankfully, our driver noticed and gave me a small shove. We would need to wait until we were at home to get answers to our questions. Not only had I awoke from being nearly dead and the fact that my love saved my life, but my mind was awakening to the real possibility Amelia was Neemah's great-granddaughter.

LYCANDRA:

THE FOOL

Quickly I shifted into my wolf and ran from my son and his pack. That stupid fool Jakkel could ruin everything if he opens his big mouth. *Why did I ever allow myself to believe he would be able to stay away from my son's pack?* Plain and simple, he was obsessed with killing Amelia, the little whore. She was every bit the problem he professed her to be. That was proven when she killed my daughter. All we needed to do was go unseen until the full moon, and we would be able to fulfill the plan the Queen and I so carefully laid out all those years ago. But, because of his recklessness, he was yet another loose end I needed to dispose of.

It did take him twenty-four years to bring the Phoenix and Dragon Mystics back to our lands. So, it should not surprise me the idiot fouled up his responsibilities once again. His only task was to retrieve the informant and get her information. I needed to make sure the Queen did not find out about his colossal mistake. Should she discover the latest foul-up, I definitely fear it would be my head she would cut off next.

Swiftly, I ran through the tunnel back to our lair in Demeter. My wolves and I quickly took over full control of the farming village just after we made our exit from the pack lands. Since the Queen held

26

little care over what happened in the village, it was easy for us to set up our base of operations there. It seemed like ages ago when my good-for-nothing mate, the high and mighty Lord Edon, expelled me from Pack Lingwir.

Of course, his treatment of me all stemmed back to his thieving little bitch, Lylaine. If Edon had never laid eyes on her, he and I would have been mated, and the two of us could have easily ruled the southern territory. After Edon cast me aside like a piece of trash, it did not take me long to come up with a plan of removing her from the situation. It was effortless to use Marta, the simpleton, as my pawn. Should I have been discovered, all I needed to do was blame Marta and show Edon the proof of the poison. Edon always suspected someone disposed of his beloved Lylaine but never accused anyone. However, he did keep an extremely close eye on people afterwards.

Once his meddlesome Lylaine was out of the way, the poor devastated Edon was all too easy to console, and when I told him I was pregnant with his child, he did not wait to claim me as his mate. Edon said, "It is the proper thing to do. My son or daughter must be raised correctly."

Never once did that bastard ever tell me he loved me. Not once! This was why I held no guilt when I split his precious pack, taking his pack members with me. Nor did I weep when I killed the multiple members from Pack Lingwir over the years. The best part of my revenge was taking his brother, Jakkel, as my lover. Aerin never knew, but she was not Edon's child. Jakkel and I began our relationship before Edon banished me. I allowed Edon to believe I was taking one of his precious children to hurt him further, and by the Gods, it worked brilliantly.

It was both my misfortune and curse my bothersome son was standing between me and my prize. If he never mated with that loathsome creature, Amelia, it would have been all too easy to collect the lost children. When I sent word to my daughter to capture them and bring them to me, I should not have been surprised when Aerin tried to kill them first. Then she wound up eliminating herself, which was as stupid as her plan to blow up the

27

market. I swear nothing but insufferable idiots surrounded me. It appeared as though I was the only one with intelligence enough to carry out our long-overdue plan. At least the girls were safe and hidden right under my stupid son's roof. The six maidens that were impregnated during the solstice celebrations were more valuable than he knew. After I stabbed their precious wolf, it would at least keep Brevan and his band of wolves busy. They should be mourning the boy's death.

As I reflected back to the moment I ran my blade into the shoulder of that wolf, I commended myself on my knowledge of poisons. I was always exceptional when it came to deadly toxins. The berries from the deadly nightshade plant and root extracts made a quick and efficient killer combination. Hemlock was another lovely, natural poison, and it would work just as quickly. Moonflower oil on one's blade, however, was, by far, a superior way to eliminate an enemy. There were even others I used in the past, but indeed none as effective as Moonflower.

Finally, I reached our sanctuary in the north, and I shifted back to human. I made sure to dress quickly. There were prisoners who needed to be checked on, and pack members who needed further instructions. It appeared as though they were going to need to run decoy while the assassins took care of Jakkel. No loose ends!

"Gentlemen, round up the others and be back here in two minutes. Once again, we have a mess to clean up," I instructed two of my most trusted and loyal pack members.

"Yes, M'Lady." they bowed and went to comply with my wishes.

It was time I visited our most extended guest. Confidently, I strode through the house and into the back garden. Across the way was the barn that we were using to hold our prisoners. Those contemptuous creatures would all die eventually, but at least for the foreseeable future, they still held some value.

In life, timing was everything. I understood these things, and so did Queen Cosima, who decided this moment was an ideal time to visit our outpost.

"My dear, Lycandra, you seem quite vexed." Her sweet noncommittal tone always grated on my nerves, but I needed her power to pull off this plan.

"Queen Cosima, to what do we owe the honor?" I bowed, playing my part. The Queen was a tall, pale blond woman with sun-kissed golden skin. She walked with an air of grace and yet held a cold stare in her golden eyes.

"I came to see how things were getting along. From what I hear, you have run into a spot of trouble. Tell me, where is your high-spirited daughter?" She coyly asked.

"Tragically, she made an error in judgement, and lost her life." I attempted to brush off her death as though it were nothing.

Her majesty moved quickly at my words to stand before me in her terrifying glory. "I warn you, Lycandra, we will not receive this chance again for another thousand years. Do. Not. Foul. Up. Our. Plans! I would hate to see you lose your life." The Queen's power pressed down upon me, forcing me to comply with her wishes.

I choked out my vow, "I swear to you, I will not fail."

"Lycandra, you better not. I will not be denied. I am sending my Sylphs to acquire the girls you left in your son's care, and I do not want you to touch a hair on their heads. Do I make myself clear? I need to assess which holds the Alpha child."

"Yes, your majesty, as you wish."

"Good, and one more thing. I am leaving you half of my guards. It seems as though you need the assistance, and they will keep me informed of your progress." Queen Cosima smoothed her clothes and motioned for her guards to take up posts in my encampment.

I bowed again. "Thank you, your majesty. We are not worthy of your generosity."

"No dear, you are not, but you have it nonetheless." Queen Cosima turned on her heel "Remember, no more *mistakes*, Lycandra." With her reminder firmly in place, she left me standing alone in the garden.

I briskly walked through the door of the barn, and marched up to the last cell on the left. I slowly crouched down in front of the bars glaring at the pathetic creature inside. "Well, my dear, it seems as though your children are a bit more troublesome than I originally thought or was led to believe. Either way, as promised, they will die," I spewed out to the wretched creature huddled in the back.

"Lycandra, do not think you can scare me with empty threats. We both know you cannot touch them. They are beyond even your reach," The creature spat back. Perhaps there was fight left in her still.

"You were a foolish girl then, and you are even more foolish now. Your children have returned to the island and mark my words; by the time I am finished with them, they will be begging me to end them. The only reason you are still alive is because I need your blood to enter the temple. You are nothing but a mere key." The intimidation of this creature was all too easy and only provided mild amusement.

"Leave her alone, you witch!" Behold, it was yet another one of my guests who felt they possessed the right to disrespect me.

"Silence, you pathetic mouse, or you will wind up in the same state as your mate." Even behind bars, these insolent pieces of filth thought they were entitled to a voice. One would have thought they learned something when they saw what fighting me would get them.

"Miss Prudence, shh, quiet now. Come away from there," stated another one of them, who held a lilt in his voice.

I stood from my crouched position and moved to the cell of the woman. "I would strongly advise you to listen to the boy. I am no witch." I allowed myself to partially shift for a terrifying effect. "I am a wolf!"

Terror struck her face, and I strutted out of there laughing. If those lost children were anything like those I currently held captive, then I would have no troubles whatsoever once I got them into my hands. No trouble at all!

SLOANE IVAN CRANSTON:

AISLING

*A*fter I borrowed a horse from the stables at the council hall, I stopped at Lady Nova's coven and left a note for my cousin, Jackie asking when I might meet with her. She was still in mourning over the loss of her father, Newton Peabody. We didn't have any idea where the others, like Jackie's mom and the others were being held, but my gut feeling was Jack knew.

As I rode, my mind was whirling with everything we'd learned. How odd was it Jack Cranston was Brevan's uncle, Jakkel? There was only one person who possessed a knack for getting under the bastard's skin, and that was Ami. However, Ami was tied up with Mathias' life and death situation, so we would have to wait before we could use her unique gift to agitate him into some type of confession.

When I finally made it home to the packhouse, I dismounted the horse and headed straight through the front door. My first stop was the kitchen. In times of stress, people either ate or paced. Aisling did both, and so my sound logic found her seated on top of the counter with a berry pie and whipped cream. No, not a slice of berry pie but the who pie covered in whipped cream. As soon as she noticed me walk into the kitchen, Aisling set the dish down, jumped off the counter, and ran over to me.

"Sloane, oh, thank the Gods, you are alright. I could not stop worrying over all of you," Aisling cried as she wrapped her arms around my neck.

"There's my girl! Come on baby, don't cry." I wouldn't say I liked it when women cried, but I really hated it when Aisling cried. It was as if someone ripped my heart out of my chest and stomped on it.

Aisling wiped away her tears and choked out, "Has there been any news on Mathias?"

What was I going to tell her? I couldn't say Brevan ran out because he could feel despair coming from Ami. "All I know is Mathias was taken to Lord Oren's coven, and Brevan went to meet him and Ami there. That is all I know, sweetheart." I decided to stick with a version of the truth which consisted of only facts.

"Lyros, Oren's husband, came here earlier looking for Neemah. He informed me Amelia asked him to fetch her. Sloane, I am so worried. Mathias is the only family I have left." Tears started to form in her eyes again.

"Aisling, I understand because I feel the same way about Ami, but he isn't your only family. You do know that, don't you?" I needed to make sure she understood she had me as well. "I love you more than the air I breathe, and there is nothing that is ever going to tear me away from you, okay?"

Aisling nodded her head, but questions remained in her eyes. "But Sloane, we are not mated yet. What if you change your mind? What if you decide you don't want to be with me after all?"

"You are now and will always be my girl. It doesn't matter if we are fifty or one hundred and fifty. I will love you just the same." I rubbed her arms to comfort her. Aisling started to calm, but nothing would completely erase her concern until she saw Mathias was alive and well.

"Aisling, why don't you come up to my room and sleep with me for a while. I swear I will behave myself and act like a proper gentleman. You shouldn't be alone right now, and I don't think Mathias would wring my neck for making sure his sister was well taken care of. Besides, I would love just to hold you while we lay in bed. What do you say?" My brain was frazzled, and the only way I could clear it, was to rest.

Aisling sniffled and wiped her eyes. "Alright, but what if I do not wish for you to be a gentleman?"

Oh, dear sweet baby Jesus, please no. I promised Mathias I would wait, and here she was, all soft, vulnerable, and tempting.

"Sweetheart, we are both exhausted. Let's go get some rest, and then we can look at things with new eyes." I chose to do the right thing, but damn, wasn't it hard, along with other things.

I grasped Aisling's hand, and side by side, we walked up to my room. Once we were inside, I closed the door and stared at a face I could never get tired of looking at. She and her brother Mathias shared some similar features. They both possessed the same hair and eye color and were lean muscled, but Aisling was the beautiful feminine version of her brother. One particular feature they differed on was their noses. Aisling's was an adorable, turned-up, petite, button nose where Mathias' was more robust and more pronounced. I wasn't comparing the two of them, but it was hard not to notice their similarities and differences.

"Sloane, would you help me loosen my corset? I am afraid I have had it on far too long today, and it is beginning to cut into my sides," Aisling pleaded and my resolve crumbled even further.

I needed to imagine cold water. Yeah, that was it. As I pictured swimming in freezing water, I told her to turn around. Carefully, I untied the bottom of the corset and gave a slight tug to loosen the laces. When I finished, I went over to my wardrobe and pulled out a large hunting shirt.

"The bathing chamber is the first door on the left. You can go in there to change out of your dress." I handed her the shirt while trying to think of things I could do to help me maintain my promise.

While Aisling was in the bathing chamber, I stripped out of the clothes I was wearing, making sure to leave on my boxers, and climbed into bed. I managed to get Ami's friend, Drew, to send me some from his shop. By all accounts, he and the seamstress he worked with did an exceptional business. Drew and I managed to find some neutral ground between the two of us. I supposed it was because he was with Lord Oren. Drew, finally being in a relationship that made him happy, allowed him to relax and be more approachable.

Aisling returned in only a few minutes. Hell, she even looked sexy wearing my shirt. She'd let her hair down, and I finally got to run my hands through it. It was as soft and silky as it appeared to be. Her hands began to stroke my chest. I closed my eyes and took a deep breath to help me keep my composure. Unfortunately, it didn't help because all I could do was smell her sweet honeysuckle and warm sunshine scent.

"Sloane, are you going to at least kiss me?" She requested with her quiet, unassuming voice.

I opened my eyes and gazed deeply into hers. What I saw when I peered into those endless depths was Aisling's all-consuming love for me. I silently thought, *sorry Mathias*, then cupped her face in my hands. I leaned in and kissed Aisling with all the passion I held in my heart for this incredible creature. Her lips responded and moved with mine so effortlessly, it was impossible for me to resist her any longer. I could feel the real want and need in her kiss. Her hands ran over my shoulders and down the center of my back. Slowly, I traced every sensual soft curve of her luscious body. Aisling was a goddess with the way her hips and breasts molded to my touch.

As our kisses became more fevered, she began to undulate her hips against my rigid length. While every instinct in me told me to simply take her, I needed to remind myself she was far too precious to treat as though she were some girl I picked up at a frat party. I reached up under the shirt and caressed her perfect ample bosom. I teased and pinched each of her hard nipples between my practiced fingers, and as I did, Aisling arched her back in response.

In a move which defied all previous logic and caution, I tore through the shirt she was wearing and kissed my way down to those perfect breasts. I took my time and devoted plenty of attention to each one as I suckled, kissed, and licked them. My wolf rose close to the surface, and I allowed it to share this time with me. Although, not officially, Aisling was our mate, and I would no longer deny myself or my wolf the right to claim her.

Aisling was all woman, and she was all mine. I reached down between her soft, damp folds, and stroked the hard nub of her clit. She let out a moan and a growl, which told me her wolf was present as well. The bulge between my legs was going to need to find its release, but not before I made sure she was prepared to take its full thickness. I kissed and licked my way down from her plump mounds past her stomach to her intoxicating, soft, moist honeypot. Her scent alone nearly brought me to orgasm, but I needed to taste her feminine juices. Carefully and slowly, I licked and suckled her sex as she began to cry out in pleasure.

"Sloane, Please... I need... Please..." Aisling panted out as her body writhed from my ministrations.

Without a single word uttered, I crawled back up her body and kissed her passionately. I released my throbbing hard cock from my boxers and placed it at her entrance. Aisling kissed me again with her fiery passion, and I slowly began to penetrate her untouched womanhood. It was going to be her first experience, and I needed to make sure I treated her as though she were made of glass. The last thing I wanted to do was hurt her in any way. When I reached my full length within her, I stopped and stared at her.

"Aisling, my darling, are you alright?" I paused my ministrations because she let out a gasp.

"Yes...do not stop!" she breathlessly growled out.

I rolled my hips to make it more comfortable for her, and soon our passions increased once again. With much more vigor, I moved as I thrust in and out of her. God, she felt terrific. We were joined as one, and I couldn't be more thrilled. All the while, I could feel her muscles contract with pleasure. Soon I released myself to all the miraculous, immense, and all-encompassing sensations. My animalistic tendencies took control of me. When I found my release, I sunk my sharpened teeth into the soft flesh of her shoulder. Aisling was all mine, and she bore my claim.

SLOANE IVAN CRANSTON:

THE RING

As Aisling and I laid in bed, basking in the afterglow of our first time together, I heard from out in the front of the pack-house a carriage was coming down the drive. Immediately, I realized the only pack members due home were my sister and her mates.

"Aisling, sweetheart, there is a carriage coming. It could be Brevan, Ami, and Mathias," I quietly whispered into her hair.

I didn't want to leave our private cocoon of intimacy, but I wouldn't deny my girl the opportunity to see her brother. She'd been incredibly worried about him ever since Emmer and the others returned. Mathias was in good hands. If anything had gone drastically wrong, Ami would've absolutely sent word, of that I was sure.

Aisling quickly sat up. "Sloane, perhaps it is Mathias. I need to go down and meet him," She spoke with a hint of desperation in her voice.

"I wouldn't expect anything less. You can use my spare dressing gown. There is no way you will be able to put your clothes on before they reach the front door," I suggested with a slight smugness in my voice. I realized Mathias would be less than pleased to see his baby sister in my clothes, but she was mine. He would just have to get over it. I wasn't sure what good I'd do under the circumstances, so I figured

36

I would stay put. Which was presently the room that now contained Aisling's beautiful scent.

Aisling went over to my wardrobe and pulled out both dressing gowns. "Sloane, they might need help bringing him upstairs. Please come with me?"

Instantly my resolve began to crumble, so I arose from the bed and walked over to take the dressing gown Aisling was holding out for me. It completely amazed me how she looked so undeniably innocent. Her quiet demeanor and softly spoken words were why she was so incredible with the pack children.

Once we were both adequately covered, I took her hand and led her downstairs to the entry hall, which was always lit. It didn't matter if it were night or day. Marta once explained to me she kept it that way so "pack members could always find their way home."

Marta was another problem which perplexed Aisling these days. After Brevan learned of Marta's less than stellar judgment during the time Brevan's father was Alpha of the pack, she'd been removed as the current Head of the House and 'retired.' Aisling often went to visit with her, which in and of itself, would seem like it was a harmless event. However, each time I saw Aisling afterwards, she would always comment on how sad Marta was and wished she could do something to help her. It was a problem I was searching for a solution to.

Aoife had already made it to the front steps of the packhouse before I'd even opened the front door. Nearly the moment the carriage came to a stop, my sister jumped out and flew up the steps.

"Aoife, help!" Ami exclaimed.

"Amelia, what is the matter? You look all flustered, and you are absolutely dripping." Aoife examined my sister a moment longer, then slapped her hand over her mouth, "Never mind, you need to get into a cold bath immediately." The appearance of recognition on Aoife's face worried me momentarily.

Aoife then turned to Aisling. "Aisling, make sure your brother and Brevan get upstairs safely. I need to run Amelia into the house, NOW!"

Aisling nodded her understanding, and Aoife ran with Ami in tow, straight through the door and into the house. Brevan was left alone to help Mathias up the stairs himself.

Aisling immediately hurried down the steps and to her brother's unoccupied side. She raised his arm and slung it over her shoulder to help take some of his weight. Brevan grabbed the other side, and the pair of them managed to get Mathias up the stairs and through the front door. As I closed the door, I stepped up to Aisling's side and motioned for her to let me take her place.

Just as she was about to move, so I could take her place, there was a knock at the front door. I waved the three of them on and went to answer it. When I opened it, the carriage driver stood before me.

"So sorry to bother you, Master Sloane, while you are trying to get Mathias settled. Lord Oren gave me a parcel and ordered me to make sure you received it," he explained, holding out a small wooden box. As I took the driver's package, I thanked him for making sure it arrived safely and waved at him as he left to return the carriage to Oren's home.

After I closed the door, I opened the box. Inside was a ring, containing a beautiful oval peachy-pink stone banked on either side by clear stones held by a rose gold metal. As I inspected the center stone more carefully, I noticed inside the stone was a fire-like glow. It was, without a doubt, the most exquisite piece of jewelry I'd ever seen. Oren was utterly brilliant! I placed the ring back in the box and shoved the box into the pocket of my dressing gown. I needed to hurry along and catch up with Brevan, Mathias, and Aisling.

I climbed up to the second floor before I'd caught up to the three of them. "Aisling, why don't you let me take over for you? Sorry, I took so long, but the driver wanted to make sure he could send word back to Oren that you all made it home safely." Okay, so it was a big fat lie, but I wasn't going to say, *'oh, I needed to get your engagement ring from him.'*

Aisling released her side, and I took over, supporting Mathias, as she walked in front of us. We'd just reached the steps to the third floor when Mathias asked a question that brought Aisling to a grinding halt. "Aisling, who does that dressing gown belong to?"

"Mathias, I do not think it is exactly relevant at this particular moment. We need to get you upstairs." Aisling reacted with an air of nonchalance.

Mathias lazily turned his head in my direction and glared at me. "Sloane, is there anything you would like to tell me?"

"Nope, not a thing. Besides, you still need to get some rest," I replied while Brevan watched us and smirked as he tried to hold back his laughter.

Mathias wasn't going to just simply let the question drop as he managed to pull us to a halt even in his weakened state. Brevan propped Mathias against the wall and stepped to the side, so Mathias could have a clear view of Aisling and myself. Aisling and I knew we would need to face the 'Mathias firing squad.' There was no way around it if we wanted to get him upstairs.

"Now, Mathias, I am a grown woman, and you have to understand what I choose to do or whom I choose to be with is none of your business," Aisling retorted with a glare in her eyes and a warning in her tone.

"Aisling, you are my baby sister. I love you and only want what is best for you but, so help me if he hurts you, I will kill him," Mathias countered, and it wasn't just a warning, it was a promise.

"Mathias, I know how protective you are of your sister, so perhaps I can ease your concern," I told Mathias and turned to Aisling. After I bent down on one knee, I proceeded. "I wanted to do this in an entirely different way. I wanted to shower you with flowers and have a candlelit dinner for just the two of us. All the romantic things women want under these circumstances. However, Aisling, you are wholly, perfectly, and unconditionally the most amazing, beautiful, kind, and caring woman I have ever met." I took a deep breath and pulled the box out of my pocket. "I was wondering if you would do me the great honor of becoming my bonded mate?" I popped the question I'd wanted to ask her so many times before but couldn't because I didn't have this one little item to show her how seriously I was in love with her.

After I placed the box in her delicate hand, she shakily opened it.

As Aisling peered inside, tears began to form in her eyes, and she dropped down on both knees. "Oh, Sloane, it is the most beautiful ring I have ever seen. Yes, yes, a thousand times, yes, I will become your bonded mate."

I reached into the box and slid the ring on her finger. In the next moment, I kissed her with all the love and passion I held in my heart. When cheers suddenly broke our kiss, I discovered unbeknownst to me, we'd managed to draw an audience. Marta came out of her room and hurried over to the two of us.

"Oh, you two dears. You must allow me to arrange your ceremony," She cried as she hugged the pair of us.

"Marta, I would love for you to do that," Aisling cried out, and how could I argue. Marta was a mother to many of the pack members, and Aisling was very close to her.

"Alright, everyone, the show is over. Sloane, we need to get Mathias upstairs," Brevan urged with a concerned edged in his voice. Mathias had already been through an ordeal and needed bed rest.

I retook my position as Aisling gave Marta one last hug before we formed our line again. Mathias turned his head in my direction, "I knew you would do right by her. You just needed the right motivation." He spoke with a hint of humor in his voice.

"Mathias, the last thing I want to do is piss off my sister's mate. Besides, I'm more afraid of her than I am of you. She is scary when she's angry," I replied jokingly and then remembered what Ami was capable of. Ami was definitely the scarier of the two.

AMELIA (AMI) JANE GRAY:

BAD TIMING

*A*s soon as Neemah gave us the all-clear to leave, Brevan escorted her to the carriage Oren allowed us to borrow. She was going to head back to the packhouse first to make sure no one would get in the way of getting Mathias up to our apartment.

Brevan, Mathias, and I were all in our own carriage and headed home. Mathias might've awoken, but he was still weak as a newborn and would need assistance getting up three flights of stairs.

As we traveled through the streets of Tenebris, I kept a close eye on Mathias while I thought about Neemah's words. He was finding it challenging to stay upright, and every so often, he would list to one side after the carriage would hit a hard bump in the road. Neemah called me her great-granddaughter while we were at Oren's home, and those words just blew my mind. I was so focused on Mathias and Neemah's bombshell that I didn't even notice I began to perspire.

We were three-quarters of the way home when my next indication of something strange was going on hit me right in the abdomen. I felt a burning ache, which was slowly building inside me, and the light-bulb inside my brain finally recognized what was happening. Talk about unfortunate timing, I was hitting my fertile cycle in a big way.

When the carriage came to a stop outside the packhouse, I noticed

Aoife and Aisling waiting for us to arrive. I opened the door and jumped out as quickly as I could, headed right for Aoife.

"Aoife, help!" I pleaded.

"Amelia, what is the matter? You look all flustered, and you are absolutely dripping," She commented and then clasped her hand over her mouth. I saw the moment of recognition on her face as she started to put two and two together.

"Never mind, you need to get into a cold bath immediately." Aoife wrapped her arm around my shoulder and turned to Aisling. "Aisling, make sure your brother and Brevan get upstairs safely. I need to run Amelia into the house, NOW!"

The next moment, Aoife whisked me through the door, and we ran up three flights of stairs to our apartment. She was moving so fast I thought she might tear my arm from its socket. As we entered the apartment, she slammed the door behind the two of us, headed right for the bathing chamber, and dragged me with her.

"Amelia, we need to get you into a cold bath. Mathias needs to be settled in, and he cannot smell you right now," Aoife declared hurriedly.

"Aoife, I know. Why the hell is it so damn hot, though?" I asked in frustration. I heard older women speak about hot flashes, but this was ridiculous.

"That is why I am running you a cold bath. With all the emotional trauma you must have experienced in the last twenty-four hours, your body is all confused. We need to cool you down and open up every window up here, or Mathias will not make it to the bed." I heard the concern in Aoife's voice.

"Aoife, I feel strange." I glanced over at my friend and warned her.

"Oh, dear, hurry up. There is no guarantee a cold bath will work, but it is the only thing we can do right now. Your fertile time has come, and we need to slow you down just a bit. If we can lower your body temperature, then perhaps you will not want to jump both Brevan and Mathias before Mathias is even settled in bed." I loved her for the trouble she was putting herself through. Aoife, having gone through this multiple times herself, at least held an idea of how to handle the situation, whereas I absolutely possessed no clue.

I stripped off my clothes and slid down into the coldest bathwater I'd ever felt in my life. "Holy blue-lipped baby, this bathwater is cold!"

Aoife yelled to me from the apartment area, "Stay in there as long as you can stand it."

I heard her as she bustled around the apartment, opening every window and door in the place. When she was finished, she closed the bathing chamber door and let me know she would be back in a minute.

Aoife came back with as many scented oils as she could carry. "Amelia, I am going to warm some of these over a candle. We have just enough time before Brevan and Mathias finish climbing the stairs. They are at the top of the stairs on the second floor." She was trying to mask the smell of my scent, and I crossed my fingers it would work. The last thing I needed was to feel guilty because I couldn't control myself.

I was just about to get out of the freezing cold bath when I heard the apartment door open and close. Brevan, Mathias, and Aisling finally made it upstairs, and they were coaxing Mathias in an attempt to get him into bed. Mathias, on the other hand, was having none of that. A small argument ensued between Mathias and Aisling, which ultimately led to a compromise of Mathias stretched out on the sofa with pillows and a blanket.

Aoife, on the other hand, made sure the door to the bathing chamber was shut tight and took up a guard position in front of it. "I am sorry, Brevan, but you cannot go in there right now," she stated apologetically.

Brevan's next words came out as a growl, "Aoife, why am I being blocked from my mate?"

She was a smart cookie, though, and didn't hesitate to answer in her own sassy way. "Brevan, listen to yourself. That is why! Now, pull yourself together, wait fifteen more minutes because I have a broom, and I am not afraid to use it."

I heard Brevan's all too sexy growl even though the door was

43

closed, and all my lady bits responded. Aoife told him fifteen minutes, hell, I wasn't going to last fifteen seconds at this rate.

I heard a squeal from outside the door within the next minute, and then the door burst open. Brevan stepped inside the room with his nostrils flaring. Oh, he most definitely picked up my scent. He slammed the door shut on Aoife and, in two very long strides, was at the edge of the bathtub. With movements swifter than I'd ever seen before, Brevan lifted me out of the bath and set my naked body on the counter with the washbasins.

"Amelia, it was already too late inside the carriage," Brevan growled and kissed me with a fiery passion that would've melted the ice from atop Mount Everest.

Brevan didn't take his time as his kiss ignited my own passions. I reciprocated every touch, taste, and emotion I received from him. I ripped his shirt from his body, not slowing a moment to care about destroying an article of clothing. I needed to feel his skin upon mine. I wanted to touch him, all of him.

Brevan managed to remove the remaining bits of his clothing so fast, it was almost as though they spontaneously combusted. Instantaneously, he lifted me, flipped me over, and with unyielding vigor, slid himself inside me. He rapidly moved his large, rigid shaft so powerfully, I nearly came instantly from the sensations it caused. This was not tender lovemaking. It was hard and fast, blatant desire. That moment was such a wave of intensely overwhelming feelings, I quickly lost myself in the raw, pure, animalistic hunger which raged inside me.

I lost all care of the fact that there were other people out in the apartment. It'd begun, my week of being completely insatiable, and there was no stopping it whatsoever.

SLOANE IVAN CRANSTON:

BLOODLINES

$\mathcal{W}$e finally managed to get Mathias upstairs and into the apartment he shared with my sister and Brevan. He and Aisling disagreed about the bed or the sofa, but when Brevan moved Aoife out from in front of the bathroom door and barged in, well, let's just say the sounds of sex were all any of us needed to hear.

Aisling settled Mathias on the sofa, and we were just about to make our way out the door when Mathias stopped her.

"Aisling, I need to ask you something, and I realize with the sounds coming from the bath chamber, it is not ideal, but it is important." Mathias gave his sister a pleading look.

"Sure, what is it, Mathias?" Aisling made her way back over to her brother's side.

"Mother's ring, to be honest. I was saving it for you, but since Sloane managed to get you one of your own, I was wondering if you would mind if I gave it to Amelia? You and I do not have much left from our parents, and if it was something you wanted, I would find something else, but I wanted to know how you felt about it." My sister absolutely had a considerate mate in Mathias as well as his fierce protectiveness.

"Mathias, I think it would be lovely. I could not think of anyone

45

more deserving. Have you told her about our father yet?" Aisling gave her blessing and then piqued my interest with a question of her own. What about their father did they need to unveil?

Mathias shook his head. "Not yet. I was going to when I gave her mother's ring. Not many people in the pack remember these days because you and I blend in so easily."

"Okay, you two, what is it about your father that not many remember? Not to be rude, but I'm standing over here listening to you both, and hell, I'm a bit flummoxed about your entire conversation." I needed to remind them I was still there.

Aisling returned to my side almost immediately. "Come on, Sloane, I will explain downstairs."

She took my hand and guided me to the door. "Mathias, I will have something sent up for you to eat. Please make sure you rest, and if you need anything, let me know."

We left the apartment and headed downstairs to my room, hand in hand. Truth be told, I got a thrill just from holding her hand and walking with her. We'd done it before, so many times as I'd courted her and walked with her through the pack's secret garden. Neemah stopped us as we were headed down the stairs, and she was headed up.

"Good, there you are young man. Now, I do not need to go looking for you. I need to see both you and your sister once she is out of her fertile time. I cannot have my great-grandchildren walking around this island completely blind. What kind of great-grandmother would that make me? Not a very good one, I tell you," Neemah began to rattle off, and then suddenly, her words registered with me.

"Neemah, you must be mistaken. There is no way Ami and I can be your great-grandchildren. First off, we weren't wolves until Brevan initiated us. It kind of disproves your theory, don't you think?" The old girl was a brilliant healer, but she sounded three sandwiches short of a full picnic right then.

"Do not sass me, young man! I am too old for that nonsense! You do as you are told, and I will explain everything later. Just make sure you and your sister show up together. I hate having to repeat myself,"

Neemah scolded, and I felt like I'd been reduced to an eight-year-old child.

I placed my hands up in surrender. "Alright, Neemah, you win. When she is out of her heat, she and I will come and find you."

"Good, that is more like it. Now, you two run along and make me some great-great grandbabies." She winked and slapped my ass.

"Neemah!" Aisling exclaimed, as Neemah laughed heartily.

"Oh, if I were only young again. Go on, run along. I have work to do." Neemah waved the two of us off and continued to make her way upstairs.

Once we were inside, I closed the door and motioned for Aisling to sit on the bed.

"Sloane, how can it be possible? Neemah is your great-grand-mother? I have known her my entire life and thought I knew who her family was. I fear she may have slipped in her thoughts." Aisling's concern rang through in her question.

"I'm not entirely sure, but I suppose I will find out after Ami is no longer *busy* with what she is doing if you follow what I mean." I wasn't going to be quite as in your face with the description of Ami's condition. Sure, I could've said 'heat' but really, what would be the point? We both knew what was going on with my sister.

I needed to circle the conversation back over to the discussion from upstairs. There was something Aisling needed to tell me about her father, and whatever it was, it was making her extremely nervous.

"Sweetheart, what haven't you told me about your father? Why is it so important?" I almost pleaded as I sat next to the love of my life and placed her small delicate hands in mine.

"Sloane, our father was an Alfar from the northern territory. It is why Mathias and I are so fast and agile. Although Mathias downplays his skills, so as to not stand out amongst the other wolves. Our father died when Lord Edon, Brevan's father, sent my father out as an emissary of sorts. It was supposed to be a peaceful trip to see the King and Queen of the Alfar. All my father was asked to do was deliver a message. From what I know, father delivered the message, and then he was returned to Lord Edon, no longer alive. It was Marta who told

47

us to hide our lineage, so people would forget. For the most part, she was correct, but a few pack members remember. Brevan, for one." Aisling explained.

"Aisling, I don't care if you're half goat. You are now and will always be perfect exactly the way you are." Aisling was the most incredible soul I'd ever known.

"Sloane, you do not know what this means to me." She began to tear up as I pulled her into my arms.

"Oh, please, don't cry, baby, you know I suck at cheering people up when they cry. Besides, I don't quite understand why it would be such a big deal, other than it appears the Alfar are involved with Jakkel and Lycandra in some way. But it really shouldn't affect how others in the pack see you or Mathias. They've known you two your whole lives." I rubbed her back as I attempted to soothe her nerves. It was utterly true. I did suck at that sort of thing.

"Sloane, thank you! It never ceases to amaze me the kindness and understanding in your heart. Especially after you told me about your past and how you were raised along with what you did to protect your cousin. You are truly remarkable, and I am the luckiest woman to have found such a strong, loving partner." Aisling sniffled out her thoughts and curled up against my chest.

She thought she was the lucky one in this relationship, but in truth, it was me. I'd never grow tired of her in my arms, the sound of her laughter, or the smile on her beautiful face. She was my girl. From the day I laid eyes on her, I knew Aisling was it for me.

"Hey, beautiful, why don't you go ahead and get dressed properly this time. You need to check on the kiddos, and I need to sift through these papers again. I can't help but think Brevan and I've missed something." Not that I wanted to let go of her, but something was needling at my brain.

Aisling sighed, "I suppose you do have a point, and the kids do look forward to their playtime in the *daycare* as your sister calls it."

She moved off of my lap and began to collect her clothing off the floor. "Aisling, why don't you leave those? Actually, why don't you bring a few more things over here? Say, your entire wardrobe?"

She ran back over to me and jumped into my arms. "Sloane, you just made me the happiest girl again. Twice in one day, that is a new record!" She peppered me with kisses, which I happily accepted and smiled at the lovely creature in my arms.

When I let her down, I playfully spanked her backside. I suggested if she needed help moving her things, perhaps she should talk to Aoife to see if they could gather some of the house staff to assist. After Aisling left my room, I meandered over to my desk and began to sift through the papers which were brought back from Pack Lumen.

I was searching for the letters Brevan deemed nonsense. What perplexed me was they seemed like nonsense or ordinary letters from pack members on the surface, but my gut was telling me differently. There was something more to them, and I just needed to figure out what. It was time for me to become a first-class sleuth and decipher the puzzle which was laid before me.

SLOANE IVAN CRANSTON:

THE CYPHER

$\mathcal{W}$hat laid before me was a puzzle worthy of Sir Arthur Conan Doyle. The letters themselves seemed fairly innocuous upon first glance, but what I noticed and what was needling at me was the number in the upper right-hand corner along with the letters that were underlined. The one with the letter L, was currently in front of me, and it read as follows:

$\mathcal{L}$ - VIII
    Lady Aerin,
    We are no longer within the ability for the cattle to graze on our lands. We will need, very soon, additional areas that are not infested by zealots. With zealots everywhere, we cannot allow them to journey far. Lately, Gerard looked for land where we should be allowed to have the cattle graze. The land he found was by Lady Astraea's estate!
    Sincerely,
    Turk.

. . .

50

*A*s I viewed the letter, I noticed some of the individual letters were underlined. The syntax and overall grammar of these letters seemed to come from someone who was not well educated. It all appeared odd, even to my untrained eye, so I pulled out another letter because it depicted similar markings and read:

R - IV

Lady Aerin,

Please direct your attention towards your new pack babies. The young are sure to be a handful. If help is required, Xander alluded Keri would be able to help; just as soon as Paul finished with his chores. Another option would be Janice. Either of these people would be qualified for such a task and in turn would kindly care for the children. I just thought you should know.

Respectfully,

James

I must've stared at those letters for hours because, by the time I looked up again, Aisling was returning with her arms full of clothes. I immediately jumped up from my seat at my desk and went to help her.

"I am sorry, Sloane, I did not mean to disturb your concentration," She apologized.

I took some of the clothing out of her arms and placed them over on the bed as I replied, "Please, you never disturb me. Besides, I needed a break. I've been staring at these two letters, and I can't put my finger on why they bother me. There's just something strange about them."

Aisling set her pile of clothing down on the bed and moved over to my desk. "Do you mind if I have a look at them?" She inquired. Lo and behold, I found myself grateful for any assistance I could get.

"Please, feel free. I know there is a puzzle there, but it's driving me crazy to try and figure it out," I answered and some of the frustration I felt leaked into my tone.

51

As Aisling took a seat at my desk, I heard glass breaking and then a blood-curdling scream. It came from either down the hall or downstairs. Quickly, I went to my wardrobe and pulled out my sword.

As I moved towards the door I turned back to Aisling, "Stay here and lock the door behind me. Please, don't open it again until you know it's me on the other side. Brevan and your brother shouldn't be down even under these circumstances, so I want to make sure you're safe." Aisling nodded her agreement, and I swiftly flew out the door.

Rapidly, I moved through the second-floor hallway until I came to the apartment where the six pregnant women were living. The door appeared as though it'd been forced open, whether from the inside or outside, I couldn't tell. In the next moment, Emmer appeared at my back.

"I have Cash and Riley checking the perimeter of the house," Emmer declared and went to move into the room when I stopped him.

"Emmer, look at the door. It's been forced open," I pointed out what I noticed and Emmer acknowledged my findings as he slowly and carefully opened the door.

The pair of us entered the apartment cautiously. The door creaked as we pushed it open all the way. The sight of the room before us was completely trashed, and the window on the far wall was smashed. The glass was on the floor just under the window, leading us to assume, whoever broke into the room came in through the window and yanked the door open.

"Emmer, I think whoever broke in, is still in the house," I stated based on my observations of the empty room.

"Come on, we need to check the rest of the floors. I do not know about you, but I heard someone scream." Emmer motioned for us to leave, and we both exited quickly to find the source of the scream.

We went downstairs to the entry hall and checked the front of the house first. After careful observation, the two of us agreed nothing was disturbed. As we headed to the back of the house and entered the kitchen, Aoife was standing over Marta lying unconscious on the floor.

"Aoife, sweetheart, what happened?" Emmer asked his wife.

"Emmer, I do not know. I just left to go feed the twins, and Marta was the only one in here. She told me she wanted to look and see what there was on hand for baking because she was planning a surprise for Sloane and Aisling. The next thing I knew, I heard her scream and came running back down to find her here on the floor." Aoife's account of the events was all we had to go on.

"Sloane, see if you can find Cash and Riley. Something is definitely going on, and we need to find out what it is." Emmer as Brevan's beta commanded and I immediately left to find the pair of guards who were sent to investigate.

After I'd run the perimeter of the house twice, I finally found Cash and Riley in the barn. Cash was in wolf form, and Riley was following close behind in human form.

"Riley, hold up a moment," I yelled so they would stop moving and allow me to catch up to them.

"Sloane, what is it? Cash has picked up a slight scent and is trying to follow it," Riley informed me.

"Emmer wants an update. We found Marta in the kitchen, lying unconscious on the floor. It appears as though whoever it was may have gone down the backstairs in order to get out of the house," I relayed to Riley as Cash continued to sniff the ground.

A question suddenly popped into my mind. I remembered Cash was one of the pack's best trackers next to Emmer. "Riley, why is Cash having a hard time keeping the scent? It was he and I who went through the rubble in the marketplace after Aerin blew it up, so I know his sniffer is one of the best."

"The scent is being masked. I suspect it is because they took those six pregnant girls and are using the girl's scents to hide their own." Riley's assessment of the situation was confirmed by Cash, in wolf form, giving a head-bob.

"Alright, I will let Emmer know. Don't do anything drastic. We need to be smart and careful about this before we do anything. If there were enough of them to make off with six girls, then you absolutely don't want to take them on by yourselves." My concern for my fellow pack members was met with complete agreement as they both continued on to follow the only real lead we had.

I made my way back into the packhouse and found Emmer and Aoife still in the kitchen. Marta was just beginning to wake up, and Aoife was trying to keep her calm while Emmer shifted into his wolf to see if he could pick up a trail on the backstairs. It appeared Emmer came to the same conclusion that I'd just done in speaking with Riley and Cash.

When Emmer returned, he shifted back to human form and redressed himself. I often thought pack life was a bit weird at times. No one ever flinched, even slightly, at the naked bodies, which tended to be present at any given time due to everyone shifting from wolf to human and vice versa. Needless to say, it was something I was working on getting over.

Aiofe's eyes rose and gazed upon Emmer. "Honey, did you find anything?"

"Just the scent of the girls. Sloane, did you get anything from Riley or Cash?" Emmer questioned me.

"Cash is having a hard time following the trail. Riley informed me the scent of the girls is being used to hide the scent of the perpetrators. My assumption would be we are dealing with more than one person because it appears as though they took the girls and ran. So, if we follow that train of thought to its logical conclusion, then whoever we are dealing with is not only fast but strong and agile." My assessment was quickly agreed upon by Emmer.

"Your conclusion makes sense. Did you tell Cash and Riley to use caution?" Emmer asked, and I responded with my patent-pending eye-roll. Okay, so I haven't lost all my bad habits. Emmer got the picture without me saying a word, thank heavens.

The timing of their break-in was peculiar at best. I suspected someone knew about Brevan, Mathias, and Ami being out of commission for the time being. Knowingly, they decided to take advantage of the fact that three of our strongest members were down for the count, so to speak. My next thoughts were, *how would anyone outside the pack have known?* and *do we have another mole?* Both reasonable assumptions which needed to be figured out.

After I left Emmer and Aoife to deal with Marta, I headed back upstairs to my room. I needed to sit down and solve one puzzle before I moved onto the next. As I climbed the stairs, I found myself cursing my sister's timing but quickly realized there was no way she would've known anything was going to happen. When I knocked at the door and announced myself, Aisling flung it open a half a second later.

"Sloane, I am glad you are alright. What happened?" Aisling possessed a nervous edge to her voice.

"Someone broke in and kidnapped the six pregnant girls who came over from Pack Lumen. Cash is outside trying to track their scent while Emmer and Aoife are in the kitchen with Marta. Sweetheart, whoever it was, knocked Marta out and left her on the floor down there. She's pretty confused and shaken up right now." I attempted to break the news as gently as I could, especially since I knew how Aisling felt about Marta.

"Sloane, do you think she will be okay?" Aisling wondered as she bit her lip.

"I think she'll be fine once she's seen by Neemah. Marta might wind up with a slight headache, but that will probably be the extent of it." I pulled her into a hug to help calm her nerves. Aisling's capacity for caring was boundless, and she worried about everyone.

Once she calmed enough to think clearly, she pulled back and told me what she'd done while I was helping Emmer.

"Sloane, come look at this first letter about the cattle." A sort of excitement filled her voice as she pulled me over to the desk.

When we got there, I leaned my sword against the wall, and she continued. "See what I did! In the letter, there were certain words with underlined letters, so I pulled them out and wrote them down in the order they appeared."

She showed me the parchment she'd used to write them on. The letter's orders were: O – W – F – W – W – V – L – Z – W – Z – W – A – J – L – G – L – W – S – D – H – Z – S.

As I stared at the written letter and the letters Aisling wrote down, something in my mind clicked into place. I thought to myself, *'It couldn't be that simple'* and began writing out the alphabet.

"Sloane, honey, what are you doing?" Aisling asked as she'd undoubtedly saw the look of recognition on my face.

I replied excitedly, "Watch, and I'll show you!" I continued, "This is the standard alphabet. A – Z. Now, if you factor into account the number in the upper right-hand corner, which is the Roman numeral for eight, then the alphabet for this letter begins with S and ends with R; so, it would appear like such: S-T-U-V-W-X-Y-Z-A-B-C-D-E-F-G-H-I-J-K-L-M-N-O-P-Q-R."

"Okay, but how does it help us?" Aisling still looked confused, and I continued with my explanation.

"Sweetheart, it's an old school cypher. It means that the normal letters once you match them up to the modified alphabet should spell out the hidden message." My explanation began to make sense to her as Aisling started to follow along.

"So, what does it say?" her excitement bubbled over.

I took a moment to translate the letters and what I came up with was absolutely what I thought. It was a hidden message inside the letter which said: *'We need the heir to the Alpha'.* Once I figured out the cypher, I translated the other letter doing it the same way I'd done with the first one, only shifting the alphabet over four, so it began with W and ended with V. This one said: *'The sacrifice will be on the next super moon.'*

"Aisling, I've got to find all the letters that look like this. I need to get them translated and to either Brevan or Emmer." She nodded, and we began the hunt for the letters containing the hidden messages.

Puzzles were my thing, so I had every intention to find as many of these letters as I could and translate them as quickly as possible. There was no doubt that I'd have my work cut out for me.

SLOANE IVAN CRANSTON:

THE MONSTROSITY

After the discovery with the letters Aisling and I found, there was a total of twenty hidden cyphers. Over the course of the next few days, we then organized the rest of the papers and placed them into individual piles. Our objective was to make heads or tails of them. I primarily focused on decoding the letters in my spare time. I still continued training with Cash in the mornings and my legal studies on top of this project. It'd been only a brief period of time, but the workload was becoming quite extensive.

Aisling was lending a hand when she could. She, too, went on with her own training, running the 'daycare', and was organizing our binding ceremony. To top it all off, she was still moving her belongings into my room. Aoife suggested we should take over the room next door and add it to our space once the new building was finished. One night both women were discussing the possibilities of adding onto our apartment while I was working and asked me what I thought. Apparently, I gave the wrong answer when I said, "whatever will make you happy," because I received a playful slap on the arm followed by a chorus of "MEN!" *Honestly, how do we guys win in either situation?*

Construction on the new building was moving along quickly.

57

Brevan employed the construction workers from Lady Nova's coven as well as some of the town's folk from Tenebris. Emmer was overseeing the construction crew's work. He basically was as tough a foreman as he was a drill sergeant. The building was initially projected to be finished in a month. At the rate they were going, it appeared as though they might be completed a week ahead of schedule.

Last evening, as I paused my decoding of the letters so I could fetch something to eat, Emmer stopped me and asked how things were going. He'd heard I made a discovery with some of the confiscated items from Pack Lumen. I explained I'd managed to decode approximately half of the letters, and would inform both he and Brevan once I completed them. All we'd be able to do for the foreseeable future was wait until those were finished. Besides, Brevan, Mathias, and my sister were still all MIA for the time being.

I made my way down to the training room for my usual daily ass-kicking with Cash. On this particular morning, however, Emmer was present and was awaiting my arrival as well as the ladies who were also training.

"Good morning, everyone! If I could have your attention, please," Emmer opened with before he continued.

"Normally, we would have you all do a three-mile run before your combat training begins. Today, we will get to forgo that." As soon as he'd finished, the word 'forgo', excitement broke out in the group, but I knew Emmer a little too well by this point. There was no way we were going to get off that easy.

"Alright, settle down! Do not get too excited. Along with the other guards, I have completed what Amelia and Brevan called an *obstacle course*. Instead of the three-mile run, you will be put through what I am calling *The Gauntlet*. Now, move out!" Yup, I'd been correct. Drill Sergeant Emmer was back, and he looked just a bit too pleased with himself when he'd made his announcement.

As I approached him, I paused for just a moment to speak to him. "Emmer, you realize you were just mean. Getting their hopes up like that in one breath, then dashing them in the next."

Emmer's smug grin was my confirmation he'd done it on purpose. "I would never do anything of the sort. I merely pointed out no one was going to have to run three miles today." I guessed denial wasn't just a river in Egypt, nor was his sarcasm lost on me at any point.

Once we all assembled at the newly constructed Gauntlet, my jaw fell open. I thought, *Damn, Emmer was only given a few ideas and then ran with them.* As easy-going as Emmer was at times, he definitely possessed a sadistic streak when it came to combat training.

There were moss-covered logs, rope climbing obstacles, a climbing wall, ground crawl, rope bridge, mud pits with rope swings, and last but not least, a full-on victory tower complete with a challenging climb on one side, and the person would rappel down the other. I took a page out of my sister's book and made a mental note to kill her for implanting the idea into Emmer's head.

Emmer made his way center stage and started to speak. "Since chivalry is not dead amongst our pack, I believe it only fair for the men here to step up and tackle the new beast before the ladies."

Aisling stepped up, and to her credit, directed her statement at Emmer himself. "While we ladies appreciate the grand gesture, I believe we will tackle it the same as any of you."

My girl was everything a woman should be and then some. God, I was proud of her. I knew Mathias wasn't exactly thrilled with the idea of her training, but that was where I strongly disagreed with him. If Aisling and the other women knew how to defend themselves, then, in my opinion, it made them somewhat safer in these dangerous times.

"Very well then, how about you step up and run it first?" Emmer threw down the challenge.

Emmer and Aisling walked up to the start line, and when he dropped his hand, she took off. Before anyone could blink an eye, she'd cleared the hurdles and was onto the moss-covered logs. After only slightly losing her balance once, she moved to the stomach crawl and got hung up in there because the back of her shirt caught on a nail. All in all, she managed to clear the obstacles in a relatively short time and only paused a brief moment as she approached the tower.

As she paused in front of the tower, I could see a strained expression come over her face. While she'd made the course look relatively easy, I could see the toll it'd taken, and Aisling was beginning to tire. I yelled, "Come on, babe, you got this!" and the ladies followed my lead. They all began to cheer her on because, honestly, if one succeeded, then they all might succeed.

Aisling focused, and with one last burst of energy, scaled the tower, ran the rope bridge, and rappelled down the other side. My girl didn't just complete the course, she'd totally turned it into her bitch. Pride swelled within me as she jogged over to my side.

"Baby, you were amazing!" Pride exuded from my voice for what she accomplished. I took her into my arms and kissed her nose as I congratulated her for a job very well done.

"Thank you, handsome. I cannot wait to see how well you do." A smile lit up her face. I suspected she was hoping for me to do well but not quite as well as she'd done.

"Now, that is how it is done. Everyone line-up and prepare for your turn!" Emmer barked out, and we all fell in line, including Cash, Riley, and Finn.

I managed to make it through the course, and I was now going to dub it 'Emmer's personal torture playground'. He was just a little too smug about the monstrosity they'd constructed. Even Cash, Riley, and Finn were breathing hard when they finished. I was counting down the days until Brevan would be back and resume Alpha of the pack. Perhaps, with any luck, he'd make the horrible thing go away.

AMELIA (AMI) JANE GRAY:

MIXED BLOOD

*I*t turned out having one's fertile time didn't actually last a week. It was more like five days of constant, wet, sensual, hot, intimate sex with two incredibly virile, well-endowed, sexy men. Mathias was fully recovered from his injury by day two. Between him and Brevan, when the morning of day six rolled around, I was beyond satisfied. Hell, it amazed me I was even able to walk. I slipped out of bed and crept into the bath chamber, closing the door behind me. The last thing I wanted to do was to wake the two men who were still asleep.

There were only two thoughts on my mind. The first was to pee, and the second was I needed to bathe. After the last five days, I needed a long hot soak in the tub—NO men allowed! Quietly, I clicked the lock shut, and began to fill the tub before I took care of my bodily needs. Don't get me wrong, I loved my guys, but sometimes a girl's gotta do, what a girl's gotta do. This girl needed some serious alone time.

An hour later, I felt like a new woman. My hair was washed, and the long soak did my body better than a massage by a Swiss masseur. After I unlocked the door to the bath chamber, I slid out into our sleeping area. I stood there for a moment as I lovingly smiled at my

61

two gorgeous men. I then quietly moved over to my wardrobe and slipped on my dressing gown. I headed across the room and opened the French doors to air everything out. I breathed in the cool morning air and filled my lungs with the scent of morning blossoms and the freshness of the outdoors.

My next two objectives were keaff, the wonderful coffee-like substitute here on the island, and food. I managed to exit our apartment with my guys still out like a light. I made my way down the backstairs and into the kitchen, where I found the entire kitchen staff buzzing with activity.

"Hi, everyone. Looks like I still live," I chirped as I entered the kitchen.

Aoife was the first one to turn towards me. "Amelia, how are you?"

I thought it was a bit of an odd question but answered anyway, "Hungry, actually. Any chance of getting some food and keaff?"

"Of course, but I mean seriously, how are you feeling?" Aoife asked again and walked over to me.

"Should I feel any different than I did before? Other than way less turned on. It was kinda freaky, to be honest. I mean, it took everything I had in me to not rip Brevan's clothes off on the way home. Now, though, I feel like my normal self." The look of concern vanished from Aoife's face, and she visibly relaxed.

"Oh, thank heavens. It is not good when a female wolf has to deny those urges. When I saw you, I really became worried. I was not sure you would be able to reduce your temperature. That is just one of the side effects of denial," Aoife explained, and I must've visibly gulped because she smiled over at me reassuringly before she continued.

"Do not worry. If you feel fine now, then I suspect it is just so. Besides, the likelihood of you having more than one child your first time is slim." Aoife's statement brought me up short.

"Aoife, what do you mean more than one child? Like twins or something?" I asked because I was slightly panicked.

"Well, when a wolf's body is as fevered as yours was, multiple eggs can drop, but I am sure you will be fine. Do not worry about it." She brushed off her explanation and went to fix some breakfast for me. I concentrated on breathing while I tried not to fall over. Aoife was just playing with my head. Wasn't she?

When Aoife was finished, I loaded up two trays full of food. One tray held plates of eggs, bacon, sausage, and fresh fruit; the other tray held cups of keaff, cinnamon rolls, pancakes, which the kitchen staff made with my recipe, along with whipped honey butter and berry syrup. The real trick was getting it all upstairs without dropping anything. Even with my waitressing skills, it was going to be difficult. Luck was on my side though, Mathias appeared just as I was picking up the second tray.

"Good morning, my angel." Mathias hugged my waist from behind and kissed my ear after he greeted me.

"Good morning, handsome, you're just the man I was looking for." I gave Mathias a chaste kiss on the cheek. "Would you mind terribly giving me a hand?" I requested as I pointed to the second tray of food.

Mathias returned my chaste kiss and lifted the tray of food I motioned to. We managed to make it back to our apartment as Brevan was leaving the bath chamber. As we set the trays down in the sitting area, Brevan sauntered over and placed a kiss on my temple.

"Good morning, my little wolf," he affectionately greeted me, and I smiled up at him.

"Good morning, my favorite Alpha," I replied.

"I am the only Alpha, Amelia," he countered and I laughed.

"I know, and that's why it's a no-contest, hands-down win for you. You'll always be my favorite." I smirked and responded with a wink.

Brevan chuckled and picked up a plate of eggs. "Somehow, your logic almost makes sense... Almost." He continued to pile on bacon, sausage, fruit, a cinnamon roll and grabbed his cup of keaff.

"I need to go meet with Emmer and find out what has been going on in our absence. The two of you stay and enjoy your breakfast," Brevan announced before leaving with his food.

"Guess it's back to the real world for us," I mumbled and almost pouted.

"It is alright, my angel. We need to have a talk anyway. Brevan is just giving us some space because there are some things I need to tell you about myself and my family. It is something I should have told you prior to our binding, and I meant to bring it up before you hit your fertile time. But, now that we are trying to have children, I really need to tell you everything." Mathias shook his head.

"Mathias, what is it?" I questioned him as he pulled me into his lap. Screw the keaff; my mate was more important.

"Amelia, there is a reason why I hold back in training and why I am so much faster and more agile than the others in the pack. Aisling and I came from a blended lineage. Our father was an Alfar who defected from the northern territory. My mother fell in love with him while he was still under the King and Queen's rule. For them to be together, he defected, and they were bound." Mathias explained, and I tapped my finger on my chin.

"Mathias, pull back your hair, please?" I requested, and he knew I was playing with him by my smirk.

I examined his ears as he did as I asked. "Nope, no pointy ears, and I've seen the rest of your delicious body... I mean your physical appearance." Mathias rolled his eyes at me.

"Now, you listen to me, love, the simple matter is I don't care who your father was or your mother for that matter. Am I grateful they got together? Absolutely! Because if they hadn't, then I wouldn't have you. I love you exactly the way you are." I still couldn't fathom the fact I needed to repeat myself, yet again.

"It wouldn't matter to me if you were covered in purple dots, with one eye and one horn. You'd still be you!" I added just to drive my point home.

"Amelia, I am half Alfar! What if our child or children come out with some of their more distinguishing markings? Like the ears, as you pointed out. What then?" He wasn't concerned with himself. He was more worried about his children, who weren't even born yet.

"Mathias, if it happens, then we will deal with it but there is no sense in worrying about *what if's.*" I used air quotes to emphasize my point. I reached over and took his hand. "It will only drive you crazy." Mathias relaxed and used his thumb to rub the back of my hand.

With his other hand, he reached into the pocket of his dressing gown, and pulled something out. "Amelia, I would like to give you something which belonged to my mother. I wanted to give this to you sooner, but as it belonged to my mother, it was only right to secure Aisling's blessing before I passed it along to my mate."

Mathias opened his hand and what laid on his palm was a stunning, rainbow-hued, glowing, white stone ring. He slid it onto my finger, and I kissed him softly on the lips.

"Mathias, it's lovely. It was your mother's?" I incredulously asked and couldn't believe how well it fit my finger.

"Yes, it was the only item my father managed to bring with him when he left the North. The stone is called *Glowing Mother's Tears* and is only found on the Alfar's side of the mountains." As I looked at the stone, it reminded me of a rainbow moonstone.

"Thank you so much, Mathias. I love it!" I practically squealed, and I meant it.

"Amelia, I also need to tell you something else," Mathias appeared hesitant.

"Okay, what is it?" I countered back with curiosity lacing my voice.

"Earlier, when I awoke, Brevan was already awake, and he was dressing to go search for you," Mathias stated, and nothing so far surprised me.

"Well, there's nothing unusual about that. I kind of expected one of you to show up while I was down in the kitchen." So far, I wasn't following why his declaration was so important.

"I told Brevan not to worry because you were just downstairs, specifically, in the kitchen," Mathias continued, and I was starting to understand.

"You knew where I was before you'd even seen me with your own eyes?" I remarked in surprise.

"Exactly! I am not sure how, but I could tell where you were. It is something which went way beyond our bond," he exclaimed.

"Well, that's weird. I don't really mind you knowing where I am. It just means I won't be taking any sneaky shopping trips into Tenebris with Drew." I was trying to make light of the situation.

"Definitely not! I remember the last time you went shopping in

Tenebris. While I was not thrilled about playing guard to the woman who absolutely enraptured me, there was no way I was going to leave you unprotected. The same goes even more now!" Mathias declared and squeezed me tight.

"Mathias, not that I don't love being in your arms, but our breakfast is getting cold. As for the *new bond* thing we have going on, maybe it won't last, or maybe it will. Either way, is it really a problem?" I was curious to know because I truly didn't mind it. It wasn't like it went both ways, but I wanted to know if he'd been troubled by it.

"No, it is not an issue for me. I just wanted you to know as it was something I just noticed this morning." Mathias stated, and he seemed to actually be pleased about it.

I scooted off his lap and thought about what Mathias told me. On some level, I wondered if it was something to do with his enormous blood loss. When it happened, I was the only known universal blood donor, and we put together a make-shift I.V. to replace what he'd lost. What if my blood mixed with his half Alfar genetics caused some strange alternate bond between the two of us? Regardless, there was another deeper bond between Mathias and me, which wasn't there before, and I for one, actually relished it.

AMELIA (AMI) JANE GRAY:

WORKING WITH SLOANE

$\mathscr{A}$fter Mathias and I finished our breakfast, we both dressed and headed out of our apartment. I was on my way to see Sloane, who I felt somewhat guilty over. The last time I'd seen him was when we were faced off against Jack. I hadn't even given him a second glance when I'd taken off with General Pax and his Gargoyles.

When we reached the bottom of the third-floor steps, I paused and gave Mathias a quick, chaste kiss, and turned towards Sloane's room. I rounded the corner and saw Aisling with her back to the wall. Sloane was in front of her with his arms stretched out on either side of her head. The scene was very cute, and I felt the need to clear my throat as I announced myself.

"Sloane, get a room!" I laughed out loud.

"Ami!" Sloane exclaimed. He kissed Aisling before he came over to me and hugged me. "Nice to see your mates didn't wear you out too badly."

"Nice to see you too," I replied and hugged him back.

When Sloane released me, I went over to Aisling and gave her a hug as well. "It's good to see my brother is taking excellent care of my favorite sister-in-law."

"Well, if he was not, I know all I would have to do is let you know." Aisling smirked and giggled as she spoke.

"You know it, girl!" I'd gotten the urge to do a fist bump but quickly realized Aisling probably wouldn't know what it was.

"I really must be going now. The children need to be organized into their groups, and then I have to get to the training room. I will see you in a while, Amelia. Bye!" Aisling began to walk off when I noticed her hand.

"Freeze you!" It wasn't quite at a yell, but it was enough to pull her to a stop. "Get back here and show me your hand."

Aisling turned and beamed the biggest smile. She practically skipped her way back to me, and I grabbed her hand. "Aisling, that ring is amazing, and it perfectly matches your skin tone. Oh, I'm so happy for you," I gushed and hugged her again.

We stood there a moment longer, and she told me how Sloane popped the question. When I thought back, it made sense why it took so long for them to get up to our apartment. After another quick embrace, my brother and I watched as she left. I waved at her retreating form before turning my attention to my brother.

"So, want to clue me in on what's been going on around here?" My question was merely out of curiosity, but he yanked me inside his room and quickly closed the door behind the two of us.

"Ami, in the five days the three of you have been sequestered, the six pregnant women who came over from Pack Lumen were kidnapped. I've also discovered hidden messages in some of the papers we brought back from Lady Aerin's house. Neemah dropped a bombshell when she told me that you and I were her great-grandchildren, and, to top it all off... Emmer finished your damn obstacle course. "

"Wait, what? Back up a second... Who was kidnapped?" I needed to slow Sloane's roll.

Sloane and I sat on his bed as he recounted the events of what happened with the kidnapping, which included Marta getting knocked out. I was relieved to hear the only thing she suffered was a bump on the head. What disturbed me, though, was the fact, someone or someone's managed to break into the packhouse and take the girls, right from under our noses. As I paused a moment to mull over the information, something dawned on me.

"Sloane, do you think they used some sort of concealment spell like the one I can use?"

"Ami, I simply don't know. Cash, who is, as you know is one of the best trackers in the pack, found it incredibly difficult to track their scent. Then there was Marta's story. She recounted seeing the girls *floating* out on air. It's like we're dealing with David Copperfield or Harry Houdini. I suppose a concealment spell would account for some of it, but what about the scent. I'm not an expert on scent tracking, but I think that would be extremely difficult to do and from Cash's frustration I think it's a fair assumption."

"Sloane, I don't know enough about magic to know if it's even possible, but we both know someone that does," I remarked suggestively and waited for him to pick up on my train of thought.

"Ami, do you mean Astraea?"

"Sloane, that's exactly who I mean. We both know she's been around long enough. If it was even possible for something like this to happen, then she'd be the one to ask."

"You have a good point. I'll write her a letter and ask her about it," Sloane agreed.

"Now, what about those hidden messages?" I asked to redirect the conversation.

Sloane pulled me over to his desk and took out the letters he'd been working on. As I glanced them over, I realized they were cyphers, just like my dad used to have me do when I was growing up.

"Sloane, these are classic cyphers. My dad would have me do them. He always told me it was our special language. At first, he made them easy so I would learn how to do them, but he gradually made them harder. Some even held double meanings."

"Ami, what do you mean by *double meanings?*"

"Well, he'd do the original message, but he started including things like directions to where my reward was. He always could motivate me with Oreo cookies, especially the double stuffed ones." Which reminded me of their rich chocolate, the cream filling, and made me instantly salivate. "Damn it, now I want an Oreo, and I just ate breakfast!" I sort of pouted as I thought about the addictive cookies I'd never eat again.

"Relax, killer, I'm sure there is something in the kitchen you can have when we head down. For now, I'm more interested in what you said about double meanings. Do you think we could blow off training today and work on these? Otherwise, I might not be able to finish them." Sloane's comment was one of concern. He really did want to get them done, and I always did like solving these sorts of things.

I started thinking about the times my dad would have me solve puzzles. It was a nostalgic feeling as I remembered one of the cyphers led me to my very first *big girl dress* as he titled it. The actual reward was a father-daughter dinner out at a fancy restaurant where I ordered my very first Shirley Temple. I think it was his way of acknowledging I was growing up. The memory made me smile.

I looked at my brother and agreed we'd skip training for today. I'd gotten a gut feeling the letters were more important than swinging a practice sword. We started by spreading out all twenty pieces of paper and quickly ran out of room. His living quarters were just too small for this task, so gathered them together and brought them up to my apartment, where there was far more room.

On the way to my apartment, we ran into Finn and explained what we were doing. He promised he'd take over the training for the women today, but I needed to get my ass down there tomorrow come hell or high water. As we climbed the last flight of stairs, we couldn't help wonder what we were going to find hidden amongst the words of the letters in our hands.

AMELIA (AMI) JANE GRAY:

NEEMAH

When Sloane and I reached my apartment, we glanced around and decidedly came to the same conclusion. There was absolutely more room but not enough flat surfaces available at the moment. We set the letters down on Brevan's desk, then moved the sofa and coffee table to the walls. This left us plenty of floor space to spread everything out on.

We placed the letters in the order we thought they might've gone chronologically. Sloane and I concluded we should decode them first then search to see if there was an underlying message amongst them. Sloane marked the letters he had already managed to decode. This eliminated half of them right off the bat.

After a couple of hours, Sloane and I'd managed to decode another five letters when the door to the apartment opened. Neemah was searching for the two of us and mumbled something along the lines of, "Why did it have to be on the third floor."

"Hi, Neemah, was there something you needed?" I inquired because I hadn't seen her since Mathias was injured.

"Yes, dear. A chair would be lovely." Both Sloane and I stared at her, and being the gentleman he was, Sloane retrieved Neemah the chair from behind Brevan's desk.

Neemah patted Sloane's arm. "Thank you. Now, tell me what the two of you are working on here. I do not think I have seen so many papers around this place since Edon was here trying to hide your lineage."

Neemah possessed a crazy way of just blurting things out. It was almost as if the filter between her brain and her mouth was worn out, and she just said what she thought. Her words jolted my memory, and suddenly, the phrase *great-granddaughter* popped into my head. Sloane must've had a similar experience because we both peered at each other with a look of realization.

"Neemah, the last time I saw you, you said I was your great-granddaughter. Not to be rude, but since there isn't a life or death situation going on, would you care to elaborate further? I mean, before I became part of Pack Lingwir, I hadn't shifted into a wolf, and clearly, you are a wolf, so...." I allowed the sentence to trail off in hopes Neemah would fill in the gaps.

"Not here, dear. I need you and your brother to come with me to my cottage. You might as well bring your mates along. I know you will wind up telling them regardless." Neemah glanced over at Sloane and sighed, "Bring that female of yours too. The fewer times I have to repeat myself, the better." She continued to sit there and gawked at both of us. "Well, get a move on. I am not getting any younger, you know."

The two of us stood together, then Sloane and I moved toward the door. "Neemah, do you need some help getting downstairs?" Sloane's question was met with a scoff.

"Dear boy, do I look like an invalid to you?"

Sloane swallowed and shook his head. "No ma'am, not even slightly. I just thought you might like to be accompanied down the stairs by someone as handsome as myself. It's probably best if I don't, though. I wouldn't want Aisling to become jealous. You know how it is... new couple, beautiful goddess of a woman; it's the classic story." Sloane could be sly when he wanted.

Neemah loudly chuckled, "Alright, for that one, I will allow you to accompany me downstairs. At least you were original."

Neemah took Sloane's arm and we all walked out of the apartment. On the way down we ran into Mathias who was on his way up. I gave him a brief explanation of the mess on the floor upstairs and told him Neemah wanted all of us to come to her cottage. Mathias was as curious as I was, he agreed to collect Brevan and Aisling and meet us there.

Neemah insisted we exit out the back, citing "The shortest distance between two points was a straight line." I couldn't exactly argue with her logic because it was definitely a true statement. We walked past the pack's private garden to the construction site where the new housing for the additional pack members was being constructed. I made a mental note of our direction and got a good view of how far along the new building was coming. It appeared as though the crew was moving incredibly quick.

As we were just clearing the construction site, Brevan, Mathias, and Aisling caught up with us. We continued to walk at Neemah's pace up to the tree line of the forest. That was when I saw her home.

Neemah's cottage was a small, log cabin styled house. In the front garden, she'd planted lavender, sage, and fireweed on one side of the path. On the other were vegetables like tomatoes, peppers, carrots, and cucumbers. The cobblestone path was graced with an arbor which supported climbing roses of many colors.

When we reached the front of the cottage itself, Neemah opened the door and invited all of us inside. As we entered, I discovered a cozy, warm living space. It wasn't large, but she made it feel like it was homey. All of the windows were framed with brightly colored curtains, which allowed as much light as possible to come into the space. On the left side was her kitchen area, and on the right was the living area. The kitchen held a small stove, sink, and a two-person table with a vase of wildflowers in the middle.

The living area held a sofa and a wooden rocker; both were focused towards the fireplace. On the mantle were some small mementos I assumed Neemah collected throughout the years. In the middle of the floor was a handwoven rug that completed the cozy feel of her home.

Neemah took a seat in the rocking chair and gestured for us to follow her lead. Three of us sat on the sofa, including Aisling, Sloane, and myself. Brevan and Mathias took the two chairs from the kitchen and brought them into the living area, so they could sit.

"Now, where to begin," Neemah mused, "I suppose I should start with your parents. Your father's name was Xantho and your mother, my granddaughter's name was Melisandre. The two of you were born nearly a year apart from one another, give or take a month. Your mother was so excited when she learned she was going to have another babe right off. She so wanted the two of you to be close friends." Neemah began to get a glazed look as though she were playing a movie from back in her memories. "I remember the day she told me she was pregnant again. Sloane, you were only a few months old at the time." She pointed to Sloane and then continued. "Melisandre wanted to make sure being pregnant so soon after her first child would not hinder the second one in any way. I assured her she would be fine and gave her some herbs to help keep her from becoming ill."

Neemah began to rock in her chair, and while she paused, I snuck in a question. "Neemah, it all sounds wonderful, but how do you know Sloane and I are your great-grandchildren? Couldn't it be possible you have us mistaken for someone else?" I really needed to bring up the obvious issue because no one else was.

"Oh, sweet girl, you give me a moment I will tell you everything I know," Neemah chided, and I zipped my lip.

"You both need to understand your lineage is very mixed. By that I mean, humans and the Lycanthropes have intermingled in our line throughout the generations. Your father was the last Phoenix Mystic and carried the ability to pass those powers along to his offspring. Xantho was raised in the fishing village of Ori, where he met Melisandre. He, for all intents and purposes, was or appeared to be fully human. Your mother, while she was not the Dragon Mystic, she was his heir, and it gave her the ability to pass those particular gifts along. She was however, a healer like me and did showcase those abilities quite well. Magic flows in our veins going back generations beyond me. So, when the two of you turned out to be who you are, your mother knew she needed to hide you both until you were of age. Melisandre, at first thought, she would have been able to conceal you in the farming village of Messis. Since I knew you were not shifters the day each of you were born, it was a distinct possibility to use Messis as a hiding spot. If either of you turned out to be Lycanthrope, then you both would have shifted within the first few hours of coming into our world, but neither of you did." Neemah's explanation was such a scattered roundabout one, it was difficult to follow.

Neemah then stood from the rocking chair and moved over to the corner of the living area. She lifted two of the floorboards and pulled out two thick books. Once she'd safely extracted the books, she replaced the floorboards and walked to stand in front of both Sloane and myself. Neemah handed Sloane one book and myself the other.

"What you hold, Sloane, is the history of our family. It tells you the who, what, and when for each member. Included in *the what* are any special gifts they might possess. Amelia, what you hold is the last book left from the library of the Acolytes of the Phoenix. It contains documented spells used by each of the mystics that came before you." Neemah shockingly pulled out the medallion she wore hidden around her neck. *Holy shit-balls!* She was an Acolyte and managed to keep everything hidden for many years.

"Now, to make a long story short... Sloane, are you paying attention?" Neemah scolded my brother as his focus shifted from the book in his hands back to Neemah.

"Sorry, Neemah, but the book you gave me is amazing. You have my full attention now," He apologized for getting distracted.

"As I was saying, after Amelia was born, word filtered down to Edon the two of you were in danger from those who wanted to steal your abilities. Edon sought out me and your parents. The four of us concocted a plan to hide you two in the non-magical world until your twenty-fifth year. Alexander and Marissa were chosen as your guardians because Alexander was a member of the Order of the Dragon, and Marissa was an Acolyte. Alexander was gifted with a small amount of magic and learned a few spells, one of them was a concealment spell. Marissa tragically could not have her own children due to an accident that happened to her at a very young age. Needless to say, your parents were not thrilled at the idea of giving away their babies, but as any good parent would, they chose your safety first." Neemah paused long enough to head back to her rocker and sit down.

"We Acolytes gathered enough magic to send the four of you through a portal. While we created the portal, Edon gathered as many members of the Order he could to protect us while our backs were exposed, for lack of a better turn of phrase. That night, just as we finished creating the portal, the Alfar attacked us. They, however, were not alone. The Alfar were aided by wolves. Wolves, we now know, who were loyal to Lycandra. Edon and his brothers fought valiantly. But, due to the sheer numbers, the Order members and Acolytes, save myself and one other from that fateful night, were all slaughtered. Xantho did his best to aid and protect everyone for as long as he could. Sadly, one well-placed arrow managed to pierce his heart, and he was one of many who fell during the slaughter." Neemah took a deep breath before she continued.

"After Edon and I noticed two wolves following Marissa and Alexander through the portal, Edon made it a point to drag me from the temple, which saved my life. I witnessed the wounds which were inflicted upon him before he ran back into the fray to rejoin his brothers. The wounds Edon suffered were from an Alfar blade. I do not see how he could have survived. Those blades are coated in a rare venom that slowly kills the victim. Melisandre, we could only presume was dead as there has been no sign of her or her corpse since then, nor did we manage to find Lord Edon's body. I can only assume he or the pair of them ran through the portal to follow the wolves who made it through before the magic ran out, but those thoughts are sheer speculation on my part. The rest of this tale you already know." Neemah ended her story, and I sat there and attempted to digest what I just heard. One thing was certain, it was absolutely quite the story.

AMELIA (AMI) JANE GRAY

SHE'S GOT THE LOOK

I started to tap the book in my lap with my fingers. I was just simply having a hard time swallowing the story we'd all heard. Up to that point, I'd managed to accept a lot of weird things, but this was where it stopped.

"Neemah, your account so far has really been interesting. Thank you for the books but, I think, I've hit my threshold of the supernatural. Not to mention, you still haven't explained fully why Sloane and I never shifted. Great, there were non-wolves in our lineage, so I guess it technically means the pair of us both possessed recessive genes that got together and did the tango. I'm sure the odds of that happening to both of us are slim. It would be the equivalent of hitting the genetic lottery. I may not be a science expert, but even I can figure that one out." I spouted. I realized my words were a bit harsh. I was done with all the supernatural bombshells.

"I'm sorry, Neemah, I'm simply going to need more proof than your word on the subject. You're a wonderful healer, and I commend you on your impressive knowledge. Still, all of it is way beyond anything I'd be willing to take at face value." My conclusion was met with a grin that insinuated Neemah approved of my skepticism.

Neemah paused, then directed her gaze to the men in the room.

77

"Boys, please close the shutters and pull the curtains closed." Sloane, Mathias, and Brevan did as they were asked while Neemah sat in her chair and stared at me. "I have to admit, I expected one of you two to be skeptical, but I expected it from Sloane."

I shifted my gaze towards Sloane, who'd just finished closing the curtains in the kitchen window. "Neemah, Ami is just being cautious, and right now, I honestly can't honestly blame her. I have to confess she isn't the only one who has their fair share of skepticism." Sloane retook his seat next to me and squeezed my shoulder.

Once the cottage was dark, Neemah stood and lit some of the candles around the room. "Neemah, I'm all for mood lighting, but could you please explain what's going on?" I asked because I'd become even more confused.

When Neemah finished lighting the candles, she strolled over to one of the closed doors and knocked three times. "No, I cannot explain, but my guest can. You seem to not want to believe your great-grandmother, so, perhaps, you will believe someone who is not." Neemah sat back down, and the door opened. The man who stepped out was a complete shock.

"Lyros, what the hell are you doing here?" Stunned, my question came out a bit more like a demand for information rather than a request. He carried what appeared to be a framed painting covered by a drop-cloth.

Lyros strode over and rested the painting against the fireplace hearth. When he looked up at me, his face was sorrowful but also apologetic. "Amelia, I wanted to tell you sooner, but I figured the less you knew, the safer you were. Your mother was my oldest and dearest friend. I recognized you as her daughter the moment I laid eyes on you. You look just like her, only your hair is darker, and your eyes are a different color." Lyros paused and lifted the cloth off the painting. What I stared at was me, only it wasn't me. God, the woman in the painting could've been my twin.

"Lyros, this is the evilest joke anyone has ever played. I didn't think you were capable of something so cruel," I spouted off in anger. I liked

Lyros, and if Oren knew what he was doing, Oren and I would need to have some very harsh words.

Brevan glared at the image and I knew both he and Mathias felt the anger and hurt which ran through me. "Lyros, explain yourself at once!" Brevan demanded.

Sloane stood and walked over to the painting, knelt down, and examined it carefully. "Guys, this painting is old. I'm no art expert, but the cracks in the paint indicate age, or at least it does to my mind. There is also some patina and yellowing on it. I don't think it's a joke, Ami." Sloane's news abruptly ceased my anger, and it was instantly replaced with curiosity.

"Lyros, she's my mom?" sadness rang through my question.

"Yes, little one, she is. I painted it just before she and your father had their binding ceremony. It is one of the reasons why I was so insistent on doing your portrait. The other reason is, I am your godfather. Both yours and Sloane's, that is. I hoped Neemah and I would be able to ease you into the information, but the clock is ticking, and there has been some disturbing news." Lyros broke off and peered over at Brevan, then Mathias. "I hope you two have an excellent plan in place because, according to the Wood Nymphs, Melisandre is alive and being held prisoner by none other than Lycandra." When Lyros concluded, I felt elation, anger, and confusion all at the same time.

"Why would she keep our mother alive this whole time? I don't get it. Once Sloane and I were gone, we were out of her reach. What would've been the point? How did the Wood Nymphs hear about her being alive? Could they possibly be mistaken?" My head spun with just too many questions and not enough answers. Once Sloane deduced Lyros wasn't playing some kind of mean prank, and there was tangible proof Neemah was actually my great-grandmother, my brain automatically accepted her as family.

Neemah seemed satisfied we understood who and what she was, then tried to give me an explanation to my recent barrage of questions. "My only inference is somehow, Lycandra found out Melisandre is one of two keys who can open the hidden temple. For some reason, she needs access to the temple, which is frightening enough on its own. The temple is the magical nexus of the island." Neemah paused, put her finger to her chin, and thought a moment before she continued. "It could be plausible Lycandra, over the years, attempted and possibly succeeded in plotting out the labyrinth. Hmm... If she has successfully plotted the labyrinth and has the key, then there has to be some sort of astrological or magical event coming." Neemah rubbed at her temples. "Gods, I really am hating my old brain these days. I just do not remember what I used to."

Lyros placed his hand on her shoulder. "Neemah, you have done more than anyone could have hope for."

I stood and moved over to Neemah. When I reached her, I knelt down in front of her. "Neemah... Gran, I'm so sorry I didn't believe you. To be honest, I'm still having a hard time swallowing most of it." I was still struggling with how to address her. However, I was trying.

Neemah patted my cheek. "You are a good girl, and you are stubborn, just like me." She chuckled, "It is all right."

"Neemah, do you know the way through the labyrinth?" Brevan inquired, and I could tell he was thinking something by the tone of his voice.

"No, I have long since forgotten it." Neemah's answer made my heart drop, but the sly old healer wasn't finished. "I can do you one better, though. In the book Sloane holds, the very back is a map through the maze. It is hidden within the back of the book's cover between the stitched area."

"Brevan, don't you know the way?" I urged because it would've made sense to me.

"No, my little wolf. It is a secret only the Acolytes kept," Brevan explained.

"We also never allowed those with the map to be the keys," Neemah elaborated further. "That way, if one was taken, then the other was safe."

I contemplated for a moment and realized it was actually a good security precaution. The trouble was we held in our possession the map, but we didn't have a key. We were still missing too many pieces, and the clock was counting down to the full moon.

"Neemah, thank you for telling us what you know. I still feel like I need to pinch myself. You're actually my gran! And Lyros, you're our godfather. It's overwhelming!" A tear ran down my cheek. Family was everything to me, and here I was with two people who were family to both Sloane and me. I took another peek at the face on the painting and could swear the woman in the picture was giving me a knowing gaze. It was as though she knew one day I'd be seeing it. I made an important decision at that moment. If it was at all possible, I'd find a way to free her from Lycandra's hold.

"Brevan, Mathias, Sloane," I stood and continued. "I am speaking now as a member of the Council of Tenebris. I'm formally calling together the council. It's time we all got together and put our cards on the table. Tomorrow night we meet in the council hall and figure all this shit out. Every scrap of information, every whisper, every detail, we need to comb through and figure out what the hell is going on. It is also imperative that we come up with a strategy based on the note which was unceremoniously dropped off at our binding. We'll need maps as well, I think. Enough of this shit is enough."

Brevan stepped forward and stared into my eyes. "You've got that expression."

"What expression?" I questioned.

"The face you have when you are about to kick someone square in the ass." He replied, and the statement couldn't have been more acurate. I was going to make damn good and sure I did it with as much information as humanly or inhumanly possible.

"I suppose we better get the rest of those letters decoded then, Sis," Sloane commented, and he was right. He and I needed to get back to work.

"I agree. As soon as we get back to the house, I'll compose a letter to call the council together and—" Brevan cut me off before I could finish.

"I will call the council together. You need to focus on the decoding. Neemah, would you be amenable to joining us tomorrow night for the meeting? Your input would be most welcome. Lyros, you should explain to Oren your involvement in all of this before tomorrow. I am sure he will have a fair amount of questions for you." Brevan took charge and left me to gather the book of spells Neemah had given me.

We all moved to leave but not before I hugged Neemah and Lyros goodbye. I told each of them I would see them tomorrow night. Even though my head still swam with everything I'd just learned, I felt better with the knowledge I wasn't alone in this. Not anymore.

AMELIA (AMI) JANE GRAY

MYSTERY

$\mathcal{A}$s the group of us left Neemah's cottage, I noticed Aisling was hanging towards the back of our group. She'd remained unusually quiet while we were all being educated on the surprise linage that Sloane and I shared. Unaware of what was going on with her, I slowed my pace and walked alongside her.

"Aisling, you okay? You look pretty lost in thought here."

"I am fine. Just thinking." I'd never seen her so tight-lipped. Something was running around in her mind. I was just going to have to pry it out.

"Hey, talk to me." I nudged her with my elbow.

Aisling slightly turned her head to peer at me. "I understand why you made sure my brother and Brevan were there. Brevan is a council member like you, and Mathias is your advisor, but why me? It is not like I make any of the decisions or have any influence with the council or the pack."

I gently pulled her to a stop and yelled up to Mathias, "Mathias, you're fired. I'm taking your sister as my advisor."

Mathias yelled back to me, "Does that mean I do not need to show up for the council meeting tomorrow?"

I laughed, "Nope, you still have to go!"

83

Aisling playfully nudged me, and we chuckled together. "Seriously, Aisling, what's bothering you?"

"I am worried for the both of you, Amelia. You and Sloane. It seems as though every time we turn around, something else creeps up and we are running out of time before the full moon. I cannot stand the thought of something happening to either of you, especially due to some old, evil hag who is simply out for power."

"Aisling, what does your schedule look like for the rest of the evening?" I'd begun to have a brilliant idea and wanted to make sure I could get Aisling on board with it.

"Well, when we get back, I need to check on the children. Then, I am headed off to meet with Marta about the binding ceremony for Sloane and me, but afterwards, I am free. Why do you ask?" I'd piqued her curiosity.

"I've come up with a brilliant idea, if I do say so myself." I gazed over and winked at her. "Why don't you come help Sloane and me when you're done. Not only do we need to finish decoding those letters, but in my opinion, we need to put them into some kind of chronological order for any of it to make sense. Plus, I'd like to examine the items which were confiscated from Pack Lumen. Perhaps, I can find something everyone else missed. It's worth a shot anyway, and the more brains we have working the problem, the easier the work is."

Aisling gave me a huge smile at the idea I just presented to her. She appeared as though she liked my reasoning and confirmed as much when she agreed to come. I took her by the arm, and we talked the rest of the way back to the house. I started to see what it was about Aisling my brother fell in love with, and it made me glad they'd found each other.

Once we all reached the house, I waved at everyone and told them I was headed to the kitchen. My goal was to arrange to have meals delivered, so we wouldn't need to stop what we were working on. When I found Aoife in the kitchen, I gave her the abbreviated version of what was going on, and she confirmed it wouldn't be an issue to have the food brought up. We chatted a moment longer, and I hugged her as I left. I totally loved the fact I'd managed to make female friends in the pack.

The back stairwell was the fastest way up to our apartment and was right off the kitchen. As I made my way quickly up the stairs, I made a last-minute decision to take a small detour. I'd not seen Marta since the whole debacle began, the night of her unfortunate confession. I loved Marta and wished things turned out differently. I knocked lightly on her door and hoped I'd catch her while she was in. Luck was on my side as Marta answered and beamed a smile at me.

"Oh, my dear, it is lovely to see you," Marta greeted and gave me a warm embrace.

"Hello, Marta. I've missed you." It was the truth, and I felt a lump form in my throat.

She patted me on the back a couple of times and ushered me inside her room before the tears could start. The last thing I needed to do was find myself standing in the hallway crying.

Marta closed the door, and I scanned her room. It was the typical pack room with a few exceptions. There was a beautiful handmade quilt on her bed with bright colors, predominantly whites, yellows, and oranges. Her curtains were white with yellow rose buds, and on her nightstand was a vase filled with fresh flowers. The overall effect gave the room a bright, cheery feel.

"How have you been?" I'd grown a daughter-like affection for the woman who was concerned about my wellbeing. She was one of the first people I'd met in the pack, and her warmth was indelibly seared onto a piece of my heart.

"Oh, I have been keeping busy, and, now with Sloane and Aisling's binding ceremony coming up... well... it has given me something to do." She replied, but I could see the hurt which still laid between the words.

"Marta, I've actually come here for a reason. The first is, I really have missed seeing you each day. Somehow, it's just not the same without you in the kitchen or scolding Mathias for his shenanigans." She gave a soft chuckle at the mention of Mathias. "But I also wanted to ask you if you'd consider being a nanny for me. As you may or may not have heard, we're trying to have a baby and last week was my cycle, so there's a good chance I was able to conceive—"

Marta cut me off with a squeal and pulled me into a vice grip. "Oh, my sweet girl, of course, I will. You know I have helped to raise the orphaned children in the entire pack, including Aisling and Mathias. Oh, you have just made me so incredibly happy."

When she pulled back, there were tears of joy in her eyes. Who could ever possibly believe the woman in front of me possessed a mean streak in her body? I knew, with every fiber of my being, I made the right decision in this situation. Granted, I hadn't told Brevan and Mathias yet, but I knew deep down in my heart it would be one instance where I was sure they wouldn't mind. We all loved Marta, and while Brevan, as Alpha, had no choice but to remove her as head of the house, it certainly didn't mean she couldn't be our nanny.

After I'd finished talking with Marta, I continued my way upstairs until I reached our apartment. Inside, I noticed Brevan managed to squeeze behind his desk. Sloane was working on decoding the next letter and Mathias was reading the book related to my lineage. I set the book of spells down on the coffee table which was still pushed up against the wall and went to help Sloane with the letters.

As Sloane and I toiled away with the decoding, Aisling joined us and examined each letter carefully. "I agree, Amelia, I think we should attempt to put these in chronological order. You can tell which are the older ones versus the newer ones based on the wear and tear."

Sloane answered Aisling, "Good idea! You should start with the ones we've already done and fill in the blanks as we complete the remaining letters." Aisling nodded and got to work arranging the letters and translations carefully, making sure not to mix any of them up.

Brevan finished the letter to the council members and release himself from behind his desk. I looked up apologetically, and he shook his head. It was his way of letting me know what Sloane and I were working on was far more important than his comfort. On his way out of our apartment, he announced to everyone he would stop by the kitchen and have Aoife send up something for our supper.

What caught my attention, though, was when Brevan held up an individual letter and winked at me. I guessed it was the letter to Cedrik explaining they would like to induct Mathias into the Order of the Dragon. We were all doing our part in piecing together the mystery that laid before us.

Revelations were in abundance all day. There was still more to come as we toiled away at the puzzles before us. I didn't have a good feeling about any of this but knew, in my heart, it needed to be done. I just hoped the information revealed would be helpful.

AMELIA (AMI) JANE GRAY:

EVIDENCE

$\mathcal{M}$athias set the lineage book down and left it open to a specific page. He then picked up the spell book and began to search through it. Even though my entire focus should've been on what I was working on, Mathias' actions grabbed my attention.

"Mathias, what are you doing?" I couldn't help myself, as curiosity took hold.

"I am working on figuring out something. I cannot explain at the moment because I am not entirely sure I am correct, however, I will let you know once I have an understanding myself." Mathias explained, which was good enough for me.

I returned to decoding the letter I'd been working on when Brevan returned to our apartment. "The notices to the council members are on their way. I have got Cash and Riley delivering them. They were instructed to await confirmation before returning home." I nodded in understanding, as did Mathias, Sloane, and Aisling.

Brevan went to work assisting Aisling as they organized the letters while Sloane and I finished the last few left. Once we'd completed all twenty letters, we discerned that they fell in order as follows:

1. It will take place at the Equinox.

2. We need the heir to the Alpha.

3. A sacrifice of the innocents is required.

4. The Queen has found what she was looking for.

5. We will soon rule, patience.

6. Send him a proposal of unity.

7. Will the six be ready?

8. Bring two girls on each of the full moons!

9. The time is near.

10. I have been called to Queen Cosima's court.

11. The sacrifice will be on the next super moon.

12. Has your brother responded?

13. Humans have been found in the Northern Sea.

14. Jakkel has returned home.

15. Bring the humans here! Do Not Fail!

16. They must not bind! You must stop them.

17. The Queen sensed old magic.

18. Kill all except the boy and girl!

19. Use the alchemist.

20. The Queen's Sylph has found a new puppet.

As I read them over, I found my eyes locked on the first two along with numbers seven and eight. I connected a few dots and realization dawned on me. Nausea hit and I ran to the bathing chamber. Immediately, I locked the door behind me and knelt in front of the only place I could safely allow myself to be. Every last morsel that was in my stomach wound up in the toilet. Those poor girls were impregnated with Brevan's babies and they were going to be used as sacrifices. I was utterly disgusted at the thought, angry at Brevan for what he'd allowed to happen and scared to death for the missing six girls.

A knock came at the door, "Amelia, let me in, my little wolf."

"Go away, Brevan. I don't want to see you right now!"

"Please, Amelia, do not do this."

"GO. AWAY!"

While I used a cloth which I soaked in water to clean up my face, a fist slammed into the door. I held onto the washstand to make sure my stomach wasn't going to send me back to kneeling in front of the toilet again. I knew who stood on the other side of the door, and there was no way I could face him in my present state. If I did, I wouldn't be responsible for my actions.

I heard Mathias' voice. "Brevan, give her some time… Aisling, go get Emmer. NOW!" I heard the door to the apartment open and close before Mathias continued.

"Brevan, calm yourself. We are family, and she knows this. Brevan, brother, DO NOT DO IT! SHIT! AMELIA, STAND BACK!" The warning from Mathias came a second before Brevan kicked open the door to the bathing chamber.

My magic went into self-defense mode, and I was covered in what looked like blue flames. If Brevan wanted a fight he was going to get one. The look on Brevan's face was pure fury and it was absolutely my cue to finish this before it even started. I pushed two balls of magic into my hand and tossed one right after the other at his chest. They'd knocked him out of the door frame and allowed me to exit the room.

"Amelia, where do you think you are going?" Brevan growled at me.

I spun and glared at Brevan directly into his eyes. "Anywhere but here!"

Emmer burst into the room and saw the stalemate which was taking place.

"What, in the name of the Gods, is going on? Why is Amelia all blue? What the hell, Brevan? Why do you look as though you want to rip someone's head off?" Emmer asked and stared at the two of us for an answer. It was Mathias who filled him in on what was going on as I didn't flinch from my stance.

Sloane came to stand next to me. "Ami, I love you, and I've got your back, but nothing is going to be resolved if one of you doesn't calm the fuck down."

"You want me to calm the fuck down? I'll calm the fuck down when our precious Alpha, explains how the hell six very young women wound up pregnant with his children, and he never bothered to mentioned it. Oh wait, I know. He's using the good ol' line of, *I swear I don't remember*, which is the lamest excuse on the planet. Or, how about, *They meant nothing to me,* which is even worse. Go ahead, Brevan, explain to me how the six missing girls from YOUR pack wound up impregnated with your seed. The evidence is as bold as bold can be!" I only paused a moment because I wasn't even close to being finished. I just needed to take a breath.

"What's even worse, is all those unborn children are going to be used as sacrifices. Sacrifices that are apparently going to be done on the next full moon because that's when the super moon is. So, no offense, Sloane, I love you too but telling me to calm the fuck down!" I shook my head. "It isn't going to happen." I glared even harder at Brevan, if that was even possible, as my anger rolled off of me. "When I said I didn't want to see you, I meant it, Brevan. What's the matter? No one ever told you NO before? Newsflash, Alpha! This girl not only told you NO, she just told you how much of a NO it was. So, DEAL with it!"

The silence in the room was deafening. When no one moved or spoke, I turned and stormed out of the apartment. I managed to get halfway down the hall before Mathias caught up with me. He didn't say a word. He simply just walked along beside me. I descended the back stairs, marched through the kitchen, and out to the back garden. There I finally stopped and freed the scream I'd been holding back. In doing so, I released the magic I'd built up over my skin. In the sky above me, the shape of a blue magical dragon appeared.

I collapsed onto the grass, and Mathias sank down next to me. He pulled me into his lap, and as he did, the magical dragon swooped down, creating a circle of blue flames around the two of us, and slowly dissipated. I wept on Mathias' shoulder as my heart broke. He just held and rocked me in his arms without saying a word. I didn't need or want any platitudes or words of condolence. Simply and plainly, I just needed a good damn cry. I cried to release what was left of my anger. I cried for the missing girls. I cried in fear of not being able to stop their nightmare. Most of all, I cried because I knew in my heart, above all else, I'd just deeply hurt a man who loved me more than anything he'd ever cared about before.

As my tears slowed, the circle of blue fire died down around us.

Mathias coaxed me back into a standing position. He cupped my face in his warm hands and wiped the remainder of my tears away with his thumbs. I gazed into his face, and all I saw there was warmth and love. Mathias held no judgement towards me, and for that, I was grateful.

Suddenly, from out of the sky, General Pax swooped down and landed beside me. "M'lady, is everything alright here? I saw the magic in the sky and became concerned you all might be in some sort of trouble." General Pax studied my face, "Are you hurt? Is Lord Brevan alright?"

Mathias spoke, so I didn't have to, "General Pax, I do not believe we have been formally introduced. I am Amelia's other mate, Mathias." Mathias released my face and extended his hand to General Pax, who took it. "My sincere apologies for worrying you. It honestly is a matter of a more personal nature and nothing for the honored guard of Tenebris to worry about."

General Pax nodded in understanding. "My apologies then, M'lady. We have begun to monitor the skies ever since the incident with Jakkel and Lycandra. Should you find yourself in trouble, we will respond to your signal. M'lady, take a piece of advice from an old man. Whatever it is that has you in such a state, take heart in knowing those who love you will continue to do so regardless. The heart has a miraculous way of forgiving. One day when you are ready to hear it, I will tell you my tale, but for now, I bid you farewell." General Pax bowed and shot up into the sky.

Mathias moved to my side and placed his arm around my back. "Let us go for a walk, my love. When you are ready, we can talk." I let Mathias guide me into the pack's private garden. It was a place of peace and harmony amongst nature and a place for one to reflect. At the moment, what I needed was peace and quiet.

MATHIAS:

MY AMELIA

I placed my arm around Amelia's back and led her to the garden. The sun was beginning to sit on the horizon, and there was a special place I needed to show her. Sure, I wanted nothing more than to whisk her away and take away the pain she felt, but it was just something I simply could not and would not do, especially since I understood it all too well.

She probably did not realize it, but Amelia changed Brevan fundamentally. In the months previous to her arrival on our island, Brevan started to go downhill. More and more, Emmer was summoned to go collect Brevan from one place or another. However, the current problem at hand was not about trying to figure out what in the name of the Gods happened with Brevan. It was all about giving my Amelia a moment of peace, so she could collect her thoughts.

I guided her to the very back of the garden under the weeping willow which dominated the space. After I released her waist, I took a seat and leaned against the trunk of the tree. Next to me, I patted the ground to signal for her to have a seat.

"Mathias, what are we doing here?" Amelia's question was filled with sadness.

"We are here, waiting. There is something I would like for you to see." I patted the ground again, and Amelia took the seat next to me.

Amelia sidled up against me and rested her head on my shoulder. While we waited, I felt her pain ease with each moment as the seconds passed. Neither of us spoke because words were not needed. She knew I loved her more than my own life. I would do anything for my Amelia, and that included taking on our own Alpha if I needed to. Did I relish the thought of potentially destroying the family we created? No! Family meant everything to me, but Amelia meant that much more.

It was then, the time when the light of day just barely kissed the dark of night. The time of day, when the stars shone brightly one by one in the new night sky, as they began to appear. Around us, small light began to flicker and dance. I nudged Amelia with my shoulder, "Sweetheart, look," I whispered.

Amelia picked her head up off my shoulder, and her eyes became wide. "Fireflies?" She turned her head as she asked her question in an excited whisper. I nodded and pulled her into my lap. Gradually more and more of her 'Fireflies' appeared and played within the leaves of the willow. It was a show of dancing lights within the curtain of the drooping branches surrounding us. At one point, Amelia held out her hand and allowed them to land on her palm. As they did, I felt her heart lift just a little bit more.

Once she released them to fly back with their friends, Amelia turned and straddled my legs. Slowly she leaned in and kissed me with a fevered desperation that I felt all the way to my manhood. I did not want to stop, but angry sex was not what this was about. Gently with my hands on her arms, I pushed her back.

"Amelia, we do not have to do this. I brought you here to help ease your pain, not take advantage of your saddened state."

"Please, Mathias, make love to me. I need you to make love to me, so hard I forget even my name." She pleaded with an intense sadness.

I stared into her depthless eyes and lost all resolve. With her words, I could deny her nothing, nor did I wish to. She reached around my neck, and with her fingertips, she began to stroke the back of my neck. I found myself hard with the desire to please my mate. I pulled her back down to me, our lips crashed together, and our tongues danced in their own seductive rhythm. As I slid my hands underneath her top, I felt the soft-fevered skin of her womanly curves.

Amelia moaned into my mouth as I caressed her stomach and moved up to her ample mounds. I felt her hard nipples protrude through the fabric of her undergarment. I pinched and flicked with the attention each one warranted and deserved. She began to grind her center against my stiffened desire.

In one swift move, I lifted her off my lap and laid her on the soft, fresh grass surrounding the two of us. I wrenched my shirt off over my head, and my love followed my movement, exposing her perfect upper half to me. Amelia's milky white skin drew me in with the seduction of her utterly aroused scent.

I kissed and licked my way up her stomach to her perfectly shaped breasts. With one hand, I managed to undo the clasp and freed them from their binds. Each flawlessly formed globe fit perfectly into my hands. I licked, suckled, and nibbled their pointed peaks, and with each movement, Amelia's breathing hastened.

I completely indulged myself in taking my time as I worked my way over every delicious curve. It may have been selfish, but at the moment, I did not care. What I cared about was pleasuring my mate, my love, my life. I went in for one more lust-filled kiss and was not disappointed as Amelia kissed me back with as much feeling as I gave to her.

Because, I previously learned every spot on my woman's body to bring her pleasure, I put my knowledge to good use as I left her plump, luscious lips, and worked my way back down her body. I placed my hand between her legs and could feel her heated arousal through her clothing. As I rubbed at her sex with the palm of my hand, Amelia lifted her eyes to eagerly gaze at me.

"Mathias, please," she panted out breathlessly.

Without a care for the material, I tore away the obstruction that laid between me and the jewel I sought. As I hungrily gazed upon her beautifully sweet spot of sexual pleasure, my own arousal grew even harder. I was so stiff, it was painful to leave it within the confines of my own clothing, but my release was only secondary to the need I felt coming from my mate. I kissed and licked her inner thigh as I worked to free myself.

Once I released myself, I moved to the oasis that was calling my name so melodiously. I inhaled the intoxicating perfume of Amelia's womanhood, and it was more than I could stand. I found her sexual piercing and teased it with my tongue, sending pleasure waves throughout her entire body as she arched her back in response. I licked and suckled her love-bud as I brought her to the edge of orgasm. Before she fell over the edge of oblivion, I would pull back and slow my ministrations. She tasted far too sweet for me to allow her to find her own release quickly.

Gently, I slid my two fingers into her center and found the spot inside that drove her to wild abandon. As I bent and flexed my fingers, Amelia's passioned cries grew louder, and she thrust her fingers into the earth to hold on. Slowly, I brought her back down for the second time.

"Mathias, I need you inside me now."

I flipped her over as she maneuvered herself onto her hands and knees. When I placed myself at her entrance, I thrust inside and grabbed onto her hips. Oh, she was so ready for me. Every ounce of wetness slicked my thick, hard, throbbing member. With each movement in and out of her center, it began to clench around me and tightened her grip with her expounding arousal. I reached around with my hand, flicked her hard nub, and she rewarded me with her cries of rapture.

We made love in nature, and nature took hold to push forward our wolves. My teeth elongated and sharpened as Amelia's back and neck arched. She wanted this from me, and as we climaxed in the same moment, I sunk my teeth into her soft flesh. Her body shook against mine as we found our release and crumpled onto the soft earthen bed beneath us.

The bite I gave her was far more profound than my initial claiming of her, and my wolf refused to let go. It took some coaxing from my human half to release the bite, but when it did, I licked the wound clean. I felt Amelia deep in my soul. She was a fundamental part of me. Our bond went far beyond the usual mating bond. When she gave me her blood to save my life, it changed my connection to her. Yes, we could feel when each other was happy or sad through our emotional tie, but on top of that, I always knew where she was.

As we laid in the soft grass, even though I was completely spent, I remained inside her while I held Amelia in my arms. Our time in the garden calmed her. Even though I could tell she still held anger in her heart towards Brevan, at the moment, she felt loved.

"Mathias, I have to go talk to him. Don't I?" Amelia's question was merely rhetorical.

"You know the answer to what you seek. I do not think you need me to tell you what you should do. However, if you asked, I would stand by your side. I believe we both deserve an explanation."

"What I said was so absolutely horrible. How do I even face him?" She inhaled sharply, "I'm not sure I can."

"My sweet Amelia, do you remember what General Pax said?" She turned her head to look at me. "He said the heart has a miraculous way of forgiving. Brevan will forgive you for your words, but you need to give him a chance to explain. I am not defending him whatsoever, but you did not know him before he met you. The pack was growing increasingly concerned about his wellbeing. On more than one occasion, Emmer was summoned into town to collect Brevan from different inns due to his excessively inebriated state. It would take him days to recover, then he would be fine for a while until the next time it happened. You, my love, changed everything. He does love you, of this, I am certain."

Amelia sighed, "Alright, I suppose sooner is better than later. Let's get it over with."

I laughed, "There is my girl, only we have one problem. I sort of shredded your pants." My words caused her to giggle hysterically, and I laughed along with her. It felt good to have a smile back on Amelia's face.

LORD BREVAN:

IT IS NOT POSSIBLE

$\mathcal{I}$ was frozen in place. Amelia's ire towards me was unlike anything I ever felt come from her before. The words she spewed tore my heart in half. If it were just anger, I would have been able to deal with it, but it was so much more. It was her disappointment and disgust, which rattled me right to my very core. Every last drop of those raw emotions was for something I held no knowledge of doing.

She just stormed out of our apartment. Mathias only spared me the smallest of glances before he left to follow after her. I stood there, faced with three people I would rather not harm, but they were the barricade between myself and my mate. Emmer, Sloane, and Aisling lined up shoulder to shoulder in front of me and my exit.

"Emmer, move. NOW!" it was a guttural command.

"I cannot do as you demand, Brevan." Emmer never denied a command from me before.

I was not going to ask again and moved to step forward when Sloane cast the spell, "Naur rind."

Flames spewed forth from the palms of his hands and encircled me. The fire ring prevented my forward movement.

"How dare you defy your Alpha?"

98

"Brevan, look, it's not as if we're defying you. It's more like we are giving both you and Ami a chance to cool off. Especially Ami. Right now, she's extremely upset, and you forcing the issue with her isn't going to help. I know what she said must've hurt like fuck but come on, man, see reason on this one." Sloane spoke hurriedly. He no more wanted to hold me there than see his sister so despondent.

"Brevan, brother. I need you to get your head screwed on because we need to figure everything out. This way, you can possibly provide Amelia with a reasonable explanation. One that she could live with, because right now," Emmer shook his head, "she is far too hurt to see anything but the pain. Take it from someone who has a mate as strong-willed as your Amelia. She loves you, my friend. Just give her the time she needs."

From down on the lawn out in the back of the house, I heard a scream so wretchedly heartbreaking, I knew it was Amelia. Instantly, Sloane released the fire ring, and I moved to open the glass doors to our balcony. Emmer, Sloane, and I stood there while we observed the streaks of blue magic as they flew up into the sky to form a dragon. I peered down and watched as Amelia collapsed onto the ground weeping with her head in her hands. Mathias moved in behind her and cradled her in his arms just before the dragon swooped down, encircling the pair of them in blue magic before it disappeared into the ether.

Without another word, I backed into the apartment, moved to the sofa, sank down, and placed my own head in my hands. I felt the pain running through Amelia, and even worse, I knew I caused it. Emmer and Sloane were correct. I needed to allow her the space she required. As much as I wanted to erase everything causing her pain and unhappiness, this time, I could not.

"Note to self; don't ever piss off my sister," Sloane spoke to no one in particular, but he was correct nonetheless.

A small soft hand was placed on my shoulder, and an ever softer voice whispered to me. "It will be alright, Brevan."

I gazed up into the sympathetic eyes of Aisling. "How can you be certain?"

"Because I know you, Brevan, and I know Amelia. The pair of you are strong, stubborn, and unreasonable at times, but you both also have the largest hearts of anyone in the pack. Besides, I have a thought about all of this." Aisling held an expression on her face and in her eyes as though she remembered something.

"What have you recalled neither Emmer nor I could remember?" I inquired, genuinely intrigued.

"Well, if you factor in the missing girls and their due dates. Making the logical assumption, their actual due date is the next full moon; it would mean the conception of those children was six months ago. Do you know where you were roughly six months ago?" I shook my head because I, in all honesty, could not remember anything that would create the situation causing six separate pregnancies.

"Brevan, you were at Pack Lumen for the Spring Equinox festivities. Well, you and half the pack were there. I wound up staying behind with Aoife and Naima to look after the children. When the rest of the pack returned home, you, Cash, and Liam did not. Mathias and Emmer went to collect you three the next morning."

I stared at Aisling in disbelief, "How do you remember so far back? I have no recollections of these events."

Aisling threw me an exaggerated smirk I knew Amelia would have given me, "Brevan, I have a unique gift of my own. It is not just Sloane and Amelia who can perform unique things around here. I remember everything."

Sloane gawked at Aisling. "Everything?"

Aisling nodded, "Everything. Everything I read, see, and hear."

Sloane whistled, "You have an eidetic memory. You're pretty impressive. Although, I suppose I shouldn't expect anything less. You're amazing, even without it."

Emmer snorted, Aisling giggled, and I used Amelia's trademark eye-roll. That stunning woman of mine absolutely made an impression on me. I redirected the conversation back to what Aisling could remember.

"Aisling, why would you even bother to remember something so bleak? Back then, I was coming home blind drunk every other night.

Those were such dark days for me," I reminded the woman who stood before me.

Aisling returned my previous eye-roll. "Mathias made it a point to mention to me the alchemist from Lady Nova's coven was there when he and Emmer went to get the three of you. He told me, and I am actually quoting, *'It was strange because the vampyr skulked off out the back as we entered the house. It was almost as though he did not wish to be seen.'* " Aisling paused and took a breath. "Brevan, do you not see? You may not be solely responsible for all six if my calculations are correct. In truth, you were not mentally responsible regardless."

Emmer followed Aisling's thought process clearly. "Aisling, do you realize what it is you are implying?"

She nodded in affirmation. "Yes, look at what we know. First are the decoded letters." Aisling moved to where they were arranged in order and began to shuffle them around. "We numbered them one through twenty. However, what if the order is incorrect? What if the first one is actually, *I have been called to Queen Cosima's court.* Next, *The Queen has found what she was looking for.* Followed by, *The time is near.* Then, what if we put letters six, one, seven, three, two and twelve in the middle of these letters? If those are correct, it leads me to my next point; the timeline. The Spring Equinox was six months ago, and a werewolf pregnancy takes six months. Then there is the alchemist's involvement, which we already know about because of the incident at the merchant market. The icing on the cake was the conversation I had with the dad of one of my daycare kids. Grady and his parents were some of the refugees from Pack Lumen. I know you are not aware of it, but his father was talking more openly with me the other day when he came to retrieve his son. He told me those girls were worshiped by Aerin's trusted guards. I do not believe all of those children are to be sacrificed. The decoded letter does say *A sacrifice of the innocence.* I am merely connecting the dots, but what if that means the mother's innocence. It could be taken either way."

I truly underestimated Aisling, just as Amelia implied. The women of my pack were forces to be reckoned with all on their own. Ever since Amelia's influence, each of them constantly surprised me more and more every day.

Emmer interrupted my train of thought. "Aisling, if you are correct, Liam and Cash may also be responsible for some of those children." Aisling gave a single head nod in agreement.

"And here I was thinking I was the one good at puzzles. Sweetheart, you're amazing." Sloane walked over and kissed Aisling on the cheek, then froze.

"Shit! Shit, shit, shit... I'm such an idiot!" Sloane started to ramble and pace. "If only I possessed your memory. Think, damn it. Think."

"Sloane, brother, what is it?" Emmer questioned as I was still far too enraged with myself.

"I read it or heard it. Everything is beginning to fit together, and I can almost see it." Sloane stopped his pacing and snapped his fingers. "I heard it. I heard it from Cedrik and Astraea. The night Ami and I were summoned to their home. They read us a prophecy about Ami and I. Boy, Ami's right. We need to put all of these people and pieces together." Sloane started to pace some more.

"I am going to send additional word to the council members. We need everything, and I do mean everything. No more hiding bits and pieces. For the sake of our families, we have got to figure it all out before the full moon, and secrets are what has held us back. Perhaps, I will deliver the messages myself," Emmer growled. He was equally frustrated with everything as well. "And I think I will make a special stop at Lady Nova's home." His statement was barely audible.

"Emmer, do not do anything rash," I voiced as he headed for the door.

"You know me, Brother," Emmer retorted.

"Absolutely, it is exactly what I am afraid of," I quipped as he exited through the door.

In truth, I did not have any right to talk. I highly doubted Amelia would have recognized me six months ago, and it was Emmer who held my pack together back in those days. If it were not for him and his leadership abilities, I profoundly suspected I would not have had a pack to return to. I owed Emmer far more than he realized.

Aisling left only for a few moments to collect the other documents we retrieved from my sister's pack. It was true. I needed to make sure I was able to give Amelia the best explanation I could. She not only deserved that much, but she earned so much more.

This time, I thoroughly examined every small detail of the Pack Lumen's documents instead of simply glancing through them. Some of what I discovered began to support Aisling's theory, which was starting to appear less like theory and more like fact. Anything that appeared to be supporting evidence, the three of us sorted into distinct piles and arranged with the corresponding decoded letter.

"Brevan?" Aisling queried.

"Yes, what is it?" I replied and gave her my full attention. She definitely earned it on this night.

"I am not sure I should mention it, but I do not think you remember." She chewed her bottom lip.

"What is it, Aisling?" I saw the concerned look in her eyes.

"It is Cash's wife, Naima. Do you remember where she is from?" Aisling questioned, and comprehension dawned on me.

"I do now." It was all I needed to say as Aisling nodded and returned to her work.

As we continued to sort through the remaining documents, my mind wandered. It may have been possible I fathered two of those children but what was not possible and what I would not allow was the loss of my true mate. I would earn back her respect if it was the last thing I did.

EMMER

TIME FOR TRUTH

I left Brevan's apartment and went directly to find my mate. Aoife was often running between the kitchen, making sure the house staff was doing what they were supposed to, and tending to our children. At the moment, she was seeing to our daughter, Laura. . Apparently, Laura and one of the newer pack children played slightly rougher than wished for, which caused Laura to fall and cut herself.

"Mommy, Grady did not mean it. It was an accibent," Laura declared with a serious expression upon her young face.

"I know, my sweet girl, and the word is accident," Aoife reassured her while correcting her mispronounced word.

"How are my two best girls?" I asked as I entered the room. Laura jumped down from her seat, ran over to me, and leapt directly into my arms.

"Daddy! Grady and I were playing today. He has some of the best games." She started and then proceeded to tell me about what they played and how she fell and cut her knee. Laura promptly pointed out the wound and told me, "It did not really hurt. I just pretended I was brave like Ami."

"You are such a good girl. You keep staying brave, and I have a

104

feeling one day you will wind up being one of her shield maidens." Those words caused her to beam up at me.

"Did you hear what Daddy said, Mommy? I am going to be a shield maid," Laura excitedly professed.

"I did, sweet girl, but you also know what that means, right?" Aoife smiled at her as she shook her head. "It means you need to work hard and train with the other shield maidens."

I set Laura down, and she placed her little hand on her hip before she responded to Aoife, "Mommy, I am still too little to do all those things. Can I go play now?"

"Alright, but no more roughhousing. Tell Grady... Oh, never mind, go have fun." Aoife laughed and shook her head as Laura ran out of the door, waving.

Thanks to the daycare, there were always two adult females to watch the older children as they played, and the children knew not to wander from the area of the packhouse. It freed up the rest of the adults to tend to the matters which needed to be taken care of. Amelia's ideas for the pack have not only made things more efficient, but the pack members were happier because they bound us together as more of a family and less as the individual society, we had become.

"Well, not that I do not love seeing you in the middle of the day, but..." Aoife wrapped her arms around my waist and let her sentence fall away.

"You know me far too well." I kissed her nose and held her in return.

"Emmer, what is going on?"

"Certain things have come to light, and they involve the alchemist from Lady Nova's coven. Somehow, I find it very difficult to believe Lady Nova knew nothing. She is one of the most powerful telepaths on the island, if not the most powerful one. I also find it terribly coincidental she managed to survive the slaughter of the Acolytes. Not to mention, how did the Alfar even know what was happening that night without inside information? Something does not add up. However, more and more evidence points to her as being involved. She knows more than she is letting on.

"Emmer, you need to be careful with what you are implying. Lady Nova is not one to be trifled with," Aoife warned.

"I know, my love, but Brevan and Amelia refuse to even see the possibility she may be involved. Brevan is also being blamed for impregnating the six girls who were taken from us, and Amelia is rightfully disgusted with the entire situation. For crying out loud, Brevan is Laura's godfather. You and I know he would never willingly do anything so awful even in his darkest days." I released my mate and ran a hand through my hair in frustration.

"Is Amelia okay?" Aoife inquired, concern lacing her voice as I shook my head. Suddenly I heard Amelia scream, causing Aoife and me to run to the back window of our apartment.

We watched as Amelia unleashed her magic in one powerful emotional burst. She created a similar magical dragon to the one she'd made the first night she became a wolf. Aoife and I shielded our eyes from the light as we contemplated the events unfolding.

"Aoife, I believe it would be wise to bring everyone inside and allow her the full use of the grounds. Then, I am heading off to Lady Nova's estate. Enough of the pain and sorrow. It is all too much!"

Aoife and I quickly rounded everyone up from outside and made sure all the children were in the daycare room. After my mate and I completed our task, I kissed her goodbye and headed out the door.

I rode on horseback over to Lady Nova's estate. I was counting on the fact it was not nightfall. Hopefully, the daylight would allow me the element of surprise, and I would be able to catch her off guard.

As I approached the front door, I was greeted by one of the human household staff. "Sir Emmer, may I ask what brings you here during the time the sun is still out?"

"You may ask, but it does not mean I will answer," I replied. "I am coming in! Get your mistress, and do not delay!" I sternly made my request.

I pushed my way inside, and the staff member grudgingly escorted me to Lady Nova's private study. He then rushed off to awaken his mistress. At least he was smart enough to realize I was not in the mood for any nonsense.

Lady Nova appeared a couple of moments later. She was wearing her dressing gown, and her hair was mostly disheveled due to her half-awake state. "Emmer, what in the name of the Gods are you doing here at this hour? Whatever you needed to say could not wait until the council meeting?"

I did not hesitate but moved with as much speed as I could muster as I pinned Lady Nova against the wall. "You may have Brevan and Amelia fooled, but not me. All of our trouble go back to when Sloane and Amelia were sent through the portal. You miraculously survived when all the others were slaughtered. How is it you suddenly needed to leave while your sisters were left to be murdered? Why is it you were conveniently not there when my brothers fell, including Brevan's father?" I paused and reasserted my strength over her. "How is it your alchemist was intertwined in all this deception, and you knew nothing about it? The others might not wish to see all the lies, but I am not so blind."

Unbeknownst to me, Nova and I were not alone. Declan and Jacqueline followed her to the library and were there while I hurdled my questions at her. I released my hold on Nova as she glanced at the stunned faces standing just inside the room. From where I stood, it was more their reactions and less my forcefulness that caused her to slump in defeat.

"Yes, Nova. Please explain because Emmer is making some very valid points," Declan surprisingly declared.

"Nova, what's he talking about? Tell him he's got it all wrong," Jacqueline pleaded.

With the saddest eyes I had ever seen on her, she answered her two lovers. "I cannot. He is right to be asking these things of me," Nova peered over at me and continued. "I must admit I am somewhat surprised it was you who figured out the holes in my story, but you must allow me a chance to explain. Not everything is what it appears."

"You have thirty seconds to start talking, or I haul you off to General Pax, where you can sit in a cozy cell with your alchemist," I warned. The full matter needed to come to light regardless of who she was on the council.

"Most of what I explained the night of Amelia's initiation was true. I did leave in a hurry because I needed to attend to coven business. I left my female companion at the temple. She was amongst those who were killed that dreadful night. The coven business I was attending to was the release of my male companion. Lycandra swore she would return him to me once I left a trail clear enough for them to follow into the temple," Nova stopped and sarcastically chuckled. "She was true to her word, Lycandra returned him but..."

"Nova, what did you do?" Jacqueline pressed as she stood there with her arms crossed.

"I did what I had to! I told Lycandra I marked the way in and carried James home. I do not think I need to tell you all, he did not survive. Lycandra and her wolves dumped him at my feet, and I carried him back here by myself. He only lived until we reached my estate. I held him as he passed into the great beyond, it was then I returned to the temple, but I was too late. Everyone was already dead, and the portal was closed."

Slowly I stalked my prey. She backed against the wall with fear in her eyes. It took every ounce of self-control to keep my wolf at bay. "You have known the entire time that Lycandra was behind everything. AND. YOU. SAID. NOTHING!" I growled out as she vehemently shook her head.

"I swear I did not. I suspected but held no proof, and I could not say anything without incriminating myself in past events. I tried to help when I could. After the explosion, I instructed Amelia on the laws of our people and her right to challenge at their trial." Nova pointed to Jacqueline. "It was I who read their thoughts and knew how to guide the questioning. I have been quietly attempting to atone for my guilt ever since the night I lost my sisters and my loves."

Declan carefully approached me and placed a hand upon my shoulder. When he spoke, he directed his words not towards me but to Nova. "Did you know the alchemist was involved? Answer truthfully because I will know if you lie."

"Declan, I did not know of his involvement until the day Brevan came here with his suspicions. He was taking an elixir to hide his mind while around me. It is why I was never able to clearly read him."

I glanced over towards Declan, and he nodded his affirmation. Nova was telling the truth. As I backed off, Declan took my place in front of Nova, "You WILL explain absolutely everything at the council meeting. If you do not, I WILL! I am giving you this opportunity for two reasons. First is because you are a member of the council, and out of respect for the position you hold, you should have the opportunity to come clean. Secondly is your friendship with Brevan. He deserves to hear the truth from you, someone he has trusted for many years."

I spun and headed for the door. "Do not worry, I will see myself out!" Once I was in the hallway, my paced quickened until Jacqueline halted me.

"Emmer, is Ami okay?"

It was not the fault of the young lady in front of me whose lover was mixed up in the island's misdoings. She was also an excellent friend to Amelia, and her concern was genuine.

"No, she is distraught and could use her friends, but you know her temper as well as anyone. Give her some time to simmer down. She will need you at the council meeting. I suggest to you, it does not matter what Nova says, you should come regardless."

Jacqueline reached over and squeezed my arm in understanding, "I wouldn't miss it for the world. It's time the truth finally came out. The good, the bad, and everything in between."

On Jacqueline's last words, I left the estate and returned to the packhouse. There was a pack to run and matters to attend to before I could return to my family.

AMELIA (AMI) JANE GRAY

UNDERSTANDING

$\mathcal{M}$athias and I left the private garden and made our way back up to the apartment. He'd given me his shirt, which fell to mid-thigh, in order for me to cover my modesty. . While my mood had considerably improved, I was still upset at Brevan for his lack of judgement. Part of me began to understand some of how it could've happened, but with six women impregnated, he was completely speechless. I could feel the guilt washing off him when I'd confronted him.

We made it to the second floor of the packhouse when Mathias pulled me aside. "Amelia, you need to give him a chance to explain. Neither you or I know how nor when it could have happened."

"Mathias, I think the how is pretty self-explanatory, don't you?" I sarcastically retorted.

"Do you really believe Brevan would have slept with six women and managed to retain no recollection of doing so? I have a very strong suspicion something else happened, at least to some degree." Mathias shot back. *Damn it!* I hated the fact, deep down, I knew he was right. .

"Fine, I will listen to his explanation. But so help me, if he even comes out with the excuse of *I was drunk* at any point, I will probably

110

lose my shit. Having worked in a bar, I've heard those same words from so many of the *guys,* as they would recall the previous night's booty call," I warned and Mathias actually rolled his eyes at me.

"What is a booty call?" Mathias questioned, and it caused me to chuckle.

"I'll explain it later, and don't make me laugh. You did it on purpose, and you know it too," I playfully scolded him.

"Come on the, let us get this over with," Mathias gave me a sweet, chaste kiss on the cheek and nudged me onwards.

We finished climbing the stairs, and just as we were about to enter our apartment, I heard raised voices through the closed door. One was Brevan, and the other one was Aisling, to my surprise. The two clear words I understood were 'alchemist' and 'girls'. My only thought was, *what the heck* as Mathias and I entered the apartment.

As we entered the apartment all conversation ceased. Mathias closed the door, and I stepped in front of Brevan. Suddenly, I realized I was standing there without any pants. Thank goodness my shirt was long enough to cover my modesty. It made it difficult to come off as indignant, so I went for slightly irritated with a smidge of impatience.

"I won't guarantee my reaction will be any better than before. But at least for the moment, I'm willing to listen, so you better make it good," I warned before he could even utter a word.

Before Brevan was even able to speak, Aisling interjected, "Amelia, I think we might have placed the order of the letters incorrectly." My head swiveled over to her.

"Show me, please," I replied, and she brought me over to view their new arrangement.

As Aisling explained the reason for the new order, she also explained the time line and the festival of the Spring Equinox. She included the other bits of information they'd been able to piece together in my absence.

"We were just discussing the possibility of the girls not fully understanding what happened to them when you two walked in," Sloane interjected. "It's entirely conceivable they could've been drugged just as Brevan was. We won't know for sure until we're able to question the alchemist. Emmer's headed over to Lady Nova's to see if he can find out any different information." He concluded before he resumed his duties of scanning through the documents.

Finally, Brevan stood and came over to me. When he reached where I was standing, he dropped down to his knees. "I swear to you I have no memory of what happened for most of that night. You need to understand I was a different man back in those days. The drink was my only comfort, and I know it is no excuse, but it is the truth." He desperately stared at me with the eyes of a man pleading forgiveness.

If I was being completely honest with myself, I couldn't possibly hold him responsible for circumstances, which, based on what Sloane just said, were out of his control. Not only that, but I wasn't even in his life back then. So, what right did I have to be angry with him, especially when he'd just admitted he was a different man before I came along? I took a half step forward and wrapped my arms around him as he pressed his head into my stomach and pulled me into his arms. As I thought through all the evidence I'd been presented with, Brevan was as much a victim as the girls were. As I let go of the remnants of my anger, one final tear fell. On that tear, I made a silent promise to myself I would put an end to all of the madness once and for all.

Mathias kissed my temple and moved to the corner seat of the couch. He picked up the two large books we'd taken back with us from our visit to Neemah's cottage. He looked like he was a man on a mission. I was content to allow him his time to figure out whatever it was he attempted to piece together earlier.

Brevan let out a jagged breath and dared to gaze up at me again. "Brevan, you do realize, even if I get completely irate with you, it won't change the fact I absolutely love you. As you once told me, we will figure it out...Together," I assured him. Brevan slowly released me and stood.

"My little wolf, I promise you I will earn your trust back. You cannot tell me you do not have any doubts. I can still feel you do. Please know you mean more to me than my own life and I will do everything in my power to make everything up to you." Dear Lord, the guilt exuding from him was completely overwhelming. One emotion I didn't handle well under the best of circumstances was guilt, and it usually was when it was my own, never mind someone else.

"Brevan, stop. When I said we'd do this together, I meant it. You're not alone in all of this, and you don't need to take on the weight of the world just to prove yourself. It's obvious with everything here, there is still more which needs to be unraveled." He closed his eyes and nodded. As he did, I felt him let go of some of the guilt he was carrying around on his shoulders.

He pulled me into a full hug and I hear him whisper again, "More than my own life."

Once Brevan released me and I managed to put on my dressing gown, we returned to the task at hand. Each document was examined multiple times by at least two different sets of eyes to make sure nothing was missed. We were all in deep concentration when there was a knock at the door.

Finn and Riley entered the apartment carrying additional boxes of papers from Pack Lumen along with some food. It appeared Aoife caught them on their way upstairs.

"Aoife informed us, if you want anything else, just let her know," Finn relayed.

"Thank you both for bringing the things we need. It's appreciated." I smiled at the two of them.

Riley was scanning around the room at what we'd been working on. He turned to Brevan and asked, ""M'lord, I do not wish to interrupt but have you considered this might have something to do with lineage?" His eyes settled on the outline we'd made with what we knew for certain.

"Explain, what do you mean?" Brevan requested for Riley to continue.

"Well, it just seems to shout out at me as I am looking at what you have already surmised. I am not sure why but something is telling me to look at the family lines."

"Thanks, Riley. That was an angle we hadn't considered yet. Well, not fully anyway," Sloane answered, and I could see his wheels spinning.

"No problem. I just hope it helps." Riley scratched his head and turned to leave.

"I do not need to remind the two of you to say nothing of what you have seen here?" Brevan cautioned, and the pair nodded as they headed to the door.

"I'll catch you two at training tomorrow," Sloane called after them while Finn and Riley waved as they closed the door.

It was going to be a late night. The only thing I could think about was tomorrow before the council meeting, we needed to visit some prisoners at the council jail. Diandra, Nova's alchemist and Jack were all tucked away in there. Perhaps they possessed some further information we were all missing.

AMELIA (AMI) JANE GRAY

TIMING WAS EVERYTHING

After yesterday's emotional rollercoaster of a day, we all wound up working late into the night. Sloane and Aisling crashed out on the couch, and I wasn't sure what time I finally climbed into bed. When I'd awoken the next morning, I felt jittery, which I attributed to the emotional overload from the day before. I decided to do the one thing that always helped me to focus.

Quietly, I climbed out of bed and dressed. I slipped out of our apartment without waking anyone and made my way downstairs to the back garden. The cool morning and serene garden made a perfect setting for some yoga. As I went through my positions, I began to feel far more centered. The more centered I became, the clearer I was able to see things and the less the jitters bothered me. No, it wasn't chocolate, cherry ice-cream, but under the circumstances, it was as good as I was going to get.

When I finished with my yoga, the thought of ice-cream still remained. My next thought was a waffle sundae with chocolate, cherry ice-cream, and whipped cream on top. The whole idea sounded heavenly. Then came the thought of warm gooey peanut-butter drizzled over the top. My sudden realization was what stopped my thought process. Was it too early to tell if I was pregnant?

115

Quickly I left the garden and jogged over to Neemah's cottage. When I arrived, I saw her sitting on the front stoop sipping her morning hot drink. "Hello child, I did not expect to see you back here so soon, and so early. What brings you by at this hour of the morning?" Neemah was obviously surprised by my unexpected visit.

"Gran, I need to ask you a medical question," I managed to puff out.

"Well, what is it?" She raised an eyebrow and quizzically gazed at me.

"Is it too soon for me to tell if I'm pregnant or not?" It was not the time for tact. I needed to know.

Neemah, rather than answering my question, grabbed hold of the handrail and stood. Once she was upright, she turned and moved towards the door. "Come on in. We do not need to be standing out here for such a private conversation. Besides, you look as though you could use a cup of keaff."

I followed Neemah inside and closed the door behind me. She motioned for me to have a seat at the kitchen table as she went to get me a cup of keaff. "Cream and sugar?" she queried, and I nodded, answering, "Yes, please." Neemah, with my mug of keaff, strode over to the table and sat opposite of me.

"Now, explain to me why it is you feel as though you needed to run over here so early with that specific question."

I explained to Neemah how I felt when I woke up and what I'd been doing when the craving for ice-cream hit me. What topped it off though, was the warm peanut butter. I liked peanut butter. I mean, what red-blooded New Englander didn't like a good ole' fashioned fluffer-nutter, but I hated warm peanut butter. Something about it when it was warm made me gag. I silently scolded myself because now I was thinking about fluff. The whipped, sugary, marshmallow goodness began to make my mouth water.

Frustration settled in as I let out a groan and put my head on the table. Neemah softly chuckled and stood to move over towards me. When she was next to me, she placed one hand on my lower back and one on the lower portion of my stomach. I felt her healing warmth pass through me from one side to the other as she focused on whatever it was she was doing. Once she finished, she retook her seat and faced me with a soft smile upon her face.

"It looks as though you are going to make me a great great-grandmother, my dear. You are not just pregnant, but you have got at least three in there."

"And you are absolutely certain?" My brain told me I needed to double-check.

"I am as certain as my name is Neemah and that I am your great grandmother," was her instant reply.

"Neemah... Gran, I need to ask a favor," I took in a calming breath. "I need to ask you not to say anything to Brevan or Mathias. The second they find out, I'll be locked in our apartment under guard until these babies are born. Right now, it's not exactly a great time for me to be doing my impression of Rapunzel."

Neemah broke out laughing. "While I do not know who Rapunzel is, child, you would be lucky to see the light of day even after their births. Fear not, your secret is safe with me. I will let you tell them both when you think it is the right time." She rose up and walked over to her medical bag, returning with some packets which she handed to me. "In the meantime, take these herbs twice a day. I would suggest mixing them in some tea. They do not taste wonderful, but they will keep both you and the babies healthy."

Neemah and I finished our keaff together. It allowed us to just simply sit and chat. I got brave as I asked her about my mother. She was more than happy to sit there and tell me childhood stories about her along with stories of her as an adult.

"Neemah, why didn't Brevan know my mother if she was an Acolyte? I mean, I'd think he would've recognized me where she and I look so similar."

"My dear, it is Brevan's story to tell you. What I can say for certain is he was a very different man back then. I suppose he was trying to get out from under his father's shadow. Brevan, even though he is and, at that time, was an Order member, did not fully start taking his responsibilities seriously until his father was gone. I hate to say it, but when Brevan realized his father was not returning, it shifted something inside him, and he began to become the wolf you know now. It was probably one of the best things that could have happened to him."

That particular revelation startled me a bit. What was Brevan like back when his father was running the show? It astonished me for as much as I loved him, I knew so very little about him. I knew and accepted the man I mated but not knowing who he was before was beginning to trouble me a bit. I kept being told Brevan was a different man before me, but how different I didn't fully understand. I was beginning to, though.

After I finished my keaff, I hugged Neemah and headed back to the packhouse. It was still fairly early, and I was almost certain Aoife would be fixing breakfast for the pack. When I arrived, my guess was spot on and proven as I entered the kitchen.

Aoife stopped what she was doing and gave me a hug. The look on her face said it all. She'd seen my episode yesterday and was expressing her concern for my well-being. I explained I was doing much better while I motioned towards the activity of the kitchen. "Can I possibly save you a trip upstairs and bring breakfast up for everyone? We all worked pretty late last night, and as a result, Aisling and Sloane fell asleep on our sofa."

My explanation was greeted with a smile along with her rounding up two trays for all the food I was about to carry upstairs. Instead of filling individual plates with food, she and I decided to do the meal family style and use large serving bowls instead. Fruit in one, sausage and bacon in another, eggs in a third, and scones in the last. We managed to squeeze in the plates and silverware along with butter and jam. Unfortunately, I realized we didn't have any room for tea or keaff, so Aoife placed them on a third tray and followed me upstairs to my apartment.

When we entered, Sloane and Aisling were just beginning to rouse, Brevan was in the bath chamber, and Mathias was standing in front of the balcony doors. Aoife and I set down the trays, and I thanked her for her help. She waved to me on the way out before she hurried back downstairs.

Mathias came up behind me, pulled me into his arms, and whispered in my ear. "Did you have a nice visit?" *Shit!* I'd forgotten he could tell where I was.

"Very nice. Neemah told me about my mother when she was a little girl. She also explained to me I was working too hard and gave me some herbs to take," I chuckled and calmed my nerves. "Even if she may have a point, I don't exactly have time to slow down right now," I finished as I smiled over at Mathias. He just raised his eyebrow at me and sat down on the sofa. Something told me he knew I wasn't telling the whole story, but he wasn't going to question me about it at the moment.

Brevan exited the bath chamber, and hesitantly greeted me with a chaste kiss. I huffed, swiftly hauled him into my arms, and greeted him properly with a real kiss, with the expectation I would immediately demand him to return it with the same love and affection he was being given. "Now, that's how you greet your mate in the morning. Don't you forget it," I playfully scolded and smiled at him.

I came to the conclusion it simply wasn't the time to tell my mates I was, in fact, pregnant. Timing these days was everything.

AMELIA (AMI) JANE GRAY

OVERCOMING OBSTACLES

fter breakfast, Sloane and Aisling left, however, not before Brevan could remind them of the council meeting this evening. I let them know I'd see them downstairs in a few minutes. I was already dressed in clothes that would work for training and didn't feel the need to change out of what I was wearing. After all, yoga pants basically worked as multi-purpose clothing.

Before I walked out the door, Mathias stopped me. He wanted to go over what he'd been studying in the books Neemah gave to us. We made plans to do just that after we completed our training.

When we entered the training room, we discovered it was completely empty. Mathias and I paused, gawked at each other, and was then startled by Finn, who came running through. "Finn, stop! Where is everyone?" It was safe to say I was completely confused by the lack of bodies.

"Everyone is at the obstacle course. Emmer has us running it first before we do any physical training." Finn ran outside in a panic. Something told me Emmer put the fear of God into him should any of them turn up late.

We made our way outside, where we saw my shield maidens along with the pack guards. They were lined up in front of the obstacle course Emmer and I'd previously discussed what seemed like years ago now.

"Emmer, you did an amazing job putting the course together. I can't wait to run it!" I exclaimed as he smiled smugly at me.

"You think you can run this without a problem?" *Ooh, a challenge,* I thought as Emmer spoke.

"Who's done it in the fastest time?" I questioned him with curiosity, and it was as though I'd thrown a damp rag at him.

"How are we supposed to time someone?" Emmer inquired.

"One moment. I have an idea." I motioned to him with one finger, turned, and ran back to the house.

Once inside, I headed directly to the kitchen and burst through the door. "Aoife, I need an egg timer!" I shouted with no explanation. Immediately she handed me an egg timer that resembled a small hourglass, and I ran back outside.

When I approached Emmer again, I held out the egg timer. "Use this!" I exclaimed. "One person stands at the finish, one person at the beginning to signal the start, and voila, timed runs."

"Amelia, what an excellent idea," Emmer's grin was slightly evil. "Since you thought of such a wonderful idea, how about you go first?"

It was exactly what I thought. Emmer laid down the gauntlet, and it was up to me whether to accept it or not. Of course, my competitive streak wouldn't allow a challenge to go unmet. "Emmer, I'd be happy to. How about you time me?"

Just as he was about to answer, Brevan showed up at our little party. "I see several of my pack standing around when they should be training. Might I ask what the hold-up is?"

Emmer and I glanced at one another then grinned. "Brevan, brother, consider yourself recruited."

We guided Brevan to the designated starting point as we explained the instructions on what he needed to do. After we concluded giving our instructions, Emmer moved the rest of the pack into position, and he went to the finish line. I'd done some stretching, then moved into position. When Brevan signaled for me to go, I took off like a shot. My sole focus was on the finish line. By the time I reached the tower,

121

my muscles were fatigued. I pushed on as I reached the top, then all that was left was to rappel down and cross the line. I grabbed the rope with a quick confidence, lowered myself to the ground, and crossed the finish line a moment later.

Out of breath, I swiveled my head over to Emmer. "Well, how'd I do?"

Emmer mumbled, "Three and a half."

"What did you say? I didn't quite hear you," I smugly prodded.

"Three and a half turns is how fast you were," Emmer admitted grumpily.

"Woohoo! Brevan, I did it in three and a half turns," I yelled down to him, and he nodded to let me know he heard me.

Cash was about to line up for the next run when Mathias stepped up. Mathias might've been my mate, but he was also my training partner. There was no way he was going to allow an unspoken challenge to go unanswered. When Emmer motioned to Brevan he was all set, Brevan signaled the start.

I knew Mathias was fast but watching him on the course showed me exactly how fast he was. The only part which slowed him down even slightly was the stomach crawl. Once he'd gotten through it, he took off again. He scaled the victory tower in no time at all, as the timer in Emmer's hand just turned while Mathias rappelled down the other side. Mathias finished the course in three and a quarter turns.

"Well done, honey!" I congratulated him with a hug.

"Thank you, my love," Mathias caught his breath as he replied, returning my hug. We both spun, staring directly at Emmer.

"Figures," was all Emmer muttered before he handed me the timer and went to the front of the line.

Once the timer was reset, I motioned for Brevan to signal the start. When he did, I flipped the timer and watched it closely. Needless to say, Emmer made it across the finish in just under four turns. I would've said I wasn't impressed, but it would've been an outright lie. The truth was Emmer held more muscle and was bulkier overall than either Mathias or myself, so because of those reasons, he'd done an excellent job.

All of the guards and shield maidens took their turns using our times as the goals to beat. When Sloane's turn came around, he crossed the finish line in the same amount of time as Emmer, with Aisling tying my time. *Whew! That girl was just fast!* After everyone made it through the course, Brevan stepped up.

Mathias jogged up to the start line, and Emmer signaled when he was ready. Once Mathias signaled the start, everyone fell silent as Brevan took off. He used his sheer strength and speed as it appeared as though he were waltzing right through the course. As Brevan crossed the finish line, Emmer just flipped the timer for the third time. Brevan smashed all of our times, and he was barely winded. If I was impressed by Mathias' time, Brevan made me speechless.

"Wow!" was the only thing my brain could come up with as words eluded me.

"Brevan, my brother, you have not lost your touch," Emmer professed while he shook his head.

"And I thought I was fast. Brevan, you crushed my time," Mathias confessed as he slapped Brevan on the back.

"Well, I could not let you have all the fun," Brevan beamed. "Emmer, well done on implementing Amelia's idea. I like it!"

After another round of congratulations, we all moved to the training area. However, Brevan paused the training. "Riley, Cash. I need you two to hang back for a moment. Amelia, Emmer, and Mathias the same goes for you as well." We all halted then redirected our movement over towards Brevan. "It is time for Mathias to retake his dominance test. While I understand it is highly unusual, I have come to realize that for a long time now, Mathias has been holding himself back within the pack." Brevan walked over to Mathias and placed his hands over Mathias' shoulders. "Brother, if you have learned anything from our Amelia, it should have been to be who you are."

We all shifted to our wolves and went to line up. I was surprised by Emmer, who nudged me to the end of the line taking his old position. Since I was in wolf-form, I was unable to argue the point, so all I could do was go with it. Mathias was the last to shift into his wolf then slowly approached Riley.

Brevan, in his wolf-form, nodded, and the dominance challenge began. Riley was first up, and the two of them put up a fight against one another, but in the end, Riley submitted. Cash was next, and with a sense of déjà vu coming over me, I watched as Cash and Mathias asserted their dominance. After what felt like an eternity, Cash submitted to Mathias. Which just left Emmer and me. Before Mathias faced off against Emmer, I'd gotten the impression Brevan had a mental word with Emmer about aggression. Probably in hopes of preventing another situation similar to what'd happened with me.

For the next hour, Mathias and Emmer went round and round with one another. Neither of them were inclined to back down. Their showdown probably could've continued for another thirty to forty minutes, but Brevan stepped in and called it. Brevan was content to place Mathias equal to Emmer and me. I quietly admitted to myself I was disappointed about not facing Mathias, however, I was proud of Mathias for not hiding who he was any longer.

Today was a day of overcoming obstacles, in more than one way!

AMELIA (AMI) JANE GRAY

TEAMS

$\mathcal{W}$e all changed back and redressed. There was still regular training to contend with, even though we'd spent the last couple of hours dealing with Mathias' dominance placement. Before we entered the training room, Brevan pulled Cash over to one side to speak with him privately. I wasn't sure what all of it was about, however, I assumed if it were something important, Brevan would let us know.

My ladies were already partnered off, working on hand to hand combat with Finn when Riley joined them. I was extremely impressed with all their progress within the week I'd been occupied with other affairs. Mathias and I went through each pairing, making corrections in stance and posture as we saw fit. We paused the hand to hand only momentarily, to give a demonstration for the ladies. One of the items each of them needed to work on was body language tells. I decided to give them some examples, "Did your opponent drop their shoulder before they threw a punch? Glance down at their feet as they move. Do they shift their weight in an obvious manner?" It was vital each of them picked up on all those little nuances.

A fantastic surprise was Maeve came in as a last-minute addition to the group. Where I wasn't available for a consult regarding the decision to allow her to join, Emmer made the executive decision. Even with the loss of Diandra, who was currently sitting in the council prison, it still left us with sixteen maidens in total. As expected, Aisling was head and shoulders above the others. Her ability to move fluidly made it nearly impossible for her peers to keep up with her. The other three who had stood out from the beginning and continued to shine were Sadine, Milestra, and Helaine.

With a loud, firm voice, , I gathered their attention, "Great job, everyone! Could I please get you all to form a single line facing me?"

While everyone moved into position, I called Finn, Riley, Cash, and Mathias over to me. "Correct me if I'm wrong in my assessment, but Aisling, Sadine, Milestra, and Helaine are the stand-out students within the group?" The three men nodded their agreement before I continued. "So, in total, we have sixteen women. What I'm thinking is setting up our standouts as team captains, then dividing up the remaining ladies, and we would have even teams."

"Do you plan on having them choose their teams round-robin style?" Cash inquired.

"No, it becomes too childish, and there's always one who is chosen last, which makes that person feel horrible. I suggest we start with the four weakest and work up from there." The three of them mumbled amongst themselves for a moment before coming to a general consensus.

Suddenly, I saw realization dawn on Mathias, "You plan on putting one group with each of us."

"You've got it. The smaller groups allow us to each work with the ones who are having trouble, while the strong ones help support and push those with the issues. By naming team captains, they can also help in bringing up the weaker ones. The overall effect should mean better performances from everyone." Not one of the men who were standing with me could argue the logic.

"Amelia, Aisling has more than enough going on at the moment. It would not be fair to her team," Mathias stated, clearly having a point, but I'd already thought about Aisling's busy schedule.

"I know, that's why I'm personally going to work with Aisling's team, whoever they turn out to be. I'd also like to voice, I would love to see Maeve on Aisling's team as well. She's the newest and needs the most work. I've been watching her today, and I see potential there. It just needs to be coaxed out." Mathias raised an eyebrow at me, Cash shrugged, while Finn and Riley laughingly cleared their throats.

In unison, they all remarked, "Agreed!"

I turned and faced the ladies, who were all waiting patiently for us to sort out the plan going forward. "Could we please have the following ladies step forward? Aisling, Sadine, Milestra, and Helaine." The four ladies stepped forward out of the line. "First, I would like to personally congratulate the four of you on a job well done. You four have shown exceptional progress, and as such, I'm awarding the four of you the title of team captain. Aisling's team will be working with me, Sadine's team will be working with Mathias, Milestra's team will be working with Cash, and Helaine's team will be working with Finn and Riley. The reason behind the last pairing is because of their rotation schedules for patrol. Some mornings you might have Finn, other mornings it might be Riley. However, rest assured, Finn and Riley work exceptionally well together, and if there are any issues, they will communicate those with each other to see to your success."

A hushed excitement broke over the ladies as we broke them into groups of four. Once everyone was split up, my group consisted of Aisling, the Team Captain, Maeve, who needed the most help, Lana, had lightning-quick reflexes with hand to hand, and last but not least Shannon who happened to be excellent with a bow and arrow.

I walked over to my group and smiled widely. "Ladies, I realize you are all excited. However, I'd like the four of you to stick around as I have my own personal training with Mathias. He and I will be working with weapons, and I really think all of you would benefit from observing. Right now, though, please go and get your mid-day meal, and I'll meet you back here in thirty minutes." I dismissed my group but held Aisling back.

"Aisling, I know you have a great deal on your plate at the moment. If this becomes too much, promise me you'll tell me. I'm asking a lot from you."

She reached over and hugged me. "If you can manage everything you have going on, then I can certainly handle all of my responsibilities. Besides..." she pulled me close to whisper into my ear. "Anyone who can do all of this while they are pregnant is absolutely someone I need to admire." When she leaned back from my ear, she smiled.

My jaw dropped open. "How did you... I mean, I haven't..." I was completely unable to form a full sentence.

"Do not worry, Sister. Your secret is safe with me. I have just always been able to tell these sorts of things ever since I was little. Not to mention, I do not think it would be wise to tell either of your men right now. They would lock you in your room, and we would not see you until afterwards." Well, Aisling's assessment was nearly identical to my own.

Mathias jogged over to the two of us. "You two look as thick as thieves. Are you both heading over to get something to eat?"

Aisling and I glanced at one another, then back over at Mathias. ""We were just discussing scheduling, but I suppose you have a point, especially since you and I have our training directly afterwards," I commented.

The three of us walked to the dining room as we discussed the issues we were facing regarding our schedules. As we ate, we worked out how we'd shuffle everything around, so everyone's training schedules wouldn't be affected. Aisling had done an amazing job setting up the adults who supervised the daycare, so she'd only need to check in periodically during the day. Aisling also mentioned she was going to speak with Marta regarding the binding ceremony. She wanted to confirm Marta could pick-up the majority of the planning, which would alleviate her schedule from any conflicts.

My own schedule was just as complicated. However, I figured since we were all working on the current problem named Lycandra, I could still factor in my normal council issues. We also figured out I would be able to keep up with my personal training schedule. Plus, the schedule with my smaller group would keep my plate full but was still manageable.

The only additional issue for Mathias was his patrol schedule. He planned on working with Emmer, so it wouldn't interfere with anything else. I was curious where his new dominance standing would put him in the grand scheme of things, but it was a question more suited for Brevan than Mathias.

As we finished our mid-day meal, I came to the conclusion our teams were going to work out well. I was looking forward to demonstrating weapons to the group I was working with and felt like they were going to pick things up quickly.

AMELIA (AMI) JANE GRAY

HISTORY

Aisling, Mathias, and I made our way back to the training room where Emmer was awaiting our arrival. Shannon, Lana, and Maeve filed in shortly thereafter, causing Emmer to shoot us a befuddled look. We were followed by Mathias' group as well as Finn's. It was then, Sloane entered the room, and Emmer came over to speak with me.

"Amelia, care to explain what your ladies are doing in MY training room?" Emmer was in drill sergeant mode.

I smiled sweetly at Emmer, "Well, I can't tell you what the others are doing here, but Aisling, Shannon, Lana, and Maeve are here to observe Mathias and me. I wanted them to get an idea about weaponry discipline before they actually pick up a practice sword."

Emmer pinched the bridge of his nose, "Mathias, same for you?"

Mathias nodded his confirmation and added, "Depending on how they take to it, I may or may not have them pair off with a practice weapon and begin their actual training."

Emmer yelled over to Finn, "Let me guess, your group is here for weapon's work?"

"How did you know?" Finn playfully retorted as some of the guards filed in for their own weapons drill.

I batted my eyelashes and pouted just a tiny bit, "Emmer, you're the best weapons master there is. If I have to, I'll go get my secret weapon and convince you this is a good idea."

Emmer crossed his arms, "Your secret weapon? What's that?"

I laughed, "Laura. She has you wrapped around her little finger."

Emmer let out a genuine belly laugh, "Oh no, not my Laura! Fine, you win, but you know my rule. If you are in my training room, you are training. The ladies get thirty minutes, then we will pair them off and start their weapons work."

"Fair enough." Mathias and I agreed simultaneously.

Quickly we gathered our groups around to observe and explained Emmer's rule. Nerves and excitement ran through their expressions. Regardless, I could easily tell each of them was looking forward to the newest step in their schooling.

Once we were all separated and we selected our practice weapons, the fighting dance began. Mathias and I were instructing as we went along, pointing out each other's tells and striking at the same time. If I were being honest, demonstrating while performing was more difficult than just simply sparring. I needed to not only focus on what I was doing but also on the explanation of why I was doing it.

When the thirty minutes elapsed, Emmer interrupted and instructed the ladies to pick up a practice weapon. He paired each of them off with one of the guards, then shouted: "BEGIN!" Mathias and I were back to simply sparring with one another. It felt good to really work my muscles and move as I dodged and attacked. It became its own Zen-like state when we sparred. When I called a timeout between Mathias and me, I dared to glance over at Maeve. She was partnered with Ulmer, who was being incredibly patient with her. He was showing her how to hold the sword, what kind of grip to use with it, and how she should stand. Silently, I wondered if maybe there wasn't something there between the two of them. I then realized I was doing the *let's pair everyone off together* thing and resumed my training with Mathias.

Mathias stopped Sloane and Aisling before they left and asked both of them to meet us upstairs once they'd gotten cleaned up. It appeared as though Mathias wanted to speak to us about the books Neemah bestowed upon Sloane and I. Aisling stated she needed to check in on the children and she wouldn't be able to join us, but she'd find out all the details from Sloane later. Sloane, on the other hand, double-checked his schedule and readily agreed to meet us upstairs.

Once Mathias and I reached our apartment, I claimed first dibs on the bath chamber, which prompted a wiggle of his eyebrows and the cheesy line of, "we could always conserve water". That in and of itself caused me to laugh hard enough, so I caved and shared my bath with him. I truly loved it when he was being playful. Twenty or so minutes later, we were fully pruned, cleaned, and satiated.

As we dressed, I suddenly remembered Brevan mysteriously disappeared during the training with the shield maidens. "Mathias, do you have any idea where Brevan is?" I wondered because it also dawned on me he'd been acting strangely earlier as well.

"Love, Brevan took a double patrol. He is still upset with himself over hurting you the way he did, intentionally or not. Do not worry, he will be back before tonight's council meeting." Mathias gazed at me apologetically.

"So, his solution is to what, avoid me? How does that make anything better?" Honestly, I would never understand men.

"Just give him some time to come to terms with himself. Brevan, even in his more carefree days, always felt he needed to hold himself to a different standard than anyone else. He forgets he is just like the rest of us, even if he is our Alpha." Mathias came over and gave me a sweet, chaste kiss on the forehead. "You need to finish getting dressed. Your brother will be here any minute."

Sure enough, in the next moment, Sloane knocked on the door. I ran into the other room to quickly put myself together. Mathias opened the door and greeted him warmly. "Come on in and have a seat. I think this is a conversation best held sitting down."

When I was ready, I made my way back to both of them, and we all moved over to the couch as Mathias picked up both books. His first order of business was to open the book of spells. He flipped to a specific page and placed the book on the coffee table. He lifted the family history book and flipped to a page near the front.

"Alright, so while you all were pouring over papers from Pack Lumen, I took the opportunity to peruse through these two items. If we are going to be as prepared as possible, I thought it might be wise for the two of you to understand your abilities. However, what I found was something far more interesting than just a how-to guide on magical skills." Mathias paused and swiveled his head towards me. "Do you remember the prophecy you learned at Lord Cedrik's?"

"Something about the super moon and stars raining from the heavens if my memory serves me correctly." I replied.

"Close enough, but listen to this." Mathias picked up the book of magical spells and read aloud. "The time is henceforth; when four become one, the stars shall rain from the heavens, and the lost children shall return home. In the forgotten temple lies the secret stones, yet to be revealed. Their powers of old, never told. When the giant is at her height, their light will shine, and when the wolf cries, the fires burn. The choice is theirs and theirs alone. The time of the Dark Star and Shadow is at hand. Their path is set, but choices are not yet met. When the Dragon and Phoenix arrive, it is as sure as time flies."

Sloane responded as I wracked my brain to remember exactly how the prophecy went. "It's similar, but there is more to it. It's almost as though the one Cedrik has, was purposely altered."

"Mathias, honey, may I have a look at that?" I requested, so I could see the actual written words. I was determined to make damn good and sure I committed the prophecy to memory. . The only way I could accomplish that was if I read the passage multiple times. As I quietly re-read it aloud, I paused at one of the new sections. "The time of the Dark Star and Shadow is at hand... What the hell does it mean?"

I was only mumbling to myself, but Mathias heard my question anyway. Surprisingly, he figured out the answer. "Amelia, that is about the only thing I can answer for certain." He pulled up the book, which contained our family tree. "Here, is your family's history, is the documentation of your birth as well as Sloane's. Sloane, next to your name are two words, Dark Star. Amelia, next to your name is Shadow. Now, if you follow back through your family history, the last time there was a Dark Star Phoenix and Shadow Dragon was… " Mathias took in a deep breath. "Three-thousand years ago. This would put it during the time of the war between the Northern and Southern Territories."

He gave Sloane and I a moment to digest everything he'd just told us before he continued with even more information. "If I may?" Mathias requested to see the book of spells again. He flipped to a new section where the writing was all swirly and old in appearance. "See, here is the section which belonged to the last Shadow Dragon Mystic. Amelia, I think these spells are ones you will be able to cast." Mathias then flipped open to another section he'd marked off. "Sloane, these are spells from the last Dark Star Phoenix Mystic. As with Amelia, I believe you should be able to cast these as well."

Sloane and I took turns with the book of spells going back and forth reading our individual sections. After the two of us transcribed several notes, we decided we wanted to give some of these spells a try. The best place to do it was outside. Sloane and I remembered Lady Astraea's warning about blowing up the packhouse and thought better of trying anything in the apartment. There were only certain ones we could actually practice. Still, it was absolutely worth a try.

As Sloane and I practiced, we began to draw the attention of not just the pack but also General Pax and some of his men. I finally managed to conjure up the Shadow Dragon as Sloane called up the Dark Star Phoenix. I paused for a moment when I realized the sheer awe of having two mythological creatures sitting on the garden lawn comprised purely of magic. I was breathless when I whispered, "Gwathren lug fliet", and watched as my dragon took off into the skies above the packhouse.

I kept staring up into the sky while I spoke to Sloane, "Can you believe it? I mean, I know we did this but still."

"Ami, I totally know what you mean," Sloane confirmed as he was in his own state of disbelief.

"Sloane, we need to practice these spells daily until we have them memorized." I was still gawking at my dragon.

"Agreed, I have a feeling we are going to need them." Sloane stretched out his arm without speaking any words, and the Phoenix he called up and fluttered up to his arm landing as though it were virtually weightlessly. The Phoenix's body was twelve inches long and the tail extended behind him another six inches. It possessed beautiful rich colors of reds and golds.

"After our combat training, you and I will do magic training," I suggested as I continued to stare at the magnificent creature. Sloane in turn nodded his agreement.

When I finally stopped watching the stunning creatures we'd conjured and focused on the crowd we'd attracted, I recited, "*Gwathren lug n-lelya,*" and my dragon vanished. I nudged Sloane and pointed out the crowd. He quickly followed my lead, making his Phoenix disappear.

"Sorry, everyone. We didn't mean to cause a scene. You can go about your business as the show is now over," I announced out with a sheepish smile.

The crowd dispersed, chatting about the magic Sloane and I just showcased. Because of Neemah, Sloane, and I learned we were the only Shadow Dragon Mystic and Dark Star Phoenix Mystic in the last three thousand years. It both excited and scared me at the same time. The one thing I knew for certain was history always had a tendency of repeating itself.

AMELIA (AMI) JANE GRAY

STUBBORN WOLF

*S*loane and I headed inside. On our way upstairs, we bumped into Finn and Riley, who paused to talk with Sloane for a moment. The one comment which stood out to me during their conversation was, "Man, am I glad you two are on our side!" The comment came from Riley, who genuinely looked relieved. I was glad Sloane ultimately made friends with those two. Even though each of our loves was the center of our universe, friends were just as important. Friends could say things our partners couldn't.

As I entered the apartment, I heard voices arguing over, you guessed it, me.

"I leave for patrol, and what happens? A dragon shows up in the sky above the packhouse. What were you thinking?"

"Brevan, perhaps you need to take a step back and calm down."

"You want me to calm down when our mate has only ever demonstrated that tremendous amount of power when she was under some sort of duress?"

"Yes, there are things you do not understand here."

It was all I could handle. Brevan was blaming Mathias for sins real and imagined.

"Will you two SHUT UP!" I yelled at the pair of idiots I was bound to. "Brevan, I called the dragon all on my own. No duress required. Mathias, why didn't you just show him the book where it was marked Shadow Dragon? Hello, common sense people."

The whole damn argument was stupid, in my opinion. The only thing it made me realize was there were underlying issues we needed to work out. Brevan's guilt was beginning to eat away at him, to the point where he was avoiding our family, while poor Mathias was trying to overcompensate for Brevan's own feelings. Talk about a crazy cycle. *Hello, family counseling for a party of three, please.*

I took a deep breath. "It's time for what is called a *Come to Jesus meeting.* Sit down the pair of you." I was irritated by the fact this was even necessary.

Mathias and Brevan thankfully shut their mouths and took a seat on the sofa. "Mathias, why didn't you just show Brevan the book?" I repeated my question much more calmly.

"Honestly, I did not get a chance to." Mathias' explanation was short, but I understood the underlying text as he glared over at Brevan.

I pinched the bridge of my nose. "Brevan, why did you feel it necessary to rip into Mathias before you'd even gotten an explanation?"

"My little wolf, you have only ever exhibited that kind of magic on two occasions. The first was when you were initiated into the pack, and the second was the other night." Brevan hung his head down and ran his hands through his hair. I knew he was remembering my reaction. He quietly mumbled something which sounded a great deal like, "It is all my fault."

Okay, it was my cue to kick Mathias out. Brevan and I needed a one on one conversation. It wasn't like I was putting Mathias on the outside of our family, but he wasn't the one who needed therapy at the moment. "Mathias, honey, would you please see to the carriage? We will need to go together tonight, and it's the only thing we can use to transport all of us."

Mathias stood and nodded. I suspected he was glad to be out of the line of fire. "Sure. Should I go and collect Neemah while I am at it?"

I looked at Brevan and then back to Mathias. "Yes, please. If you don't mind."

Mathias stood and kissed the top of my head before he left. I could feel he was much happier to be running errands. Part of me felt bad because I knew how close Brevan and Mathias had become since our binding. The pair of them were truly acting like brothers. I held no doubt if push came to shove, one would bleed for the other.

After the door closed behind Mathias, I continued my conversation with Brevan.

"Alright, Brevan, it's just the two of us. So, why don't you tell me what's running through your head." We didn't have time for kid gloves. I needed Brevan's head screwed on straight for tonight's council meeting.

"Amelia, all of this. Everything! It is my fault. Everything from not recognizing my sister's deception, to what has happened to you, to those six women who were taken from our packhouse. All of it is my fault." Brevan was exhausted and beating himself up.

I went over and straddled his legs, forcing his gaze directly at me. "Brevan, you are NOT responsible for everything. Yes, you're the pack Alpha, but it does not mean all of this is your fault. YOU are one man, and from what I can figure, you are just as much a victim in all this as anyone else." I'd taken a moment to reread his eyes. They told me he wasn't quite buying what I was saying.

"Listen to me. You wanted to believe your sister was working towards the greater good. Believing she'd come around and wanted to put the pack back together isn't a bad thing. It's hopeful." The look on Brevan's face was still strained while I continued. "As for what happened to me, let's discuss it. I'm the bound mate to two amazing, handsome, strong, kind men who I couldn't love any more than I do, even if I tried. Sometimes, we need to take the bad, in order to accept and appreciate the good. I honestly wouldn't change a thing that's happened because it would alter my fate. How could I possibly wish that, when, at the end of the day, I've been blessed with a wonderful family who I love and adore?" Finally, I could see my words as they started to sink into his stubborn head.

138

"Lastly, those women who were taken... I've been thinking about them. We've been so distracted with everything else, not one of us thought about *how* they actually were taken. Correct me if I'm wrong, but the Alfar do not have shadow skills, do they?" Brevan shook his head. "Yet, it was Marta who reported she hadn't seen anyone physically moving them. It was almost as if they were floating out of the building."

"Amelia, what are you suggesting?" Brevan countered.

"I suspect Lord Cedrik and Lady Astraea have an issue with the Sylphs. The way I understand it, Sylphs can inhabit a body and control the person, as what was witnessed with Liam. We know that Cedrik and Astraea are not behind things but if some of their people were, say, possessed, then it would explain the ease of the kidnapping." Brevan slightly lifted me as he shifted himself to change his position. I could see the wheels in his head as they began to turn. It appeared as though I was finally getting through to him.

"Brevan, you don't need to shoulder the responsibility all by yourself. Liam you could almost jack up to a one-off. But if you factor in the kidnapping and how it was done with practically no witnesses other than Marta. Then you need to take into account your mother's involvement. She knew the entire layout of this place, and with Diandra as an informant, Lycandra would've known exactly how to get in and out of here unseen. Do you see where I'm going with all of this?"

"My little wolf, it still does not excuse the fact that any of those children might be mine." He definitely made a point there, but I'd come up with an explanation about his terrible situation as well.

"Brevan, I've been driving myself crazy about that too. So much so, it's given me a headache. I think Aisling's correct. There's no way you'd have sex with someone and not remember it unless you were drugged. The way Nova bragged about her alchemist, I'd assume he's exceptionally talented. If we were to follow any particular logic, then the only possible conclusion is he concocted some sort of hallucinogen. Which was more than likely slipped into whatever you, Cash, and Liam were drinking that night. It might also be conceivable how and when Liam was possessed by the Sylph." I stopped and took in a deep breath.

"We also need to consider what Aerin told the members of her pack. She ordered those women were to be treated as though they were goddesses. She also explained the women and the children they were carrying would make the pack stronger. If you think about it, it would have meant the offspring of three of the strongest members of Pack Lingwir would be raised in Pack Lumen. It was a long-term game, but it would've worked. As far as sacrificing their innocence, she'd already done that when those women were impregnated, but it could also mean the sacrifice of their lives. Regardless, again, not your fault. Behind each and every turn was someone who planned this out with meticulous detail. Each and every move held a counter move and yet another contingency. There's no way you could've known." I'd finished my slight rant.

Brevan inhaled with a cleansing breath. "Amelia, I do not deserve you. You are right, and I know you are, but it is difficult to not bear the responsibility. Ever since my father's death, it has made me realize just how much he dealt with. Running the pack is one thing but the burden of everyone's welfare..." Brevan shook his head. "It is the sole job of the Alpha."

I grabbed hold of Brevan's face and forced his eyes to mine. "NOT. ANY. MORE! It may have been the way your father did things, but you are not your father. Besides, you have something your father didn't. You have Mathias, Emmer, and... You have me. This pack has changed from the one your father ran. It isn't just a group of people being held together by one man. It's a family!"

Suddenly and without warning, I placed a passionate kiss upon Brevan's lips. He wrapped his arms around me and pulled me in close. I could feel his heat as I melted into his hard, sculpted, muscled chest. Nothing would ever change this feeling for me. I relished being in his lap, pulled tight against him. When we separated, the two of us were completely breathless.

"Brevan, I'd love nothing more than to continue this." I pointed between the two of us. "However, we need to get to the council hall."

Brevan groaned as I slid off his lap. We both stood, and he pulled me back into him for a hug. He leaned over and whispered into my ear. "I love you, my little wolf."

As I tilted my head to gaze at him, I replied, "I love you too, my stubborn wolf."

It was absolutely true; he might've been stubborn, but he was mine, and I absolutely loved him.

AMELIA (AMI) JANE GRAY

THE DOWNFALL OF LADY NOVA

*A*fter, I made a small detour to put on something I'd not worn in a while, my parents' items. Brevan and I left our apartment and headed down the stairs. When we reached the second floor, Brevan gave me a chaste kiss and told me he'd be out shortly. He needed to find Cash and Naima. He wanted the two of them to attend the meeting as well, but there was something else there I couldn't quite put my finger on.

When I reached the front door, Aoife caught up to me and handed me a basket of food to take with us. "None of you will be around for supper, so I wanted to make sure you had something to take with you." Aoife was one of the kindest, most caring people in the pack. I was lucky to count her amongst my closest friends. I hugged and thanked her for her thoughtfulness, before carrying our care package with me to the carriage.

As I climbed inside, I noticed Neemah, Sloane, Aisling, and Emmer were already seated there. Mathias was riding up with the driver. I could tell he was still irritated and didn't blame him even slightly. I placed the basket on the floor and explained Brevan would be out shortly because he went to find Cash and his mate. Aisling and Sloane shared a conspiratorial look before they returned their gaze

142

towards me.

"Alright, you two, spill. What's going on?" I quizzed my two friends sitting across from me.

"Nothing, yet," Sloane quantified.

"Yet?" I countered.

"There may or may not be some suspicion about the loyalty of Cash's wife." Aisling clarified, and I glared at the two of them.

"Hey, don't look at me like that. We weren't withholding information on purpose." Sloane put his hands up in surrender. "Besides, it was my brilliant soon-to-be mate who realized it. I only agreed."

Aisling elbowed him in the ribs, and I couldn't help but laugh. "Nice, Sloane, you compliment her and throw her under the bus all in one swift move."

Sloane shrugged. "It's a gift." He winked at me and kissed Aisling on the nose.

Aisling scrunched her eyes at Sloane, "You are lucky I adore you. Otherwise, I might feel the need to pop you in the nose."

The lighthearted nature of the moment didn't negate the implications which were being made. My guess was Brevan wanted Naima interrogated by Oren. What I really began to wonder was how did she manage to avoid hiding the truth in the first place? It would be something I'd make sure to ask during a more appropriate moment. Perhaps when she was under Oren's scrutiny.

When Brevan emerged from the packhouse, he paused at the front of the carriage. I only vaguely heard the conversation between him and Mathias, but from what I could make out, he was apologizing for his behavior. It only took another moment before Brevan opened the door and scooted in next to me.

"All you young people. Someday you will learn," Neemah commented, and I laughed.

"Gran, are you going to tell me what you've learned?" I snickered out because I'd gotten the sneaking suspicion she hadn't.

"Hells bells, girl. No, I am just older and ornerier. At my time of life, holding back only causes indigestion."

It was maybe a half of a heartbeat later, and the carriage erupted

143

into laughter. Neemah was absolutely someone who told it like it was. I found myself growing fonder of her with every interaction. It certainly made for interesting family conversations.

When we arrived at the council hall, we all exited the carriage. Emmer, being the last to get out, picked up Aoife's care package and carried the basket inside. I briefly thought for a moment about what a horrible friend I was because I hadn't even looked inside to see what she packed us. My guilt-ridden thoughts quickly left when I saw Nova, Declan, and Jackie standing in the council chamber, waiting for us to arrive. Jackie came across pissed, or was it defensive? Declan wore a powerful expression that clearly said don't mess with me and Nova appeared as though she'd been crying for the last day. While that all concerned me, what stunned me to near silence was the look on Emmer's face. It looked like thunder.

"Hey, guys... What's going on?" I carefully spoke.

"You mean he didn't tell you?" Jackie pointed to Emmer.

"Tell me what?" I swiveled my head over to Emmer. Someone needed to talk soon in order to end the stalemate happening amongst us.

Nova inhaled sharply as her eyes were fixed upon Neemah. "I cannot do what you asked of me. I am too afraid," She breathlessly stated.

Neemah, confident in her stride, moved over towards Nova. While she paced Nova's hand in hers, Neemah quietly whispered, "It is time."

"You knew? All this time, you knew?" Nova blurted out to Neemah.

"Dear, I have always known, but it was not time. It also was not for me to tell," Neemah responded.

Nova sank to her knees, placed her head in her hands, and began sobbing. Neemah, in her grandmotherly way, comforted Nova as she cried her heart-wrenching tears. It appeared as though Jackie was going to move to Nova's side, but with one shake of Declan's head, she stopped dead in her tracks.

"She must face the truth on her own, dear one," Declan professed to Jackie.

Just then, Astraea and Cedrick arrived. Closely followed by Oren, Lyros, and Drew. As Astraea's gaze fell upon Nova and Neemah, she approached the pair, and placed her hand upon Nova's shoulder, showing her support.

"It is long overdue, my sister," Astraea commented, and I felt as though I was watching the three fates from Greek and Roman mythology. The crone, the mother, and the maiden.

"Would you all care to explain now what's going on?" Sloane chimed in with the irritation I was feeling.

Neemah and Astraea both nodded at Nova, and she stood up to face everyone who was assembled. Nova began her tear-filled story of the night Sloane and I were sent through the portal. This time, however, she added what she left out the first time we heard the tale of the events from that night. When Nova finished her confession, Sloane stalked over towards her.

"You stupid, selfish woman. Do you realize Ami and I could've been killed that night? Do you have any idea the blood which lies on your hands? How dare you sit in judgement of others on this council while you're just as guilty if not more so?" To say Sloane was pissed off was an understatement.

I couldn't argue with how he felt. It was perfectly justified, and to top it off, Sloane was right. He, however, wasn't the one I was afraid of. He might've been the one standing there yelling at her, but it was Oren who scared me. I saw his face morph from impassive to completely and utterly furious. With a lightning fast move, Oren blurred, and when he came back into focus again, he was holding Nova by the throat against the wall.

"I should rip your head from your body," Oren growled as Nova's eyes pleaded for forgiveness.

I wasn't quite sure what'd come over me, but I felt peaceful. As if the pieces of my life were snapped into place. Calmly, I walked over and placed my hand on the arm Oren was using to hold Nova pinned into place against the wall.

I spoke to him with the serenity I oddly felt, "Oren, she is your sister. Ultimately, when you examine everything and how events played out, the only person she betrayed was herself. She's lost far more than you could ever take from her." Oren's rage-filled face swiveled to me. "Let her down. It's okay."

Oren flexed his hand, and Nova crumpled to the floor. She held her throat while I knelt in front of her. "Nova, as someone your actions directly affected, I forgive you. I forgive your choices because even if they were selfish, they were also made out of love. What wouldn't any of us do for our loved ones?" I stood and backed away before I continued, "As a member of the council and a leader in the City of Tenebris, You must be held accountable for your actions, well-meaning intentions or not. Your actions cost the lives of several members within the city."

Brevan stepped up to Nova and offered her a hand. Nova gratefully took it and stood. "Nova, I agree with everything Amelia has said. As a man and your friend, I forgive you. But, as a leader of our city, you will be held accountable for your actions." I could see the torn expression on his face. The realization she could've cost me and Sloane our lives was there, along with the knowledge of how the members of the Order and the other Acolytes were betrayed. Brevan was always close with Nova and trusted her with his own secrets about who he was as a man. I could only imagine what was running through his mind, but I felt the total conflict of his emotions.

Cedrik garnered everyone's attention and motioned for the council members to take their seats, less Nova. He then called in General Pax and explained the situation. As we council members deliberated on the correct course of action, I noticed Neemah standing with Nova, and my heart broke. It was the moment I made my decision.

"I don't give a shit what the law says," I spouted out, interrupting the debate between Cedrik and Oren. "Everything stems back to the manipulation of Lycandra and Queen... whatever her name is."

"Cosima, dear," Astraea answered.

"Fine, Queen Cosima. She could be Maleficent for all I care. My point is, they're winning again. Tearing us further apart. Does Nova deserve consequences for her actions? Absolutely! But rather than throwing her in the dungeon and throwing away the key, I have a suggestion," I rattled on a bit, but I held everyone's focused attention.

"What is your idea, my little wolf?" Brevan was hopeful I held a solution to the debate.

"Replace Nova with Jackie. This way, Nova is technically removed from the council, but the seat stays with her house. Now, if Jackie should say, make her an advisor of some kind, then that is between them." I waited a moment for the suggestion to sink in. "Look at her. She's punished herself more than any of us really could. She has to live with what she did for the rest of her very long life. Who amongst us could honestly say anything we could or would dole out would be worse?"

"Dear sweet, Amelia, you are too kind for your own good," Oren replied and then sighed. "I agree with your assessment now that my anger has faded, and I can think logically. Although, while you might be able to forgive her, it may take me some time. "

"Are we all in agreement then? If so, let us vote. All those in favor of Amelia's solution?" spoke Cedrik. The group of us stated, "Aye" and Cedrik continued, "So be it."

Nova faced her punishment with grace and dignity. Jackie was sworn in as the new vampyr council leader, and her first order of business was to name Nova as her council advisor. What I didn't realize, by vampyr law, was it also made Jackie head of the coven. She was now known as 'Lady Jacqueline,' and all I could do was burst out laughing. I threw my arm around her shoulders and told her, "Welcome to the club."

Drew twisted his body towards Oren and instructed him, "You are never allowed to retire. I don't want a Lord title. Nope, No Way! It would kill my fashion business." Jackie and I laughed so hard we needed to hold our stomachs, causing everyone else to join in. Even with the seriousness of tonight, sometimes people just needed to laugh.

147

AMELIA (AMI) JANE GRAY

THE ORDER OF THE DRAGON

Once we'd ceased our bout of hysterics, we all got down to the real business of the night. General Pax momentarily stepped out with his men and brought back a long table for us to work on. Brevan pulled Oren aside to discuss something privately. I held a sneaking suspicion it had to do with Cash and his wife.

General Pax was about to leave when I stopped him. "General, please stay. I would greatly appreciate your input on what we are discussing." I suspected Pax was greatly underutilized, and with part of the meeting having to do with strategic planning, who better than a General to help us plan, especially a General with wings.

We each laid out all of the information we gathered, as well as, our educated guesses regarding how some of the espionage was being pulled off. When I got to my suspicions about the Sylph along with Cedrik and Astraea's people, I was surprised to see they'd also come to a similar conclusion. Their dilemma was how to flush out who was infected and who wasn't. Naturally, it caused a debate of another sort for the next hour. Everyone was throwing ideas into the hat while they were all being picked apart. It was Sloane who'd come up with the best solution. He suggested we use the gifts of either Oren or Nova. Accompanied by what he dubbed 'my superball', to get rid of anyone with a Sylph who was riding shotgun. I needed to remind him of Liam's ultimate outcome, but Astraea assured me her people would have a different reaction.

With his plan in place, we moved onto the books from Gran. When Sloane and I placed them on the table, all eyes went wide except for those of us who'd already seen it. Astraea ran her fingers lightly over the spellbook and Cedrik immediately flipped open the family tree.

"Let me save you the trouble. Sloane is the Dark Star Phoenix Mystic, while I'm the Shadow Dragon Mystic and there are a bunch of spells we've developed a practice schedule for, so we can learn how to use them." I'd just given them the basic rundown but Cedrik still perused through them pulling the spellbook towards him. After I decided to give him a moment, I nudged Aisling, who'd remained quiet the entire time, and nodded over to the basket of food.

The two of us noiselessly moved away from the table to where Emmer had set the basket earlier. "Alright, you've been very quiet so far, and I know not much gets past you. What are you thinking?" I challenged Aisling wanting her opinion on everything.

Aisling leaned in to speak more quietly, "I think what you did for Nova was amazingly generous. Reading over what Lord Cedrik brought with him raised a few questions for me, and I have been comparing his information with the map." She shook her head. "I can see how easy it has been for Lycandra to have us all literally chasing our own tails."

"Questions? Like what?" I probed, because on some level, she knew I'd pick up on her knowledge.

"The parchment with the prophecy. The one he explained he had shown you and Sloane. Keep in mind, my Alfar is not as good as theirs, but to my untrained eyes, it seemed as though there was some sort of warning that went along with it."

"Holy shit! You can read Alfar?" I exclaimed a bit too loudly, which caught Astraea's attention. Of course, she'd be able to read Alfar with her and Mathias' background.

Astraea quietly made her way over to Aisling and myself. "My dear, did I hear you correctly? You can read Alfar?"

I nodded to Aisling. "Yes, some. My brother taught me, and he learned from our father."

"And who is your brother, young one?" Astraea gracefully pushed.

"Amelia's mate, Mathias. Our father was a defector from the court of Queen Cosima and King Polaris. Granted, he was only one of their guards, but it still was a loss intended to make a bold statement." Aisling held her head high as she explained who their father was.

"Ah, that is right. Your father was Naffir." Astraea proclaimed as though she were remembering an old friend.

"You knew my father?" Aisling inquired, and ever so briefly, I saw a little girl longing to know more about the man who fell in love with her mother.

"Yes, I did. How about you and I make plans to sit and discuss what I know once we have settled all this nasty business with Lycandra? I would be more than happy to tell you about him from my point of view." Astraea's kind smile beamed towards Aisling.

"That would be lovely. Thank you," Aisling responded with a similar smile but then continued, "Pardon me for asking M'lady, but was I correct? Was my interpretation a warning that lies under the prophecy?"

"You are correct, little one. You are very clever, I must admit." Astraea was dodging the actual question effectively.

"Astraea, why don't you explain what the warning states. Because in my experience, if someone places a warning label on something, you should probably listen to it." I attempted to egg her on.

Astraea sighed heavily. "Very well, in short, should you and Sloane make the wrong choice, we will all be destroyed."

"WHAT?" I yelled, shocked at what I just heard.

"Shh, quiet," Astraea quickly hushed me.

I whispered sternly, "Fine, tell me what the right choice is, and I will do my doggone best to make sure it's the one Sloane and I make."

"I cannot do such a thing. Alas, I wish I could. The warning does not state what the right choice is. Cedrik did not even want you to know that much because it could influence your decision."

"Well shit, isn't this just peachy." Why is it prophecies came with warnings but never pointed out exactly what it was you were supposed to do? Damn it, I would take a pirate treasure map any day. The 'X' always marked the spot, and you knew where the treasure was.

Astraea pleaded with the two of us to not say anything further on the subject. Aisling and I both begrudgingly agreed. The three of us brought the food offerings over to the table to share with everyone present. Aoife packed cheese, wine, bread, fruit, and meats. Overall, nothing fancy, but it was most certainly welcomed by everyone involved.

After we all finished off the last morsel of food, Brevan cleared his throat. "Since Mathias is here along with what is left of The Order of the Dragon, I would ask he step forward at this time." I suspected his induction was going to happen tonight. It was the main reason I slipped on my necklace, which held my mother's pendant and my father's ring, before we left home earlier.

Mathias stepped forward, and I handed Brevan my father's ring. However, it wasn't Brevan who performed Mathias' initiation. It was Cedrik.

"Mathias, son of Naffir, mate of the Shadow Dragon. Do you promise to place yourself before harm in the protection of the Mystics?"

Mathias took a knee and responded, "I do."

"Mathias, son of Orla, brother-in-law of the Dark Star Phoenix. Do you promise to follow the ways of The Order of the Dragon?" Cedrik nodded for Mathias to respond.

"I do."

That was when Cedrik spoke in Dokkalfar. "Uin anada -o erui lug a ae, min gar- swan I an gwest – o than. An ha na- tir mage I nor- tri min vin. Im gwedhi- cin in I conn- with cin bood a I bood -o min nos. Cin vow na- I vow -o min ancent. O hi aur cin ar biho- din na cin gwest."

Cedrik pricked Mathias' finger and placed a drop of blood in the center of the stone on the ring. The image of the Dragon glowed red as the ring was slipped onto Mathias' finger and sealed his oath.

"You are now a member of one of the oldest brotherhoods. Welcome!" Cedrik clasped Mathias on the shoulder, as did both Brevan and Emmer.

After they finished, Mathias quietly made his way over towards me while I was pouring over a few of the scrolls Cedrik brought with him. "Amelia, this is your father's ring…" Mathias whispered in my ear, and I nodded.

"I do not understand?" His eyes held utter confusion.

"Mathias, I can't think of a better person to have my father's ring than you. Besides, I wouldn't want anyone else covering my back who isn't just my sparring partner but my loving mate who means everything to me. At the end of the day, I know you'll always be there."

"I love you, Amelia." Mathias kissed me ever so softly and sweetly.

"I love you too. Now, before we get all mushy and aroused… we need to get back to our plan of attack. No more getting caught by surprise." I felt his total awe, gratitude, and overwhelming love at what I'd done through our bond, but we all had a job to do and accomplish.

Sloane and General Pax began debating the merits of setting troops on the higher outcroppings of the Sleeping Mountain pass when the doors to the council chambers' doors burst open.

AMELIA (AMI) JANE GRAY

CAPTAIN J

$\mathcal{T}$hree of General Pax's men were carrying in three people I thought I'd never see again. Laudy, Milton, and Captain Jonathan Lang. They all looked like they'd been put through the wringer. Sloane also immediately recognized them as we both moved quickly over to the Gargoyles.

"Where in the name of God did you find them?" I exclaimed.

Gargoyle One answered as he carried Captain J, "They were just outside the city walls. The two older ones will need assistance. The other one I have here is not what he seems."

I leaned in closer to study his features. His vibrant green eyes were the same as they'd been when I first met him. However, his facial features shifted ever so slightly to reveal a different man beneath. The entire thing only lasted a moment. The Gargoyles carried Laudy and Milton and gently set them down as Sloane and Neemah moved over to the older couple.

"Captain J, can you hear me? It's Ami!" I lightly tapped his face in an attempt to rouse him. "Come on, Captain J, wake up!"

Captain J's eyes opened ever so slightly as he mumbled, "Nocht mo chuid féin fíor."

Brevan came to stand behind me, possibly to aid with some sort of

153

assistance, while Jackie stood next to me. Before my eyes, Captain J's features wholly transformed from the salty sailor I met back in Miami to someone I didn't recognize. However, the recognition hit Brevan like a ton of bricks as I heard him gasp. Brevan grabbed the man's hand and stared down at it. It was at that point, for the first time, I noticed the ring he was wearing. It was a ring signifying The Order of the Dragon.

"May the strength of the dragon find you and keep you safe," Brevan spoke the beginning of their secret phrase. A phrase my father once said to me.

"May the wings of the dragon bring you to your freedom," Captain J hoarsely replied and continued with, "Hello, boy."

Brevan staggered backwards in shock, which caused me to swivel my head, "Brevan, what's the matter? These people need help!"

"Amelia, he is my father. Lord Edon!" Brevan breathed out.

"Your father? I thought your father was dead," I was caught off guard by Brevan's declaration.

Captain J or Lord Edon or whoever he was passed out again. Regardless of the man's questionable state of identity, one sure thing was all three of these people needed medical attention. Since Brevan was in a somewhat dumbfounded state, I took charge.

"Sloane, you and Neemah get these three back to the packhouse. When you are there, find some beds to place them in, so Neemah will be able to properly treat them." I began with organizing the circus that'd been deposited in the council chambers.

"Ami, why should they go with you? They were my staff," Jackie piped up, and I just raised an eyebrow at her.

"Jackie, are you seriously going to stand here and debate where they should or shouldn't go? I realize all of it is a bit of a shock, but their well-being is more important than whom they stay with."

She shook her head. "No, you're right. It's just…"

"I know. As soon as they can talk, I will let you know." I hugged Jackie tightly. I knew she would be hoping one of them might have information on her mother.

"Amelia, I do not mean to interrupt, but where are we going to put

154

everyone. While the new living quarters are nearly finished, we still have a full house?" Aisling asked, and damn it if she wasn't correct.

Brevan finally shook off his shock and took over. "Place my father in your room. You and Sloane will move in with us temporarily. As for the other two, I need to know if they are a couple."

"Brevan, they are husband and wife," I confirmed for him.

"Fine, Marta is not going to like it but shuffle her in with some of the single women and give them Marta's living quarters."

"That is not necessary. Marta can stay with me in my cottage," Neemah proclaimed, which finally settled the sleeping arrangements.

"Aisling, if you wish to go with Neemah and Sloane, I completely understand," I quietly spoke in her direction, and she shook her head.

"No, I think it is best if it is just Sloane and Neemah. This way, if she needs to get to one of them, there are fewer bodies to climb over." Aisling made a good point.

Sloane came over and kissed Aisling on the cheek. "I'll move as much of our things up to Ami's apartment as I can before you get home."

"Sloane, the sofa is a sectional. It can be moved around to make a bed for the two of you. I know it'll be tight for a while, but it will only be for a couple of days," I called out to my brother.

"No worries, Ami. At least this way, we're just one big happy family." I laughed because the irony in his statement wasn't lost on me.

"Brevan, I will go ride with the driver. I know we have got the construction crew doing final touches on the new living quarters, but perhaps, I can persuade them to work just a little faster," Emmer offered. As it was, the construction people were already working around the clock to get things finished. This situation was just really forcing our hand to get it completed faster. Brevan nodded at Emmer, who then left through the door, following the group out.

I slowly approached Brevan, who'd fallen silent again. "Brevan, are you alright?"

Brevan pulled me into his arms, "My little wolf, if you only understood."

Shit! That wasn't good. I could feel the conflicted emotions

155

coming from him, and it didn't take a rocket scientist to read it on his face as well. In an instant, I realized why. He was glad to see his father, but his father was the pack's Alpha before him on the same note. I could almost see what was running through his mind.

"Are you concerned you'll have to fight your father for Alpha?"

Brevan gawked at me and sighed, "How--"

I'd cut him off before he could finish his thought, "I knew because I know you. Let's just take one problem at a time. Right now, we still need to finish up the meeting. Personally, I've got an idea I'd like to run by everyone regarding decoys and the temple. It's risky, but I think it's a better alternative than serving Sloane and I up on a silver platter. After that, we can head home and contend with our latest disaster. Deal?"

Brevan squeezed me tighter, "Deal. Let us hear your idea and see if it is viable."

AMELIA (AMI) JANE GRAY

THE BEST LAID PLANS

Over the next hour, I presented the plan I formed in my head after examining everything laid out before us. Some key points were General Pax and Sloane's ideas about using the outcroppings to place troops on. However, I amended their idea by adding my own twist to the concept.

"General Pax, how difficult would it be for say six or seven of your men to hide and conceal four of my shield maidens?" It would be key for an easier snatch-and-grab escape.

"Amelia, are you insane? None of them are ready for this kind of mission!" Mathias protested.

"Well, we'll just need to get them ready. Besides, if you think you hate that, you're really going to hate the next part, and I still need an answer from General Pax." I turned my attention towards the General.

"Should they all be around your height or smaller, it would not be difficult. Our wings allow us to blend in with the rock's coloring." General Pax confirmed my suspicions.

I nodded in acknowledgment and continued with my presentation. "We will need the General's men and our shield maidens to be in position at least a day ahead of time, so they're not seen getting settled

157

into their spots. Try to find hiding places as close to the exchange point as possible. The shield maidens will be our best equipped female archers to provide cover for when…" I took a deep breath and pointed to General Pax. "Your men swoop in and pull out the decoys and the hostages."

"Decoys, Amelia?" Lady Astraea queried.

"That's the part Mathias is really going to hate," I confirmed.

"This should be good," Mathias mumbled.

"I'm glad you think so because you're the stand-in for Sloane, and Aisling is mine. She'll need to dye her hair, but it shouldn't be too difficult." I came to a full stop and waited for the eruption. In three, two, one…

"Amelia, now I know you have lost your mind! If you think for one second, I am going to allow my sister anywhere near our potential battlefield—" Aisling hauled off and punched Mathias clean in the ribs, causing Mathias to bend over, exhale loudly and grab his ribs.

"Dearest brother of mine, I love that you want to protect me, but as you can feel, I am more than capable of protecting myself." Mathias went to protest again but was immediately silenced by a glare from Aisling before she continued. "It is my choice as to whether or not I wish to agree with Amelia's plan, and I, for one, want to hear the full idea before I cast judgement."

Aisling nodded for me to continue. "The pair of you will be dressed to conceal as much of your identity as possible. Drew, we'll need you to come up with outfits which use some cloaks and some sort of faceguard that are both breathable and movable. Declan would be an excellent consult for functionality. You'll probably be dealing with Lycandra since Queen Cosima has stayed fairly elusive during all the bloodshed. Lycandra seems to have stepped up to the front. It means she is more than aware of the style of weapons Sloane and I use. Declan, would it be possible for you to create additional weapons similar to the ones you made for Sloane and me? This way, we're keeping things as consistent as possible."

"I believe I have enough time to do so," Declan agreed.

"Ami, you know I've got you covered," Drew professed.

"Amelia, so far, your plan sound's fairly well thought out but do you have more?" Cedrik probed.

"I do," I responded and continued with my explanation right down to the smallest detail. "Brevan, Oren, the coven guards, and Pack Lingwir will form the main combatant line. In contrast, Cedrik and Astraea's guards are going to be hiding amongst the city's defenses. General Pax's men are all to be split between the city skies and the fight area where General Pax will be running the coordination." That brought me to the final part of my plan. "To further try and sell the point Lycandra will be actually looking at Sloane and me, Drew and Jackie will be standing with Brevan. Fully aware, under the caveat should fighting break out, they are to run out of there as fast as their legs can carry them." I scanned around at the group before I spoke again.

"You're all going to be the diversion. We are flipping the situation to *OUR* advantage. According to the prophecy, both Cedrik's and the one provided to us in the spellbook which Neemah provided. Sloane and I need to be in the temple. Since there is only one person I know of who has a map of the maze memorized, Nova will be coming with us along with Emmer. The smaller our group, the easier it will be for us to slip past any Alfar who might've found their way to the temple entrance."

"My dear, Amelia, using Nova as the map is a sound idea, but if you wish to get inside the temple, you not only need a map, but you will also need a key." Astraea took a breath and lowered her eyes. "I shall have to accompany you."

"Astraea, I thought you were a map, not a key." I was bewildered at this point.

Cedrik placed his hand on Astraea's arm and squeezed before she spoke again. "It is my final secret. Our reverend mother held the gift of prophecy. One, in particular, plagued her dreams right up to the day she died twenty-two years ago. She saw you attempting to gain access to the temple, but you were met by Queen Cosima and her Alfar guards. You and your brother were captured. It is where her vision stopped. In an attempt to thwart her vision, the reverend mother cast a secret key to the temple. *I* was that secret key. She told me to stay away the night you and your brother were sent through the portal. She also said I would know the time to reveal my secret. Now, is that time."

I was rendered completely speechless, so much so, it was like saying snow was cold. *Holy Shit!* was all I could think.

"Amelia, if Queen Cosima and my mother have wolves and Alfar crawling all over the entrance, how do you plan on getting by them?" Brevan's inquiry was both a strategic one and one coming out of concern.

"I've thought of that. I need four volunteers, and I can show you." Since Brevan asked the question, he stepped back, but Jackie, Drew, Lyros, and Aisling stepped forward.

"I think you all will need to be touching me somewhere for the idea to work, so find a spot and *lay your hands on meeee.*" I did a quick rendition of Bon Jovi, causing Drew and Jackie to laugh, but everyone else stared. I swear my humor was lost on these people.

Once everyone placed one hand on me, I spoke the spell I held in my mind, "Gwathren echeri." It was more challenging to accomplish in a lighted room, but our group melded into the shadows.

Astraea spoke first, "Well done, Amelia! Now, can you all move independently without being seen?"

We all went to move simultaneously but ran into the one problem I hadn't thought of. We quite literally walked into one another. Drew crashed into my side, Jackie tripped over my foot, Aisling collided with my front, and Lyros smacked into my back. All of us burst out laughing at the stupidity, and the spell was broken as I lost my concentration.

"Okay, so my plan needs a little work there, but you get a general idea."

Brevan folded his arms in front of his chest and nodded. "Your plan is the best one we have come up with so far. Except for the last bit, but if you think you can work out the issues with it, I see no reason why we should not move forward with it."

The doors to the council chamber opened as Cash strode in with his mate Naima behind him. I touched Brevan's arm and gave my head a slight shake. '*Oren, I need you to make your way around to the hall unseen and mentally listen to the conversation I have with Naima. I'm searching for deception within her answers.*' I thought as loud as I could, and my message was obviously received because Oren slipped out the side door without saying a word.

I turned on my heels, so I was facing our newcomers and greeted them warmly. "Cash, Naima, what a pleasant surprise. I didn't know Brevan asked the pair of you to come." I walked over to the two of them and hugged each of them individually.

"Apparently, Lord Brevan needed another opinion on some tactics. He thought you and Naima might have an opportunity to get to know one another better. Although, from the looks of it, you seem to be in the thick of your discussions." Cash wasn't a fool, so I needed to play my cards just right.

"Oh, you know me, put a bow and arrow in my hands, and I'll hit the bullseye each time. Ask me to plan anything though, forget it! If you want proof, just take the binding ceremony between Brevan and me." I concluded with a warm smile. One thing I sucked at was lying, so I at least tried to stick close to the truth.

"Fair point," Cash confirmed.

"Naima, perhaps you and I should step out to the hall for a moment. I believe Brevan has a few questions for Cash, and it'll give you and I a chance to chat."

"Of course, M'lady."

I hooked Naima's arm with mine as we strolled out to the hall. I wanted our conversation somewhere away from Cash. If it turned out Naima was hiding something, then the last thing we needed was a pissed off mate. This way, Brevan and the rest of the council would act as a distraction while Oren and I could weed through her thoughts.

"So, Naima, why is it I never see much of you around the pack-house?" I inquired and was honestly curious.

"Sorry, M'lady, it is just because I try to stay out of everyone's way," she answered with what I'd say was some irritation.

"Naima, it's Amelia, please. I don't think I'll ever be comfortable with the M'lady. And, whatever do you mean by staying out of everyone's way?" I countered.

"Amelia, one might say I am not exactly liked or trusted by our fellow pack members." Naima's irritation morphed slightly to sadness.

"Why wouldn't you be trusted? I mean, you're Cash's mate, so that should help soothe things over somewhat, shouldn't it?" As I pressed, I had to remind myself I needed to keep focused.

Naima actually gave me an eye-roll. "Do not tell me you have no idea why. You and I both know you are not foolish."

"Honestly, Naima, I don't. You were already mated to Cash when I arrived, and let's face it, I've been a bit busy."

Naima breathed out a sigh, "Cash and I met in the market here in Tenebris, back when Lady Aerin had just taken control of Pack Lumen. Even though we knew at the time, we were each other's true mates, we waited to have our binding because of the tense situations between the two packs. He and I did not even dare hope for a binding ceremony until word got out that Brevan and Aerin were attempting to work together. That was about one year before you arrived. Cash and I took another six months before we decided to have our binding. When I informed my parents, they disowned me, and I moved to Pack Lingwir. Ever since then, I have stayed out of people's way. Somehow, I was labeled as a gossip, which caused even more distrust, but I just go about my business and keep to myself. It is why you do not see much of me. Most days, I spend reading. Cash does not even fill me in on issues involved with the guards."

I immediately felt an overwhelming sense of guilt. 'Oren, we are done here,' I thought before I continued.

"Naima, would you like to go shopping with me sometime? I plan on meeting up with my friend Drew, who's in Lord Oren's coven at some point. We'll spend our men's money, have lunch, and just hang out."

Naima's eyes began to water. "Amelia, I would be honored."

"Good, it's a date! As soon as all this crazy nonsense is done and over with!" I gave Naima a hug and hoped like hell I wasn't wrong.

Cash soon exited the council chambers and approached the two of us.

"Everything alright here?" He frowned as he appeared concerned when he saw Naima. She was the one to answer him.

"Yes, of course. Amelia just asked me to go shopping with her and have lunch, is all." She hugged Cash tightly, and as she did, Cash mouthed 'thank you' to me. I smiled at him as I nodded.

After the two of them left a couple of minutes later, I poked my head into the council chamber.

"I'll leave the rest of the planning to the brain-trust. It's time for me to go visit some of our friends downstairs. Mathias, feel like trekking down to the holding cells with me?" I pointed, making the gesture of a circle.

"Amelia, if you are going down to see Jakkel, perhaps—"

I halted Brevan before he could continue, "You've already had a go at him and wound up doing nothing but making him bleed. This calls for psychological warfare, and him seeing Mathias alive and well along with my ability to get under his skin, might just glean us some information we weren't able to get with your methods."

Mathias moved to my side, and General Pax motioned to one of his men to join us. After he was satisfied, Brevan nodded. "Very well, just be careful. Jakkel is definitely not right in the mind."

AMELIA (AMI) JANE GRAY

IT WOULD FIGURE

The three of us made our way out of the council chamber as we followed General Pax's man down to the holding cells. I silently thanked God I was making this walk as a council member, and not how I'd first made it. The memory still brought back shivers.

That psychopath might've been known in this land as Jakkel, but I'd always know him as Jack Cranston. When we passed through the door, which led to Jack's holding cell, he started to speak nonsensical words. "Is that you, little boy?" he then laughed coldly.

The guard opened the door, and I leaned against the frame while I examined my nails. "Not quite, guess again." Jack growled, and I snagged the dagger from the guard's belt. In one fluid motion, I threw the dagger, piercing Jack's shoulder. Jack let out a shriek of pain, and I sauntered over to where he was chained against the wall. I first twisted the knife then yanked it out unceremoniously. I purposely made sure it caused an increased amount of pain.

Jack sneered, "You little bitch. I'm going to kill you."

With one hand, I grabbed hold of his face and forced his eyes to meet mine. "I don't think so. I think you are going to tell me precisely what I want to know."

164

Jack's evil cackle echoed throughout the prison, "What makes you think I'll tell you anything, you stupid little girl?"

I moved my hand over the wound and healed it before I spoke again. "Because Jack, I can literally cut you to shreds, heal you, then repeat the process over and over, and no one will ever be the wiser." I paused for a more dramatic effect, "Oh, and a side note to you, you disgusting animal. Surprise! I'm the Shadow Dragon."

Jack's cackle morphed into a defeated chuckle, "At least I have the distinct knowledge of the wolf who caused my capture is dead."

I sweetly smiled and waved Mathias inside. "Think again! He's standing right next to me, you stupid simpleton. Now, we can either have our conversation the easy way or the hard way. The choice is yours."

General Pax's guard glanced over at me and hid a chuckle. I thought to myself, *Okay, I knew I was quoting the General, but hey, if I was going to channel badass, why not the biggest badass I knew.*

Mathias followed my lead, strode up to Jack, picked him up by the throat, and slammed him against the wall. "That was rude, Jakkel. Do not ever speak to my Amelia like that ever again. I should warn you not to make me angry. You would not like me when I am angry." I tried very hard to school my face as both Mathias' words and actions dared me to laugh at Jack, while the classic television show 'The Incredible Hulk' popped into my head. It was one of those things Drew made me watch one night while we all lived together.

As I continued to pull myself together, I noticed a small barred window at the top of Jack's cell. I glimpsed through it momentarily. From the level of darkness, I guessed it'd gotten relatively late. As I focused on the darkness outside, a cool breeze drifted in and ruffled my hair. I guess the only good thing about the window was it allowed some fresh air to defuse the cell's stench.

Mathias released Jack, took a step back as we watched him slump in defeat. "What do you want to know?" Jack asked, and I felt a sense of triumph.

"Where is Lycandra keeping the hostages?" I didn't hesitate with my question.

"She's taken over most of the farming village of Demeter. They're being held—" Jack hadn't gotten to finish because he began gurgling and blood started dribbling out of his mouth.

I dared a glance at the window and noticed a bamboo-style pipe being pulled back. I pointed at the window and yelled, "ASSASSIN!"

General Pax's man who was with us ran for the prison door to sound the alarm. Quickly, I moved to Jack's side and began to examine him. After a few seconds, I noticed there was a blow dart protruding from the back of his neck. Mathias and I realized all too soon any attempt to save him would be met with failure. All we could do was watch as Jack met an excruciating death.

"Mathias, leave him. The dart is definitely laced with something perilous. I don't know about you, but I'd rather not find out what it is."

"Agreed, I have felt the effects of their poison first hand. I do not wish for a repeat performance. We will have the guards remove him and instruct them not to remove the dart."

Mathias and I backed out of the cell. There was one last person down here we needed to see, but I wanted one of our telepaths with us when we did it. As I explained my thoughts to Mathias, he agreed to go get Oren. I walked out of the holding cell and glanced down the hall. Sadly, I recognized exactly where I was.

Slowly, I walked down the hallway that led to the all too familiar cell. I reached the door and opened it. As I gazed upon the interior, I thought back to my first night here on the island. Jackie, Sloan, Drew, and I'd been dropped on the beach by Queen Lyra and her people. It was that night I'd first met Brevan, albeit in his wolf form. My heart ached to be a carefree college graduate again on vacation. A single tear fell in mourning.

Suddenly, I felt a cool breeze which broke me out of my thoughts, and I glanced over to my right. Drew ran down here to find me. I wiped at the tear before it could stain my cheek and greeted him with a sad smile.

"Hey, Ami, you okay?" Drew pulled me into his side.

"Yeah, I'm okay. Just remembering." I leaned my head on his shoulder. "Drew, do you ever think about how different our lives would be if we'd never gotten on the plane to Miami?"

Drew chuckled, "Every day, but then I ask myself, what would Ami do, and I give myself a mental slap."

His craziness made me laugh, and I poked him in the side for teasing me. "I'm serious. Look at who we've become from who we were even then." I pointed into the cell.

"Ami, except for all the Lycandra bullshit, are you happy? You've checked in with Jackie, and you've checked in with me, but neither of us has asked you."

Drew was still my boy, and I will always love him no matter what. "Drew, I absolutely love and adore both of my mates, and the pack's turning into the family they should've always been."

"You, my girl, are carefully avoiding my question." Drew bopped my nose with his finger.

"Honestly, most of the time, I am. I just miss us. I miss being able to eat cookie dough while watching a movie and trash the guys who have done us wrong. I miss waking up and seeing your face holding out my cup of coffee, telling me to get my ass in gear because we were going to be shopping all day. I miss seeing Jackie bouncing down the hall of our apartment because she drank one too many sodas and needed to pee, or she'd explode. Speaking of, where is the energetic wonder woman?"

"Oh, don't worry, she's upstairs chewing Mathias a new ass for leaving you down here alone," Drew teased.

Just like that, Jackie appeared behind Drew and me. "Were you two talking about me?"

I pulled my two friends in for a group hug. "Promise me when everything is all over, and life resumes in some sort of normal fashion, we take time to return to the old us. Even if I have to kick Brevan and Mathias out for the night, we do us. Agreed?"

Simultaneously, they both said, "Agreed," when a gentle cough interrupted us.

"I do not wish to interrupt what is obviously a precious moment between close friends, but I thought you needed my assistance with another prisoner?" Oren inquired with a smile.

Oren stood there looking all sexy as he leaned against the wall. *How the hell does he do that?* I briefly thought, and Oren chuckled. "It is a gift, my dear Amelia."

Jackie turned her head towards me, "He's right. You do think loud."

"Jackie, don't tell me you heard those thoughts as well?"

She squished up her face and pinched her first finger to her thumb, "Only just a little bit."

"Holy shit! You can hear thoughts like a real telepath?" I was stunned.

"I swear it just started. Nova's been teaching me how to control it, but sometimes there are just loud thinkers. And, honey, you're without a doubt one of them," Jackie quickly explained.

"Okay, but don't go poking around in my head, or you'll be in for a shock," I warned. Some things needed to stay private, and one of them was me imagining my mates' naked assets. Those visions were things I definitely didn't want to share. Of course, within seconds, my mind flashed to those exact images of my guys as they popped directly into my head.

"Ugh, Ami! I can never unsee those ever!" Jackie exclaimed.

Oren laughed out loud, and his laugh echoed down through the hallway. "Alright, enough playing with Amelia's thoughts. We have one more prisoner to interview."

The four of us walked down to the other end of the hall and opened the cell Diandra was being held in. She was lying in a ball on the floor. As we approached, the smell of rotting flesh hit my nose. Wouldn't it just figure, the only other person who could possibly have any information was dead?

"Come along, Amelia, it appears as though she has been dead a while. We need to report her death to General Pax and get back upstairs." I couldn't have agreed more with Oren if I tried. We all left the prison and headed back to the council chamber. We'd have to find some other way to find out what was going on with those on the other side of the Sleeping Mountain.

AMELIA (AMI) JANE GRAY

UNCERTAINTY

We returned to the council chambers and Oren reported Diandra's state to General Pax. He immediately ordered some of his men to investigate the situation. I attempted to explain to Brevan what happened with Jakkel. Brevan informed me that Mathias already relayed the information. Overall, we spent another fifteen minutes going over a practice session for those of us that would be attempting to covertly enter the temple. Oren and I made arrangements with Cedrik and Astraea to help them weed out who might be possessed by Sylphs. We came up with a viable strategy based on my explanation of what happened with Liam. It was agreed amongst all parties to meet Astraea and Cedrik at their estate in two nights. This way, they'd have time to round up those they suspected might be affected.

Our carriage returned empty after dropping everyone off at the packhouse. Brevan, Mathias, Aisling, and I climbed into the back and headed back home. I quietly chuckled to myself. Home was such a funny word. It really hadn't quite dawned on me until then that I'd started referring to the packhouse as 'home.' A home I'd protect at all costs with everything I had within me.

It appeared I wasn't the only one lost in thought. Brevan was

169

staring out his own window, concern written all over his face. I knew where his thoughts were as it didn't take a rocket scientist to figure out. His father was back, and on the plus side, Lord Edon was alive. On the minus side, no one knew if he would attempt to challenge Brevan to try and take back his Alpha status.

When we arrived back home, Mathias and Aisling went straight upstairs to our apartment. Brevan and I went directly to Sloane's room, where Lord Edon was supposed to have been placed, so Neemah could attend to him. When we arrived, Brevan paused outside the door, listened, and chuckled.

"Are you just going to stand out there, or are you coming in?" Lord Edon bellowed. He still sounded like Captain J, which slightly confused me. The one thing I knew for sure was that Neemah definitely was an excellent healer.

Brevan opened the door, together we stepped inside, and he closed the door behind the two of us. Lord Edon was sitting up in bed with his back leaning against the headboard. He was shooing Neemah away. "Good lord, woman, do I look as though I'm going to fall over?"

"You know better than anyone, I am not about to let you set a toe out of bed until I deem you fit enough to do so. Now, stop your bellyaching and allow me to do my job," Neemah spouted back.

"Hello, Father," Brevan greeted him cautiously.

"Get over here, boy. I haven't seen you in twenty-two years," Lord Edon barked out.

I took hold of Brevan's hand as we approached the side of the bed opposite Neemah. "Neemah, what is the issue with him?" Brevan inquired.

"You mean other than being more obstinate than me, I am assuming. Let me see, exhaustion, dehydration, a wounded left shoulder which became infected, and last but not least, underfed," Neemah rattled off the list as if she were going shopping.

"Should I go and get him something from the kitchen?" I questioned, trying to make myself useful, but Neemah shook her head.

"No, Aoife will be back in a moment with the specific food I requested," Neemah breathed out with some exhaustion of her own. I released Brevan's hand and moved around the bed to Neemah, placing my arm around her shoulders.

"Gran, have you seen to Milton and Laudy yet?"

Neemah nodded her head. "Yes, yes. I saw to them first. Humans are far more fragile than Lycanthrope, especially this one. They are both resting comfortably." She patted my hand.

"Alright, Gran, why don't you go and get some rest. You have a new roommate anyway, so it will take some time for the two of you to get settled. I think Brevan and I can handle Captain… I mean, Lord Edon." It was going to take some effort to remember who I was referring to.

Neemah collected her things into her carpetbag and moved to the door with no argument. "You listen here, you stubborn old wolf! If I hear you have put even a toe out of bed before morning, you will be answering to me. Do I make myself clear? Do not give my great-granddaughter a hard time either." She pointed at him as she raised her eyebrow.

Lord Edon saluted. "Yes, ma'am," he replied, and I hid my smirk with a cough.

Neemah exited, and when she did, it left the three of us in an awkward silence. Someone needed to start the conversation. So, in true journalistic fashion, I began with the questions. "Captain Jonathan Lang? Care to explain?" It was late, and I was in no mood to mollycoddle anyone.

"Girl, do you have any idea who you're addressing?" he barked back.

I stalked closer, created a blue ball of healing energy, and glared at him directly in the eyes. "The better question is, do you?"

Lord Edon let out a soft chuckle, "Seems I missed a few things since I lost you onboard ship."

"Gee, ya think? Now would you care to explain, or do I need to go find Sloane and get him to set something on fire before you start talking?" I'd so totally lost my patience pants.

"Brevan, leave us. This is a conversation between myself and Ami—"

171

Brevan cut off his father, "Anything you say to my mate, you say to me. Besides, you are no longer Alpha here. I am!"

Great, were we really going to have a pissing contest now? Seriously? They began growling at each other, and I conjured another ball of healing light, one for each hand. Before anyone could shift, I threw one ball at Brevan and the other one at Edon. "Will the two of you knock it off! You're acting like children!"

Once they each recovered from their own individual shock, I was glared at by the pair of them. At least I knew now, I held their attention. "Brevan, you are undisputedly the Alpha here. Lord Edon, you'd do well to remember those words. Now, back to my question, care to explain what the hell happened? Or, do I need to hit you with another magical energy ball?"

Lord Edon growled, "You mated my son?"

Brevan bent over his father. "Choose your next words very carefully, Father."

"Sit down the pair of you. I suppose it's time for you to hear what happened back then." Lord Edon composed himself as he realized the home he once knew was not the same place he returned to.

Lord Edon began his story with his exit through the portal. He explained he didn't pop out until well after we'd all disappeared due to the portal already becoming destabilized. "It took me months to find you. Alexander and Marissa already established themselves with you as their daughter, and Jakkel was nowhere to be found. For that matter, neither was your brother. By the time I found him, it was years later. Jakkel did an excellent job covering his tracks. If it wasn't for one of those tabloids, I'm not sure I ever would've found him. He'd already married Marsha Peabody and taken on the name Jack Cranston. They were photographed at a charity auction, and Marsha was being escorted out by two of the organizers. At the same time, Jakkel apologized for her behavior, or at least that's what the article stated. Their behavior wasn't what I cared about, though. What the article gave me were names. So, I watched and waited for the most opportune moment. It came when Newton Peabody bought the Lady Antebellum. He needed a captain, and I took on the persona of

Captain Jonathan Lang. I used the magic I possessed within my ring to transform into the figure you saw. It was only supposed to be a temporary measure, but then I met Prudence." Lord Edon paused, rubbed his eyes, and took in a deep breath. "Do you know anything about true mates?"

Without hesitation, I nodded, "Brevan is one of my true mates."

Lord Edon gazed upon me, wide-eyed. "You're going to need to explain that one to me afterwards, young lady."

"Father, are you saying Prudence is your true mate?" Brevan quizzically looked at his father.

"She is Lylaine right down to the last strand of hair on her head," he replied.

"But she was married to Newton? Oh, wait, she's the reason why you stayed? You weren't just looking for Jakkel and Sloane. You were protecting her." The lightbulb in my head finally went off.

"Aye, lass. I was, but when we passed through the portal on the way back here." He shook his head. "It didn't go how I planned."

Well, his words were an announcement from the department of 'duh.' "Wait, you speak like you're from my world. No one here speaks the I way do." I'd picked up his little tells, for example, his use of contractions.

"I needed to fit into your world or, for a more correct term, the world you were raised in. As you are well aware by now, you're in the world you were born into."

"What do you mean *how you planned*, father?" Brevan noticed what I hadn't quite gotten to.

"My plan was to sail the Lady Antebellum right directly into Ori Harbor. I was going to have Jakkel thrown into the holding cells at the Council Hall and explain to you lot exactly what was going on once we were all safe."

"Did you sabotage the radar?" I needed to know if it was planned or not.

Lord Edon shook his head and sighed, "No, I suspect it was the handiwork of Jakkel. Probably during a time when I'd taken a break. The closer we were to the portal, the more agitated he became. He never did do well around portal magic. It always made his hair stand on end."

A knock came at the door, and Aoife walked in carrying the tray of food for Lord Edon. "M'lord, I have... Oh, Amelia, Brevan, I am sorry. I did not mean to interrupt."

"Brevan, you allow her to use your familiar? Have you lost your mind?"

I pinched the bridge of my nose while Aoife froze in place as Brevan growled, "You would do well to remember you have been gone for twenty-two years. Thanks to Amelia, our pack is more than just a group of people. It is a family. Do not treat people as you once did. It will not be allowed."

I moved and took the tray from Aoife. "Thank you. Go give those babies of yours a hug and kiss from me, and please let Laura know I'll visit her as soon as I can free up some time." Aoife nodded and headed to the door.

"The two who are staying in Marta's room were asking about you. Sloane was trying to explain as much as possible to them, but you may want to poke your head in to just reassure them both." Aoife's concern about all of this was obvious.

I gave her a warm smile and nodded. "I will. Thanks again, Aoife."

I carried the tray over to Edon. "Here, maybe after you eat something, you won't be so pedantic and overly critical. Edon, as stated previously, this isn't your pack anymore, and you'd do well to remember that."

I placed the tray on Edon's lap and stepped back, "Brevan, I'm going to go check on Laudy and Milton. Will the two of you be alright?" I smirked with the implied unstated sentiment of 'if I leave' not being said.

Brevan came over and wrapped his arms around me, "My little wolf, I will see to it we are alright. Even if it kills me. Go check in on the others."

I didn't necessarily think leaving them was a great idea, but I also knew they needed to hash some of their issues out on their own. Brevan remained mostly quiet while Edon gave his explanation. From what I could pick up because of our bond, Brevan was irritated at best. However, I nodded and left the room. The conversation to follow was between father and son at this point. The uncertainty of what would happen between them was something we'd all simply need to wait for.

AMELIA (AMI) JANE GRAY

TIME IS TICKING

As I reached the door to Marta's room, Sloane was coming out. By the expression on his face, he appeared mostly relieved. "How are they?"

Sloane met my eyes. "Better, calmer. I think seeing the two of us alive and well helped. Poor Laudy was the most stressed. Milton's been handling things like a trooper."

"How much did you explain to them?" It was a critical question if they were going to be mixing with members of the pack. They needed to understand their surroundings.

"Everything. I figured best to rip the bandage off then gradually break them in." We began walking upstairs while we chatted. "They were both pretty skeptical until I showed them a ball of fire in my hands and then shifted. Once I shifted back and redressed, they both asked multiple questions. I just finished when you saw me leaving," Sloane concluded.

As we walked, I hesitated on asking Sloane the one question I knew without a doubt I needed to ask. "Sloane, how are you doing? You know, with what happened to Jack."

Sloane stopped as he turned his head towards me. "I don't know. Part of me is relieved, knowing I'll never have to deal with him again.

176

The other part of me is just numb. He raised me, Ami. For better or worse, I grew up believing Jack was my father."

I grabbed Sloane's hand and gave a gentle squeeze. "If it starts to back up on you, come find me." Sloane nodded, and we continued walking.

"We'll need to wait and see what happens come morning, I think. It's been a long night, and from what I can tell, tomorrow promises to be equally so." I just knew everyone was exhausted.

We reached the stairs up to my apartment we were all sharing. "After you." Sloane motioned with his hand, and I shook my head. I took him up on his offer, and I went up first. When we reached the door, I entered, and the first thing I noticed was a new dividing curtain.

"Mathias, if you think for one second, I am going to have my brother poking his head in on myself and my betrothed, you have definitely lost your ever-loving mind," Aisling was standing with her hands on her hips as she protested loudly.

"Mathias, what happened to the curtain?" I was confused.

"Nothing, I just removed the curtain and left the sheers. It is going to be snug enough without completely cutting off space."

"Mathias, honey, I love you but put the curtain back." Aisling stood there, smugly and Mathias moved over to me quickly.

"Are you sure? I mean it will cut off the airflow—"

I cut him off, "I don't give a crap about *airflow*. What I do care about is privacy. We ALL need it, and right now, I'm taking my privacy and shoving my ass into the bath. While I'm in there, I want all these problems sorted out. If it isn't, I promise you when everything is back to normal, and we have the apartment back to ourselves, and you're feeling frisky. Well, let's just say..." I grabbed hold of his right hand. "This is all you'll have to fix those issues."

"Amelia," he protested, but I was already walking to my wardrobe to grab my dressing gown.

"Fix it. I mean it." I walked into the bath chamber and closed the door. I was taking twenty minutes of me time, and that was all there was to it

After my bath, I crawled into bed and felt absolutely exhausted from the events of the evening. Once I wished everyone a good night, I placed my head on the pillow and found oblivion. It didn't even bother me Brevan wasn't back yet. I knew he and his father needed to deal with quite a few issues. This whole crazy day needed to end. While there were some significant strides made, there were also several stalemates and some interesting developments. My brain simply needed some time to process all of the information.

Over the next week, my training schedule was ridiculously rigorous. Each day, I was up at the crack of dawn and didn't stop until supper. I started my days with a three-mile run, then tackled the obstacle course. After that, I was training with my shield maidens and was followed by my routine with Mathias. All of those activities took place before our mid-day mealtime. After the mid-day meal was one-on-one training with Aisling. Mathias took it upon himself to work with Sloane. While I'd improved, Sloane still needed some work. The last couple of hours before supper, Sloane and I worked on spell casting and controlling our abilities. The appearance of our *gifts* often drew a crowd. I'd even caught a couple of people placing bets on who'd lose control of their abilities first, Sloane or myself.

Plus, throughout the week, I met Oren over at Astraea and Cedrik's estate, who managed to separate out twelve of their people for Oren and me to determine if there was Sylph possession involvement. I decided instead of throwing a ball of healing energy at the subject, I did more of a water balloon effect. I threw the ball over their head and let it run down. My healing powers effectively brought out five Sylphs from the twelve selected members. Astraea held a secret of her own. She trapped the creatures in some enchanted birdcages and lined them up along the wall. The members of her house who were affected by them would eventually heal, and unlike Liam, they would survive.

Astraea assured Oren and me she knew precisely how to deal with the nasty little creatures. I personally was more than happy to leave her to it. Those Sylphs just simply wigged me out. In my eyes, they were like living ghosts. It just made them feel wrong. When they screamed their high-pitched wails, every single hair on my skin would stand on end.

As Oren and I left the main house of the estate, he pulled me aside. "Amelia, again, I apologize, but I have to ask. Why have you not told Brevan and Mathias about your condition?"

Well, shit. I didn't realize he picked up on that as well. My pregnancy only briefly popped into my head just before we began earlier in the evening. "Oren, please don't say anything. Right at the moment, there has been so much going on, and with Edon's return..." I shot him a pleading look. "It's just been a timing issue."

"Promise me you will do it soon. They should know before anything happens." Oren glared at me.

"I promise. I will find the right time. Just not yet. The packhouse is still a zoo."

"Very well, I will take your word on it but make it soon."

"Soon."

We gave each other a quick hug and headed in our separate directions. I climbed into the carriage and rode back to the packhouse while Oren headed to his coven. Life for all of us was hectic.

By the time the next week rolled around, Sloane and Aisling's binding ceremony was at the top of the zoo parade. Miraculously, the contractors finished the new living quarters, and people were being shuffled around again. Marta, Aoife, and surprisingly, Laudy were all working in the kitchen together to pull off the feast for the ceremony.

I realized it took a great deal of weaving to make those flower swags which were covering everything. Aisling roped me into the decorations committee, and she welcomed my suggestion of asking Naima to help as well. Part of the suspicion around Naima was because no one really knew her. So, when we weren't training, it was all about moving people and the binding ceremony. Aisling was at her wit's end by Wednesday morning, and I needed to pull her aside.

"Aisling, you aren't superwoman. Something needs to give." Even her hair that was usually very neatly pulled back, was out of place.

"What would you like me to do? I cannot give up training because of you know what. I am working on my binding ceremony because it needs to be perfect. The children demand time. Sloane and I are moving into our new apartment, which is currently under construction by your suggestion. Where would you like me to give?" She was in a full-on rant.

"NAIMA!" I shouted without moving from Aisling. I'd just seen her pass through the hallway on her way downstairs.

Fortunately, she'd only made it down one flight of stairs when she peered up to the landing Aisling, and I were standing on. "YOU BELLOWED?"

"YES, WOULD YOU PLEASE HEAD BACK UP HERE FOR A MOMENT?"

"BE RIGHT THERE!"

True to her word, Naima was at my side only a moment later. "What is going on?"

"Aisling has taken on too much. Would you please fill in for her with the children? She needs to let something go for the time being." Naima beamed while Aisling gasped.

"Amelia, no!" She was near tears.

"Aisling, it's not a punishment, but you can't do it all. It's obvious you have too much on your plate. Even Brevan would tell you to delegate some of your responsibility to someone else." I tried to be as gentle as possible as I saw her attempting to fight back a tear.

"Aisling, I promise it is only until you can pick it back up again. I would never let anything happen to the children," Naima reassured her.

"Alright, but I will need to fill you in on a few things." Aisling wiped her eyes.

"How about we go over it all after training? I'll tell Sloane the flower committee needs to meet and call off magic practice. Besides, I could use a break from Finn and Riley placing bets," I mildly chuckled.

"They will not be happy. So far, they have cleaned up and made a week's wages since the two of you started practicing," Naima stated.

I swung my head to gawk at her, "Hey, no gossip. I saw them counting their winnings myself."

All I could do was shake my head. If they weren't such good

friends with Sloane, I might've been upset. Hopefully, they were planning on using the funds for some sort of bachelor party for him.

Surprisingly, Edon gave Sloane and Aisling their room back, once the new housing was finished. Brevan consented for them to keep on some of the contractors to remodel and make it their own. Edon also conceded after observing the pack for a few days, it really wasn't the pack he'd left behind. People were closer and happier than he'd ever seen them. The binding ceremony was on Saturday, and Edon approached Brevan the day before, stating he wanted to hand over the pack to Brevan formally. When Brevan relayed this information to Mathias and me, there was palpable relief in the air. No one really wanted to see the two of them fight it out over who was going to be the Alpha.

Brevan and Edon both agreed the best time to do it would be before the binding ceremony. That way, not only would the pack be in attendance, but so would the rest of the council. All I could say was thank goodness for small favors. The last thing the pack needed was turmoil going into the full moon.

Saturday rolled around, and as the dawn broke, I knew time was ticking away. I needed to sit both of my mates down and tell them about my condition. I quietly slipped out of bed and carried on with my usual morning routine. While I was out on my morning run, I made the final decision I would tell them this evening after the binding ceremony. I didn't want the day ruined for Sloane and Aisling, should my mates suddenly become overprotective asshats. If I was being honest, it was a distinct possibility.

As everyone was hanging the swags and flower wreaths, and arranging the centerpieces we'd made, Marta came downstairs, spouting off about last-minute changes. "Unbelievable, you would have thought after the last one they might have learned something."

I pulled her to a stop. "Marta, what's the matter? What happened?"

"The happy couple changed their minds and wish to have the ceremony and party in the garden."

"EVERYONE, FULL STOP!" I yelled, and everyone froze.

"Alright, Marta, what part of the garden do they want it in?" I inquired, so we knew where to move the decorations, along with the altar and dining table, which would now be a grand buffet.

Naturally, Brevan picked that moment to walk in with the musicians. "Brevan, hold please, we have a change."

"They did not say; all they told me was they wanted the ceremony under the stars. UNDER THE BLEEDING STARS!" Marta was about to lose her mind.

I scratched my head, trying to figure out how to pull off a perfect ceremony for my brother when Naima approached me. "May I make a suggestion?"

"Please, I'm at a complete loss," I motioned for her to continue.

"The archway that is in the pack's private garden. Move it out to a more public area. Say, just under one of the big oak trees like the one to the left. I noticed some beams left over from the construction. If we were to place them in the ground and wind the swags around them and across..." Naima's description was starting to form in my head.

"Then we can place the altar at the archway. Oh, that's brilliant!" I exclaimed.

Marta was tapping her finger on her chin as she listened to the pair of us. "How about we use the arch as the beginning of the aisle instead of at the altar?" Naima and I thought about her idea for a moment, and both of us agreed it made a better starting point.

Brevan spoke for everyone to hear, "Marta, Naima, and Amelia are in charge of moving the party outside. Everyone takes their orders from them. If you are not doing anything, then see them for a task. MOVE!"

The countdown clock was clicking down the minutes, and it was going to be a race to the end. I, for one, was going to make damn good and sure my brother's ceremony was as perfect as we could make it. The ticks of time be damned.

AMELIA (AMI) JANE GRAY

THE PERFECT CEREMONY

Thankfully, we managed to get the garden set up in time. The easiest way the three of us figured out to get everything done was to section things off. We used Riley and Finn to escort people to the area we decorated for the guests to view the ceremony. We also moved the dining table to the garden and placed it to the far back against the hedges. It would be designated as the food area and was going to be all lit up by several candles inside hurricane glasses to prevent the breeze from blowing them out. The musicians were set up on the right side of the large graveled area, and we used the rest of the space for dancing and mingling.

Once all the guests arrived, Edon and Brevan stepped up to the altar.

"Thank you, everyone, for coming this evening. Tonight, I will be formally passing along the position of Alpha to my son Brevan. These last years while I've been away, he's held the pack together, and to be totally honest, he has done a far better job than I did as the leader of Pack Lingwir."

Edon turned to Brevan and embraced his son. It made my heart somewhat lighter to know they managed to work through their

183

issues. Edon and Brevan both sliced their palms and grasped each other's hand open wound to open wound before Edon spoke again.

"Mar a rinne ár sinsir san am atá thart. Tugaim fuil iomlán an Alfa do mo mhac. Go dtuga spiorad na seanóirí tú trí do laethanta agus go mbeannaí na déithe thú sna hamanna atá le teacht."

Brevan's eyes glowed brighter than I'd ever seen, even taking into account the times we were together privately. They did light up the dark. Edon's, on the other hand, dimmed and remained the same way after he finished speaking.

Once it was over, I corralled Brevan long enough to ask him what it was Edon recited. Brevan told me the translation was, "As our ancestors have done in the past. I pass on the full blood of the Alpha to my son. May the spirits of the ancients guide you through your days, and may the gods bless you in the times to come." It was both a blessing and a passing from the old to the new.

When Brevan managed to quiet everyone down again, Sloane stepped up to the altar. He looked breathtakingly handsome in a white, mandarin-collared long sleeve shirt, a black satin vest with silver buttons, and black form-fitting leather pants. Aisling was the showstopper, though.

Aisling's dress was a simple slim A-line, floor-length, off-the-shoulder, long-bell sleeve dress with a Basque waist. Her hair was pulled back, leaving long curled tendrils strategically placed to frame her beautiful face. The back of her hair contained baby's breath, tiny white roses, and beautiful long curls. She'd taken my advice and enhanced her eyes, so they appeared even larger than they usually did. Everything was entirely her, and she just shone brightly, even in the dark of the evening.

Mathias walked her down the aisle wearing the same outfit from our binding ceremony, which made me smile to remember the happy parts of our special day. It was far from perfect, we'd been interrupted by Newton Peabody's head being tossed through the window into the hall, but before that rude intrusion, we were happy and having a wonderful time.

I broke out of my memories as Mathias handed off Aisling to

Sloane. Mathias walked over and joined me as the couple turned to face Brevan.

"Ladies and Gentlemen, we gather here on this night to bear witness to the binding of Sloane and Aisling. As someone who has been fortunate enough to see their love blossom and bloom, I can attest to these two being a union of true mates. Blessed upon by the gods and sealed by the magic, I, as Alpha of the pack possess."

Brevan pulled out the gold cord and wound it around the clasped hands of Sloane and Aisling.

"Leis an draíocht i mo chuid fola agus finnéithe anseo timpeall orainn; Iarraim ar na déithe muid a shéalú mar chairde ceangailte. As seo go dtí an tsíoraíocht."

Their eyes began to glow, as did the cord. Just as it happened with Brevan and me, it was over just as quickly as it started.

"Let it be known the binding between Sloane and Aisling has been blessed as true mates. Let the celebrations commence."

Everyone cheered as the couple turned around to face the crowd. I couldn't help myself as the tears streaked down my face. I was so dang happy for both of them. I definitely wasn't losing a brother, I was gaining a sister, and that was how I saw it.

After the couple made their way down the aisle, we all followed behind. Mathias placed his hand on the small of my back and walked with me as I wiped the tears from my face. He studied me for a moment and shook his head. I simply gave him an eye-roll and smiled. Everyone cried at these kinds of events, didn't they?

Brevan caught up with Mathias and me as we waited in the formal greeting line. It was a custom Sloane surprisingly wanted to uphold. He made a point of saying, "I want everyone to know the most beautiful woman in the pack is now my bound mate." I actually thought it was kind of sweet.

Once the three of us made it to the two of them, I immediately hugged Aisling. "Oh, sweetie, you look stunning. I'm so happy you're now my sister," I couldn't help but gush over her.

Aisling giggled, "The light blue dress you have on is lovely. Perhaps you will let me borrow it for the next pack event?"

I laughed, "Already borrowing my clothes? You got it!"

I released Aisling and hugged my brother, "Sloane, I'm so happy for you. I can't wait for us to have our first full family supper."

Sloane pulled back from me. "Perhaps, we could do it for your birthday. It's only two days away."

I wasn't going to make a big deal out of my birthday due to everything going on. It seemed silly for people to make a fuss. "Sloane, I don't know—"

Brevan cut my sentence short, "Nonsense, it is exactly what we will do. What better way to celebrate the day the fates brought you into this world?"

Because I didn't want an argument, I agreed. So, the three of us moved along, so the others in line could congratulate Sloane and Aisling on their binding. As the evening went along, everyone was having a wonderful time while they danced and mingled. On the other hand, I found it becoming harder and harder to pull my mates aside to inform them of my pregnant state.

Once Sloane and Aisling were done cutting the cake, I seized that moment to find both Brevan and Mathias. Mathias was talking with Drew and Lyros. It appeared as though someone just finished telling a joke because a beaming smile broke out on Drew's face. I scanned the faces some more to find Brevan chatting with Astraea and Cedrik. Astraea was casually motioning with her hands while she spoke.

I figured pulling Mathias first would be the easier of the two and started towards his group. As I approached, Oren came up behind me. "Are you really sure you want to do this tonight?"

He nearly made me jump out of my skin. "Oren! You nearly scared me to death!"

"I am very sorry, Amelia. Again, I apologize, but you are thinking loudly again, and I could not help but hear what you were planning." I never could be angry with Oren as he gazed upon me with sincerity.

"Oren, the sooner I tell them, the better. If something were to happen and Brevan or Mathias didn't know, I'd never hear the end of it," I explained. My plans to wait until after the full moon went out the window. I realized how upset and hurt I would feel if they kept something so tremendous from me.

"Very well, do you need any help?" Oren was concerned, and it struck me as being very sweet.

I shook my head, "The day I'm not able to speak to either one of them is the day I need to re-evaluate my relationship with them."

"As you wish, but should you need a hand, think my name, and I will find you. Ever since Lyros told me you were his goddaughter, I have felt a strong, protective urge for you. Brevan may be a good friend, but you are family. Never forget that." Oren shocked me into silence.

I threw my arms around him and quietly whispered into his ear, "Thank you."

Oren patted me on the back, and I continued towards Mathias. When I reached the three men, I apologized for interrupting but asked if I could steal Mathias away. They both nodded their assent.

Mathias wrapped his arms around me and kissed my temple, "Hello, my beautiful mate. I could feel your tension, so go ahead and tell me what is on your mind."

"Oh, I will, but I think we should probably involve Brevan. Just a quick family meeting." I smiled up at Mathias, who instantly became suspicious.

"Shall we go get him then?" Mathias inquired, and I nodded.

Mathias and I managed to snag Brevan away from Astraea and Cedrik with more ease than I originally anticipated. The three of us headed inside to the training room, where we closed the door behind us after we entered. If we'd been in a place where there were chairs, I would've suggested they sit, but since we weren't, I simply dove right in.

"So, there is no good way to say this. I'm pregnant." Might as well rip the band-aid clean off in one fell swoop.

Both Mathias and Brevan stood there silent. We stared at each other for what felt like a very long moment before Brevan spoke up, "Is that it?"

My jaw dropped open. "Is that it? Is that all you have to say? Surely you're joking?"

Brevan shook his head. "No, but nothing I can say will change anything. You would still be risking your neck whether I like it or not, even though you are now responsible for not only your own life but the life of our unborn child. Since it is the very truth of the matter, then what else is there to be said? I am simply choosing not to deal with your pregnancy until after the full moon. Until then, I am going back to the party." Brevan spun and walked out of the room. There was no argument, no joy, no emotion. *Did I enter the twilight zone?*

Mathias came over and wrapped his arms around me. "Thank you for finally telling me." As I stood there in his embrace, I felt the warmth in his heart. At least I felt it in one of my mates.

I tilted my head up to stare at Mathias. "What do you mean *finally telling* you?"

"Brevan and I figured you have known since you went to see Neemah on your own. He has been trying to figure out what to do since then to get you out of the line of fire. Even though I probably would not have said things quite in that way, he does have a point," Mathias explained as a pang of guilt hit my heart.

"Mathias, I can't back out. We all know Sloane and I have to be in the temple. There's just no way around it."

He rubbed my back, "I know, and I also agree with Brevan. Just not quite so coldly. If I did not know better, I would say he is up to something. I just cannot put my finger on it."

I moved my head back so I could see him better. "What do you mean?"

"This Brevan is the one who is calculating something. He only distances himself when he is attempting to get the full picture to see all the moves. I have only seen it a couple of times, but well..." Mathias shrugged. "It is just my best guess."

After I laid my head down on him, I nodded into Mathias' chest and realized he was right. I reached through the bond Brevan and I shared, past the numbness, and felt his dread and worry. As I thought about it, it was apparent he'd been hiding his true feelings the entire time. Mathias confirmed they suspected it since the day I'd gone to see Neemah on my own. All I knew was that Brevan skillfully managed to conceal from me his true feelings. It wasn't long ago he'd sworn to be worthy of me. These two things combined made me worry even more.

On the positive side of things, we managed to keep the ceremony perfect for Aisling and Sloane. That was what I was going to focus on for the moment. Mathias and I rejoined the party, and he remained by my side for the rest of the evening. He didn't yell or scream at me when he heard my declaration, and part of him was doing backflips over the news. The wonderful man who spoke softly to me also agreed with Brevan and was worried beyond belief.

Late in the evening, as the guests started to depart, Mathias explained that the time between him suspecting my pregnancy, and having it confirmed, allowed him to come to terms with his feelings. Not that he wasn't worried, but it was more like he was afraid he was going to display a knee-jerk reaction. Because he knew it would've been incredibly unproductive, and there wouldn't have been any positive outcomes. He wanted to enjoy the early stages with me and cherish every moment he could. Those images made me feel marginally better, yet deep down, I knew both of them were right. I wouldn't change my mind, and I wasn't going to be just risking my own life. I would be endangering our children's lives as well.

LORD BREVAN ALPHA OF PACK LINGWIR

SHITTY CIRCUMSTANCES

I felt guilty for walking out of the training room the way I did, but if I stayed, my emotions would have gotten the better of me. Even though Mathias and I suspected she was pregnant, to hear her as she confirmed it was entirely different. All I wanted was to wrap her protectively in my arms and never let go. Unfortunately, I knew all too well the words I spoke were the truth. There was no way she would back out at this point, and there was no time to change the plan.

As I opened the garden gate and walked inside, my gaze fell upon the Dragon fruit tree, and I silently cursed it. How could the fates bring such a fantastic creature into my life and then ask me to risk everything I held dear? I soon found myself on the same bench Amelia and I first sat upon and took a seat. The memories of that day were slicing clean through my heart.

I sent a prayer up to the gods, "I do not care what happens to me but please, protect my mate and my unborn child."

"Why so forlorn, boy?" I was startled by my father's voice beside me as I stood in the dark.

"Hello, Father, just searching for some quiet contemplation."

190

"I heard your prayer to the gods. I've got a newsflash. They don't answer to the likes of us."

"Do you know how strange it is to hear you speak like my Amelia?"

My father found me in the garden. It was still odd to have him home. We spent his first night setting boundaries for each other. After a few days surrounded by the pack, he saw just how much everyone had changed in his absence. When he questioned me on the difference, I explained to him it was mostly Amelia's influence. She'd blown into the pack like a powerful storm and overturned everyone and everything. His only other question to me was if I truly loved her. My immediate and unequivocal answer was "Yes, more than my own life." This was when he determined I was fully ready to take over the pack as the Alpha. He told me, "Any man who is secure enough to allow his love to lead without controlling her is a man brave enough to know he doesn't always have the answers."

Answers were what I was searching for at the moment. How do I protect my mate without stifling her? Under normal circumstances, I knew she could and would be able to defend herself. She trained harder and longer than most of my guards just to make sure she was good enough. Mathias even commented on how much harder he needed to work these days to push her. Her skills were such, even she, would take most of the men in the pack.

My father came and sat beside me. "Tell me, what's on your mind?"

"Amelia is pregnant," I just blurted it out.

"Ah, I see."

"What do you see?" My father was being intentionally vague.

"You're trying to figure out how to lock her up in the apartment you all share without losing your manhood." Of course, my father would nail the issue right on the head. I swiveled my head, so I could gaze at him as he continued. "Trouble is, your mate is more independent than any woman on the entire island. Even more so than most women from the world where she came from. Whomever she was going to choose would have to be just as strong as her. The fact she's your true mate only means one thing." I prompted him with a nod to continue. "Boy, she is your equal. It's why you're so frustrated."

191

"That is just great, Father, but it really does not help me solve the problem." I rolled my eyes.

My father laughed mildly, "Not yet it doesn't, but I bet I could help you come up with a resolution which might suit you both."

"Like what?" I asked because I became extremely curious. If there was one thing about my father I knew for sure, it was he was exceptionally wily.

"From what I can gather through the pack chatter, you have devised a strategy to confront Lycandra and plan on getting the hostages out of there." His statement made me briefly wonder who in the pack was talking about things they were not sure of. But I realized he would have only gone to one person to get that information, and it would have been Emmer.

"We do, but it all hinges on the fact we will need to run it exactly with all parties in place. One person out of line, and we will fall like dominoes," I succinctly stated. "By the way, it was not just any member of the pack you spoke with to glean such information, was it?"

He just gave me the look all fathers have, which meant, 'do not be so foolish' before he continued. "Your statement isn't entirely accurate. You have something they don't know you have, and you aren't even using it to your advantage." I must have appeared as confused as I felt. "Boy, what's the one thing that would make your mother's blood run cold?"

I sat there a heartbeat longer before it hit me as to what he was getting at. "Father, I could not possibly ask you to do—"

He cut me off, "You aren't asking a thing. I am offering it. Besides, Lycandra is an issue I should've dealt with a very long time ago. Specifically, when I found out she killed Lylaine. You kids were so young at the time, I simply couldn't take away your mother." He shook his head. "If I'd done then what I should've done, none of this crap would be happening now."

"Father, you knew?" I was stunned.

"Of course, I knew! I knew she used poor Marta to gain what she wanted. It was all about the power. The truth is, for a long time, I blamed you for many of the problems which were all mine. It took time and distance for me to realize the only person I could blame was myself. I also have a selfish reason for getting involved, but that is beside the point. What if I were to take your place? It might cause enough of a distraction that she'd be off her game. Don't forget. She believes I'm dead. I am also the only one skilled enough to hold the lead position in a fight. I assure you I haven't lost my touch even if I have taken on an interesting vocabulary," he chuckled.

As I thought over his proposition, I found I could not argue with his logic. Lycandra would be thrown off balance just with his sheer presence. This would free me up to go with Amelia's group into the temple. I might not be able to prevent her from going, but I absolutely could watch her back. Not to mention, he was the man who taught me how to fight. I knew with every fiber of my being, he could handle himself in a tight situation.

"Father, I believe you have yourself a deal. I will need to go over a few of the finer details with you, but I can see no fault with your logic."

Again, he shocked me. I held out my hand, and instead of shaking it, my father hugged me for the first time in a very long time.

"You protect those grandbabies of mine."

His remark brought me up short, "Babies?"

He shrugged. "Neemah may have let it slip your mate was carrying more than one."

Well damn! Talk about shitty circumstances. His misstep made me feel even worse for how I left her.

"You made a right mess of things haven't you?"

"How did you guess?"

"Because you're more like me than I care to admit. Get out of here and go fix it. We'll talk details tomorrow."

I nodded and stood. "Father, it is so good to have you home."

"It's good to be home."

AMELIA (AMI) JANE GRAY

THIS IS GOING TO WORK!

The next morning Brevan was up and out of bed before either myself or Mathias could open an eye. I still wasn't sure where he stood on the whole pregnancy thing, but when I finally decided to open my eyes and head to the bath chamber, he returned with breakfast for us all.

I cautiously sat on the sofa and picked up the cup of keaff, which was closest to me. Mathias arose and headed into the bath chamber cheerier than anyone had a right to be first thing in the morning. There was a weird vibe going on. I scanned over the tray holding our food, and after I became more aware as the keaff began to take effect, I noticed four plates.

I turned to Brevan. "Are we expecting someone?"

Just as I finished my question, a knock came at the door. Brevan stood and walked to the door. Mathias exited the bath chamber, and Edon entered the apartment. Brevan greeted his father with a hug and motioned for him to join us. Edon slowly and deliberately moved through the apartment while he took into account all the changes we'd made. At one time, our apartment used to be his, and I was sure it was probably strange to see it changed from what he remembered.

I knew something was up, by the appearance of Edon. Mathias

194

strolled over to the sofa and took a seat to my right. Brevan sat to my left, and Edon made himself comfortable on the end of the sectional, so he could watch the three of us. I carefully studied the three men sitting there, set my keaff down, and folded my arms across my chest.

"Okay, who's going to start?" there was no way this was just simply a 'family' breakfast.

Edon and Brevan eyed one another while Mathias gazed at me. Mathias' expression alone confirmed my suspicion his cheery mood was separate from the father and son's conspiratorial glances.

"Brevan, would either you or your father care to share with the rest of the class?"

Edon set his keaff down, "You certainly don't waste time."

Brevan continued after swallowing some keaff, "We have a minor change in our plans. I will be going with you into the temple." Brevan's declaration in between sips completely stunned me.

"Brevan, these details were already discussed in depth. Not that I wouldn't be thrilled to have you covering my ass, but Lycandra is expecting you to show up, and if you aren't there, I'm not sure the decoy will work." I countered and pointed out the obvious fact if he wasn't there, she'd know something was up.

Edon, however, interjected with his explanation, "You're right about one thing, lass. She will be expecting Brevan. But she won't be expecting me."

It clearly dawned on me how clever his unforeseen presence would work. Lycandra believed Edon was dead. The only person anyone would've seen on that side of the Sleeping Mountains, even if they sneaked back, towards our side would've been Captain J. Jakkel was killed, so even if he knew Captain J was Lord Edon, he certainly wasn't telling anyone. This was when a huge smile crossed my face.

"You clever old wolf. You're brilliant!" I exclaimed.

Edon growled playfully with me, "Watch who you're calling old."

I picked up my plate of food. "Sorry, but in comparison..." I shrugged. then winked. "Anyway, I'm all for it, but when did the two of you come up with your little idea?"

"You mean you are not going to argue about why we should not be doing this?" Brevan countered back with, and I rolled my eyes.

I shook my head, "No, are you going to answer my question?"

"Last night. What have you done with my Amelia?" his face was still skeptically gazing upon me.

I laughed, "I'm still me. Although I do have a couple of concerns. As it is, I have to conceal myself, Sloane, Nova, and Emmer. We are barely able to move without tripping over one another. I'm not sure what adding you will do to the mix. My only saving grace is Astraea can conceal herself."

My assessment was entirely accurate. Our practice sessions at first were such, we wound up in a massive pile of bodies. It finally came together over the last couple of practices where we could all move together. Trouble was, we were all still far too noisy. Any Alfar would be able to hear us while we tried to move. As I thought about adding in Brevan, my concern wasn't whether I could conceal him but how we'd manage not to trip over one another. I didn't want to set us back to the beginning.

Brevan mulled everything over for a moment. "When you meet again, I will be with you. Perhaps, a different set of eyes can help you figure out a different configuration."

"Fair enough. You never know until you try." I might've been slightly placating him just a tad. Brevan could feel my nerves regarding the change, but I wasn't fighting him on it, so he accepted it as a win. I did, however, think it was a good idea to pull out Edon as an unexpected factor. Provided we would be dealing with Lycandra.

I saw no reason why we wouldn't be able to pull it all off. That was until we got into the temple. Something was telling me the temple was an entirely different ball of wax altogether.

Once Edon and Brevan explained their detailed plans for the front lines, I felt marginally better. Mathias finished his breakfast as he sat there and listened intently to the conversations going on around him. When he finally set his plate back on the tray, he stood, gave me a quick kiss on the cheek, and began to head towards the door.

"Freeze, Mister Chipper! No one wakes up that happy with all this..." I made a circle with my hand. "Going on. Spill now, or I'll drag it out of you later."

Mathias waggled his eyebrows. "Later it is then."

Without another peep, he was quickly out the door. No explanation while he whistled and grinned like the cat who ate the canary. It ultimately left me scratching my head.

I didn't have time to linger, my schedule was booked, and I needed to head down to the training room. This morning I was working with the shield maiden archers. They needed to be as accurate as possible, and there was no time to waste. Riley, Mathias, Finn, and I selected seven of my sixteen trainees. Based on the outcroppings and where we could safely position people, seven was the magic number. This also worked out because it meant only half of my ladies were being used out on the front lines.

The other eight were serving as home defense while we were all out on what was supposed to be the front lines. Those eight were split into two groups. Mathias was taking the lead with their training along with Finn as his second.

The seven I was working with would all be using compound bows. Which meant we would be training outside. The compound bows were far different from the old-fashioned Robin Hood-style bow. There was far more force to them, which allowed the arrow's speed to travel at an incredible velocity with far more power.

Riley was acting as my second, and I was happy to have him. I learned he was one of the pack's sharpest eyes and his record was only proportionate to myself. I caught him practicing early a couple of mornings when I'd gone out for a run. I suspected once all of this was over, he'd be challenging me to a friendly contest.

Just as we were about to begin, General Pax showed up with seven of his guards. He stated they were the seven who would work with our shield maidens and felt they should get comfortable with one another. It wasn't a bad concept; besides, it gave me another idea. I asked the General if he wouldn't mind them coming by each morning for the next week. It was all the time we had left, and I needed to make sure our teams worked together like clockwork. General Pax agreed and gave his men strict orders to stick around while we paired everyone up after the ladies finished their practicing.

We explained to the seven shield maidens what they were being selected for and told them they were free to leave if any wished to back out. Not one of them budged from their spots. I was so damn proud of all of them. When I gave the order to turn and begin, everyone took to the compound bows like a fish to water.

After an hour, I halted the training. "Ladies, you're all doing well with stationary targets. Now, since you've gotten a feel for your weapons, I need to see how you do with moving targets." I moved to my bow and selected an arrow. I noticed Riley was watching me exceptionally close.

When I called over to one of General Pax's men, a few eyes went wide. Quietly, I instructed him as to what I wanted him to do. He gave me a devilishly handsome smile and nodded his head. "Ladies, a moving target is far more difficult to hit. It calls for tracking and predictability. You need to time the release of your arrow with the speed the target is traveling at, as I will now demonstrate."

Pax's man ripped one of the targets from its holder and took off into the air. When he reached altitude, I yelled, "RELEASE IT!" Instantly, the target boards began to plummet its way back down to the ground. I slotted the arrow, raised my bow, took aim, and fired. When the target hit the ground, everyone gaped at the arrow that'd pierced all the way through the target. I'd just managed to hit the bullseye's outer rim.

Helaine stepped forward, "You expect us to be able to do that?"

I nodded, "I not only expect you to be able to do it. I expect you to do it with far more accuracy than myself. These are lives we're dealing with, not targets." Sure, I was asking a lot from them, but the stakes couldn't have been higher.

Helaine turned to her sisters. "Well, girls, we will not let our commander down."

Riley walked up to me. "Are you certain we are not asking too much of them?" His concerns mirrored my own.

I shook my head and came to a final conclusion. "It doesn't matter if I am or not. Their contributions are a critical part of the plan. It HAS to work."

The Gargoyle who flew the target for me approached Riley and I. "Pardon me, M'lady, the seven of us feel we know who we would work best with. Would it be forward if we paired off with them and aided your training?"

I motioned for him to go ahead, and he made a gesture to the other six Gargoyles to move towards our shield maidens. After introductions were made, training resumed. Riley and I moved through the partnered teams while we worked with the archers to help with their accuracy. Some of them managed a partial shift and used the eyes of their wolf to track the objects. That proved to be extraordinarily successful and increased the accuracy for those who could handle it.

When their practice time was up, all seven asked if they could be allowed to continue. Pax's men agreed to stay and help them, so I saw no reason why they couldn't. Riley stated he would let everyone know to keep clear of the area. I approved their request, caveating it with the instructions they must finish before sunset. I wanted to make sure none of them overdid it because they would be repeating their training again tomorrow.

As I walked back into the packhouse, I turned and observed the paired off teams. Suddenly, I got a feeling in the pit of my stomach. It wasn't a bad feeling. It was more of a sense of certainty. This was going to work!

AMELIA (AMI) JANE GRAY

RINSE AND REPEAT

$\mathcal{I}$ was just about to leave the training room when Cash stopped me, "Amelia, you have received a couple of deliveries. They are over against the wall." Cash pointed to the far wall near the table that held the practice weapons. There were two large crates, two beautifully carved boxes, and two smaller boxes.

The two crates and two smaller boxes came with a single note from Drew:

Ami,

As promised, uniforms and concealment gear.

Be Careful!

Drew.

I immediately opened the crates, and inside was something that made me laugh harder than anything I'd seen so far. I pulled out a pair of grey and black camouflage cargo pants. I opened the other crate, and inside were sleeveless grey hunting shirts and black cloaks.

Aoife came up behind me and, without meaning to, scared the shit out of me. "Amelia, do not forget to grab a bite to eat."

I immediately stood back up and spun, grabbing my chest. "Holy shit, Aoife!"

"Amelia, I am sorry. I did not mean to startle you." She was trying to hide her laugh.

"Oh, ha, ha, very funny." I calmed my slamming heart. I hated getting jumped, which was why I always sat facing a door. However, Aoife got me good, and I needed to give credit where credit was due.

Once she stopped snickering, Aoife started over, "Can I help you with any of those things?"

"Yes, please. The items in these two crates need to be handed out to the shield maidens. The archers are outside still practicing and working with General Pax's men, so save them for last. It appears as though Drew's already marked who gets what. If we could possibly get them delivered to each of the ladies it would be great."

Aoife nodded. "Sure thing. Have you opened the other items yet?"

I smiled at her, "I was just about to." In the meantime, Emmer, Aisling, and Mathias walked in and noticed I was opening the boxes.

"Ah, I believe the rest of this is for the two of you." I motioned to Mathias and Aisling.

I opened the note attached to the intricately carved boxes.

Amelia,

I believe I have duplicated the weapons I made for you and Sloane.

I hope you approve.

Declan

I handed the slender one of the two over to Mathias and the wider, shorter box over to Aisling. "Perhaps, you should open these first," I suggested.

Mathias opened his first, and it was an exact replica of Sloane's Katana. When Aisling opened hers, I saw they were exact duplicates of my swords or were they? As I peered closer at them, I noticed the dragon on Aisling's held golden eyes. Mine were just simply carved. It made me chuckle. I couldn't fault any artist for taking a little bit of license with his creations. No one except myself would notice anyway, or so I thought.

"Mine is different from Sloane's," Mathias stated.

"How so?" I inquired.

"For one, it is heavier." Mathias swung it. "For another, it fits me perfectly."

I smugly smiled, "Declan builds to the owner. He knew you'd be carrying it. From a distance, no one will be able to tell."

"Unbelievable! Another two get one of his weapons. What am I chopped liver?" Emmer scowled.

Aoife shoved some clothes into Emmer's arms. "Come on, chopped liver. You can help me deliver these."

Aisling pulled both of her swords out of their box and swung them, feeling their weight. She gave her brother a wicked smile, "Care to have a go?"

I took a step back as Mathias grinned from ear to ear. "Just remember you asked for it."

The two of them were using actual weapons, and both were holding back but appeared to be having what looked like a great deal of fun. I moved towards the back wall and watched as brother and sister faced off against one another. It quickly dawned on me just how much Aisling actually knew. I observed her stance, how she held her shoulders, and the way she moved through what I'd shown her. She really was paying attention to my teachings.

When the pair of them stopped, I stepped off the wall. "Aisling, I'm stepping up your training. You'll be fighting me after I grab a bite to eat. Put those away and get the training weapons out. Oh, I'll also be teaching you my wall flip, so be prepared to get bruised."

I opened up the last two boxes. "Mathias, these are for you and Aisling as well." I handed the two boxes over to him.

"I will take them up to our apartment. When you and Aisling are done training, she can come and get her things."

Quickly, Aisling and I moved down stairs. We made a short stop in the kitchen for a small snack to tide us over. After picking up our training weapons, I turned towards Aisling and tossed two of them to her. "If you fight even a tenth below what you're capable of, you will get hurt." After I gave her fair warning, I began without another word.

We trained well into the evening, only setting down the weapons long enough for me to teach her my wall flip. The first few times, she landed clean on her ass. Without missing a beat, I told her to get up and do it again until she mastered it.

Sloane and Mathias worked right alongside us until it was time for supper. Sloane and I only took a short meal break then began to work on our spells. When Astraea and Nova showed up, we began to work on our group shadow walking. Brevan and Emmer arrived soon after, and we added them into the mix.

The addition of Brevan shifted the dynamics enough because, once again, we were all falling over one another. Frustrated, I called for a break and took five minutes to think things through. The definition of insanity was doing the same thing repeatedly and expecting a different outcome. How could we do things differently, so we could have it work to our benefit?

I was tired and frustrated because no ideas were coming to mind when Brevan came to sit next to me on the steps. "My little wolf, what troubles you?"

"It's not working. We are far too noisy, and we keep tripping over one another. Getting to the entrance isn't my worry. It's getting inside without being seen or heard I'm concerned about. There's no way they won't have the entrance under surveillance, especially if you take into account who we are dealing with. If it were just Astraea, myself, and Sloane it would be one thing. Astraea can conceal herself, and Sloane and I are just two, which is easy enough to make a line by having him hold my hand and leading him through. The trouble lies in adding more people." I rubbed my face in frustration.

Brevan thought through what I'd just vented to him before he spoke, "Have you tried it in another configuration?"

"What do you mean?" My brain was so tired I simply wasn't getting what he was trying to say.

"Well, for example; actually, making it a true line? Do you know for certain you wouldn't be able to conceal everyone if they were stretched out?" Brevan inquired.

"You mean like everyone holds hands in a line then cast it?" All that was running through my head at the moment was, 'Kumbaya, my Lord, Kumbaya'.

"Precisely, this would make it easier for everyone to move. The easier you can move, the more you can concentrate on your steps. As silence is tantamount, it seems like the simplest solution," Brevan commented.

I pondered on it for a moment. It was the easiest solution, but I'd never tried to conceal anyone stretched out so far away from me before. I didn't have a clue if it would even work. I stood and reached out my hand to Brevan. "Since I'm all out of ideas, let's give yours a try."

Brevan took my hand and stood. We walked over to the others who were talking amongst themselves. "Brevan's come up with an idea I think we should try. We need to make a line with Nova in the front, I will be behind Nova, followed by Sloane, Brevan, and Emmer. Astraea, I will need for you to watch and see if anyone is visible." Astraea nodded in agreement.

We all lined up as I instructed, and I spoke, *"Gwathren echeri"*. I immediately felt Nova, myself, Brevan, and Sloane fade back, but Emmer was my questionable one.

Astraea pointed. "Emmer appears as though he were a ghostly apparition."

I broke the spell and ran a hand through my hair. I suspected we were on the right track, but I didn't have enough juice to stretch the concealment that far. The only other person who could fall into the shadows was Astraea. This was when the idea struck.

"Astraea, have you ever concealed anyone other than yourself?" My eyes were nearly pleading for her to say yes.

"No, dear one, I have not," she replied.

"Have you ever tried?" I asked, hoping she'd say no.

"I do not remember a time where I have needed to." A smile crossed her face.

"Emmer, take Astraea's hand." She reached out and took hold of Emmer's hand. Astraea didn't need me to explain the spell. She'd seen me cast it and knew the mechanics behind it already.

With a far more ethereal lilt, Astraea spoke the spell, "Gwathren echeri" and just like that, she and Emmer slipped into the shadows.

When she broke the spell causing Emmer and herself to reappear, I nudged Sloane in her direction.

When I nodded at Sloane, she grasped his hand and promptly slipped the three of them into the shadows. My idea was going to work. We could use two groups. Astraea, Emmer, and Sloane; Brevan, Nova, and myself. We came up with a system of stop and go using our hands. One squeeze would signify stop, and two would mean go. This way, no one needed to actually speak, and our positions wouldn't be given away.

We all practiced into the wee hours of the morning. Just about the time the sun was about to rise, Brevan and I climbed into bed. We all agreed to meet again the following night to work on it some more. While we managed to work out most of the kinks. We still needed to make sure we were able to move around undetected.

As my head hit the pillow, I fell into a sleep of exhaustion. The next few days would be much like yesterday and last night. Simply put: rinse and repeat.

AMELIA (AMI) JANE GRAY

THE SHADOW LEGION

As the days passed by leading up to the full moon, we all worked with intense dedication. Even Edon managed to sharpen his fighting skills. He mainly worked with Brevan, and the pair of them were well matched against one another. I never thought I'd see the day where someone showed equal skill to Brevan, but it made sense since Edon was his father.

At times, I still found myself dumbfounded. There were moments where I looked upon Edon and saw Captain J and others where I saw the man who was once the Alpha of Pack Lingwir. It still made me chuckle because he refused to go back to speaking formally. Every time I heard him say "we'd" or "I'll," it brought a smile to my face. One time he caught me and wanted to know what I thought was so funny. I shook my head, gave him a peck on the cheek, and told him nothing. He called me a "strange lass," and his comment made my smile even more expansive.

Edon and I fell into a comfortable relationship. Where I wasn't quite akin to a daughter but close enough, so he didn't hesitate to pull me into his side and compliment me when he thought I'd done something well. At first, Brevan would let loose with a few low growls, but Edon scolded him as though he were five, and finally, Brevan let it go.

When we held the pairs training sessions, Mathias usually stuck to pushing Sloane to his limits. One particular day, Mathias pulled Aisling aside, whispered in her ear, and then winked. I'd instantly became suspicious, and when Aisling found the opportunity, she wound up knocking me flat on my ass.

Utterly shocked as she whooped while she jumped up and down, I swung my gaze over to Mathias. "What did you tell her?" I spoke as indignation laced my voice.

Mathias shrugged. "The same thing I have been repeating to you for months. When you tire, your left foot gets lazy and drags. It becomes easier to knock you off balance."

I ignored Mathias as I stood and dusted off my ass. "Aisling, this means no more mercy."

We both smiled at each other and began again. I only felt slightly guilty when she landed on her butt for the fifth time. Granted, each time I knocked Aisling down, she got right back up and began again. She was getting to be as good as I was. There was determination written across her face. It was a drive that brought a sense of pride, knowing she was the same soft-spoken girl who cried at the thought of my brother not wanting her. Which was nothing more than a silly misunderstanding. Still, the way Aisling was blossoming into a strong, determined woman was a wonder to behold. I was absolutely proud to call her my sister.

On the day the archers and Gargoyles were departing, every single one of the shield maidens approached me. I stood in the training room with Mathias, Brevan, Aisling, and Edon while we were discussing fallback plans should the shit really hit the fan. Helaine and Sadine were out in front of our shield maidens, and both of them were carrying packages. The whole group stopped when they reached where I stood with Aisling by my side. All of them were attired in the uniforms Drew sent over.

Helaine stepped forward. "M'lady, Aisling, since stepping forward and stating our wishes to be trained, the two of you have been our leaders. Aisling, you set the bar for the rest of us. Amelia, you have guided us, pushing and believing in our abilities even when we doubted it ourselves. It came to our attention we are not just guardians of hearth and home but warriors for peace. We are a unit led by two women we respect, and like any unit or pack, we have a chain of command. This is for *our* Alpha." Helaine handed me the package she was holding while Sadine stepped forward.

"And, this is for *our* beta," Sadine stated.

Helaine continued, "We no longer wish to be known as *shield maidens*." She smiled back at the group behind her. "We are the Shadow Legion, led by the Shadow Dragon." Each one of them took a knee and placed a fist over their hearts.

"We swear our fealty to serve and protect the peace based on your guidance, morals, and spirit," They all pledged in unison.

I proudly gazed at them for a moment, completely overwhelmed, then glanced at Brevan like, 'what the hell should I do now?' He simply nodded his head as if to say, 'it was your show.' I glanced over at Aisling, who seemed as amazed as I felt. After I shifted the package to my left hand, I stretched out my right hand to Helaine.

"Please stand." I grinned down at her as she clasped my hand. It appeared as though I would be completely winging a little speech. All of them rose when Helaine did. "Ladies, Shadow Legion, you've all worked hard, trained even harder, and I couldn't be more proud of each of you. Thank you for your confidence in our leadership abilities. I think I can safely speak for both myself and Aisling when I say we are honored. We are more than a unit, though. We are a sisterhood. Those standing next to you will always have your back in good times and bad. Friendship, loyalty, family, these are the ties which bind all of us, and it is what we are all fighting to protect."

The women erupted with a cheer, and Sadine pointed to the packages. "Please, open them. We are aware you two have special attire for tomorrow. Still, after that, we thought our leaders should be outfitted appropriately. Helaine and I went to see your friend Drew at his shop." She shrugged. "He came up with the outfits and the ring. Well, the Acolytes have their necklace with the etched Phoenix, the Order has the etched Dragon, and since we started with the idea of a shield..." Sadine's sentence drifted off.

The ring was solid silver in the shape of a shield which curved around the finger with a single letter 'A' carved into the middle. This was when it dawned on me that they knew about the supersecret groups.

"Wait, how do you all know about the Order of the Dragon and the Acolytes of the Phoenix?" I was utterly stunned.

Helaine pointed to Brevan as she grinned. "Ask your mates. Something to do with a rant of yours about *secrets and lies* being the source of all evil or something to that effect anyway."

I slipped the ring on my middle finger, and Aisling followed suit. The uniforms we held were nearly identical to theirs, only mine held gold threading in the shirt and Aisling's held silver. The cargo pants were precisely the same as theirs, and the boots, along with the cloak, seemed as though they'd fit like a glove.

As I was setting the uniform down, the Gargoyles arrived. My seven archers were getting ready to depart. Amongst them were Sadine and Helaine. They went to retrieve their weapons when Aoife came running in.

"I have put together some rations for all of you. In each pouch are cheese, bread, and some fruit. It should be enough to hold you until you return. There are also flasks of water." Aoife held the look of a worried mother.

Each of the women thanked Aoife, then went to pick up the rations and water flasks. I walked over to her and put my arm around her shoulder. "You okay?"

Aoife sighed, "This is really happening, and just like time, you cannot stop it."

I shook my head. "I'm afraid not."

Aoife gave herself another moment, then stood straight. "So be it. Amelia, promise me something."

Without hesitation, I responded, "Sure, what?"

"Promise you will all try to come back in one piece and bring my mate home to me."

I enveloped her into a hug. "I swear to you on my last breath. He will come back to you."

Aoife took a deep breath and released me from our embrace. She collected herself again, turned, and left the room.

We planned everything down to the last possible known factor we could. My group, who started out as being protectors of the home, were actually warrior women who chose the name Shadow Legion. We were heading into a fight that could alter everyone's fate on the island. I watched as the Gargoyles and archers took off into the sky and said a small prayer. "If anyone is listening, please keep them safe."

While tomorrow brought a new day, it would be a day which would be uncertain at best.

AMELIA (AMI) JANE GRAY

SUPER MOON

The morning of the full moon came, and not one of us possessed the energy to get out of bed, let alone do anything productive. Fortunately, we planned for this, as did the entire pack. It seemed as though the super moon was even more draining than the regular full moon. Aoife prepared breakfast the night before. She made berry muffins, scones, cut up some fresh melon, and already beat the eggs, so all they would need to do was quickly cook them up along with the keaff.

Sleepily, I made my way into the kitchen and took hold of the tray that was already made up. Wordlessly, she placed a pile of eggs on a plate and slid it onto the tray along with three cups of keaff. I scanned my eyes around the kitchen, and everyone was basically in the same condition. They weren't even speaking amongst themselves.

With a small smile and a nod, I thanked Aoife and headed back upstairs. After I placed the tray on the coffee table, I took hold of my cup of keaff and promptly curled up. Mathias made his way out of the bath chamber, and Brevan went in. It appeared as though I'd come up with a good idea, and Mathias grabbed the blanket off the bed. He groggily walked over to the couch and curled up next to me as he shared the blanket with me.

When Brevan emerged, from the bath chamber he noticed the two of us and took the seat on the other side of me. I shoved some of the blanket onto him, and there we stayed. Even Brevan succumbed to the effects of the super moon. It was why we'd all trained as hard as we did.

Edon mentioned a super moon held two different effects on wolves. One was where you could barely function. The other was so much superabundant energy it would give the wolves a slight edge in the fighting area. Personally, I was hoping for the latter once these effects started to wear off.

The main contingent would be headed directly to the beginning of the pass, and the rest of us were meeting at the farming village of Messis. There was a small farm just before the pine trees that led to the opening of the temple maze. We would use it as our starting point, and we'd head through the pines concealed all the way to the temple. With any luck, we'd go undetected.

The more we practiced, our two groups got quite proficient at moving without making a sound. Nova would act as a guide for Brevan and myself, with Astraea acting as a guide for Emmer and Sloane. It was also agreed once the concealment went down, no one would speak, not even a whisper. The Alfar and Dokkalfar's sense of hearing was actually so acute, they could hear a pin drop in the next room.

Around mid-day, Aisling made her way up to our apartment. She and I agreed we'd wait to color her hair until the day of. That way, it would be as close to my color as possible. Marta acquired the hair color from a merchant in Tenebris who also sold bath oils and the hair cleanser I liked to use. While she wasn't head of the house any longer, Marta was always welcome to participate in whatever way she could contribute.

Marta told Brevan in so many words, under no circumstances was she going to allow anyone else to touch our hair other than her. It must've made him chuckle because he acquiesced to her request, and she was only a couple of minutes behind Aisling. She carried with her a basket containing the hair cleanser, hair dye, and some scissors.

Marta pulled both of us into the bath chamber and held out the hair cleanser. "Both of you wash your hair. When you are finished, we will brush it out and see where we stand. I suspect Aisling will need some of hers cut off." Aisling grimaced but complied, as did I.

Her suspicions were spot on. Aisling's hair, when wet was about three inches too long. Marta took her scissors and cut off the additional length, then instructed Aisling to sit so her back was against the tub. Dye in hand, she pulled out a comb and slowly poured the hair color onto her hair, combing it through every so often.

When Marta was finished, we both towel-dried Aisling's hair, and crazy enough, it was practically an identical match. Marta then braided both of our hair identically. As she was putting the final touches on the two of us, I heard the door to the apartment open and close.

Sloane's voice, albeit muffled, filtered into the bath chamber. "I was instructed to be here. Anyone have any idea why?"

I heard a muffled "No" come from both Mathias and Brevan.

Marta opened the door but motioned for us to stay where we were and whispered for us to switch tops, which we did. "I want all three of you to close your eyes and do not open them until I say, or this will not work."

The three men complied, and when she was satisfied they couldn't see anything, Marta motioned for the two of us to exit the bath chamber and face the doors which lead to the balcony. She adjusted our positions slightly to make sure that our backs were towards the men in the room.

She then whispered in our ears, "Do not turn around until I say so." We both nodded our agreement. "Alright, open. Without moving, tell me who is who?"

Brevan was the first to voice his opinion, "Amelia is on the left, and Aisling is on the right." I held back a smile. Brevan was completely wrong, poor guy.

Sloane was next. "I agree, that's the top Aisling was wearing when she left to come up here."

Mathias took longer to answer, thoroughly studying us over from his position on the sofa. "Amelia is on the right, and my sister is on the left. Amelia has a small birthmark on her right shoulder, and it is just barely peeking out."

"Turn around, ladies," Marta instructed.

We turned and posed. Mathias cheered, "I win!" and we all laughed. Of course, it would be the one man who knew the two of us. I walked over and gave Mathias a quick kiss to his lips. His joy quickly fled as Marta interjected further instruction.

"Now, for you two." she pointed to Sloane and Mathias.

Shocked, both men replied in unison, "What?"

"Did I speak Alfar? You two, bath chamber now. We do not have all day," Marta ordered.

Sloane stood. "I don't have the energy to fight you. Besides, I know what it's about, and at least, it's not my hair who's getting bleached." Sloane smirked at Mathias, who still hadn't moved, "or cut..."

Mathias grumbled as he stood, "Marta, come on, see reason. No one's going to be looking at my hair."

Marta grabbed Mathias by the arm. "Do not sass me. If you are going to pull off your look-alike scheme, then you are next. No more arguments."

Aisling and I sat down on the sofa, laughing. The super moon might've completely drained our energy, but at least it left behind our sense of humor. We'd managed to eat breakfast while 'Hair Salon de' Marta' was open. I shared mine with Aisling as somehow there was way more food than I could manage to eat.

An hour or so later, Marta emerged. "Same thing for you three. Close your eyes and no peeking until I say." We all complied with her request.

I heard shuffling and footsteps as Mathias and Sloane left the bath chamber. Once she managed to position them where she wanted them, she allowed us to open our eyes.

I took my time scrutinizing the two of them, but Aisling was the first to speak, "My brother is on the left, and Sloane is on the right."

Brevan went next. "Mathias is on the left, and Sloane is on the right."

It appeared I was the tie-breaker as I carefully examined the two men facing the balcony. I shifted my focus from their heads and shoulders to their asses and smiled, "Sloane's on the left, and Mathias is on the right."

Marta gawked at me as the men turned around. "How did you know?"

I shrugged. "Mathias has a more muscular backside." Everyone burst out laughing at my statement.

Brevan kissed me sweetly. "You would know, my little wolf."

Marta, with a certain satisfaction, stated, "My work here is done." She spun and collected her things as Mathias and Sloane took up spots on the sofa. Before she left, Marta gazed lovingly for several seconds at the group of us sitting on the couch. "Please, be careful, the lot of you."

Brevan answered her, "We will, thank you, Marta, for everything."

Without another word, Marta left the apartment. Somehow, Marta's warning caused my nerves to roar to life. The jovial nature we all possessed only a moment ago was gone, replaced by the weight of what we were all attempting to pull off. Suddenly, my stomach began to churn, and I bolted upright, running directly into the bath chamber and expelled my stomach contents.

Brevan entered and knelt down beside me. "Amelia, what is wrong?"

All I could do was shake my head no at the moment. Fortunately, Aisling countered with her own question, "How far along is she?"

"Three, maybe four weeks," Mathias answered.

"Ahh, the timing is about right. I will go get her some water," Aisling replied.

Her inquiry and statement jarred my own mind. *Crap, I've got morning sickness.* I thought before I wretched again.

Sloane spoke up, "Would you care to clue the rest of us in?"

I managed to croak out, "Morning sick--" as my body heaved yet again.

Sloane breathed a sigh of relief, "I'll go get our gran. I'm sure she has something in her *Mary Poppins* bag for Amelia's problem."

215

"Can someone please explain what morning sickness is?" Poor Mathias was still lost.

"It's caused by pregnancy and is perfectly normal," Sloane shouted on his way out the door.

The only trouble was, it wasn't morning. It was afternoon and didn't start until my nerves started flopping about. Perhaps, the super moon was wreaking havoc with me in more than one way. I closed my eyes and attempted to calm myself with a few deep cleansing breaths. The calmer I became, the less nauseous I was.

I managed to cease throwing up in time for Neemah to walk through the door. "Seriously, child, I told you to take those herbs."

Crap, Gran was right! She'd given me some herbs to take, and they were sitting on the small table by the door. "Shit! Sorry, Neemah. I forgot."

Aisling walked in with a glass of water in hand. "Here is your water, Amelia."

"Perfect!" Neemah exclaimed.

She grabbed a packet of the herbs and dumped them into the water. Neemah swirled the glass for a moment and handed it over to me. "Drink up."

It absolutely tasted as bad as I guessed they would, but I did as I was instructed and consumed the entire contents of the glass. When finished, I set the glass on the coffee table, closed my eyes, and leaned back with my hands protectively placed over my stomach.

"Will she be alright?" Brevan inquired.

"Good lord, boy, give the herbs a moment to work," Neemah scolded, and I chuckled.

"Ah, that is a good sign. See! Her sense of humor is already returning. She will be fine, and from now on, when I tell you to take something, do it. No more of these shenanigans of, oops, I forgot. What are you, a teenage pup?" Neemah finished scolding me and shook her head.

"Thank you, Gran."

"You are quite welcome, dear. The super moon is causing all kinds of problems. I should keep a room here. Do you all realize how many times I have already been called to your house today?" Neemah grumbled as she was getting ready to leave.

"Neemah, if you need to rest, we can find a place for you to lie down," Brevan offered.

Neemah patted his arm. "Might as well. I have a feeling I will be needed sooner rather than later."

Brevan and Neemah left the apartment together. I was really beginning to dislike the super moon and wished it would end sooner rather than later.

AMELIA (AMI) JANE GRAY

MESSIS

Sloane and Aisling left the apartment a couple of hours later. They wanted to have some alone time before the sunset. I couldn't blame them. As soon as my nausea dissipated, I felt the same way about Brevan and Mathias. All I wanted to do was hold them close and never let go. My two mates, my ocean, and my oncoming storm were my world.

Apparently, I was not alone in my sentiment. I made love with both of them over the next couple of hours. As we made love, I touched, caressed, and memorized every muscle, every ripple of skin, every soft blissful curve of their lips, tender kisses followed by passionate ones. Our emotions were completely and honestly open, and not one bit of it was concern over what was to come. It was pure, unconditional love.

As we laid in bed, Brevan, Mathias, and I watched the sunset and realized we needed to rise and begin our missions.

Brevan kissed my shoulder. "Come, little wolf, it is time." He rose out of bed, and I followed along with Mathias.

After a quick cleanup in the bath chamber, I dressed in my black leather pants, a black top, and my tailored leather, sleeveless, hooded jacket. I topped my outfit off with my custom swords from Declan. They both were strapped to my back for easy access.

Brevan similarly dressed in all black, as did Mathias. However, Mathias' outfit concealed his face with something similar to what you'd imagine a ninja would wear. I gazed into his eyes, and it suddenly struck me. His eyes were like mine.

"Mathias, remember to keep your emotions in check. If you allow them to glow because you get angry, the jig is up. You, Brevan, and I all have one blue eye and one green. Aisling doesn't!"

Mathias uncovered his face, leaned over, and kissed me. "Do not worry. Aisling and I have already discussed it. We are both well aware of the eye color issue."

I pulled him close and whispered, "Come back to me. We have babies to raise."

"My sweet love, do not worry about me. We will and then some." Mathias released me and winked. He turned and left without saying another word.

"Brevan, what the hell did he mean by that?" With utter confusion, I glanced over to my other mate in hopes of an explanation.

"My little wolf, I cannot say for certain. But it was rumored upon occasion, Mathias like his father, held the ability of prophetic dreams." Brevan's explanation made my jaw drop.

"You mean he caught a glimpse of the future?" Brevan nodded.

"I told you, Mathias is special. Come, we need to leave." Brevan placed his hand on the small of my back, and I suddenly knew we were going to win this fight. If Mathias caught a glimpse of our future which held more children in it, there was no way we were going to lose. Was there?

Brevan, Emmer, Sloane, and I rode together on horseback to Messis. I still didn't know how to ride by myself and made a mental note to put it on my to-do list. It was discussed only for a moment about going in wolf form. When we thought about the logistics of carrying weapons plus clothes, and how they would come into play, the idea was scrapped.

I realized seeing Messis this way was entirely different than running through it at full speed. The quiet farming village was quaint. Although, the villagers looked upon us with trepidation. Their leeriness was only half of the issues. The villagers hustled to close their shutters and lock their doors. I knew what was happening because I could hear them scurrying through their homes.

"Brevan, what are they all so afraid of? It's not like we are here to harm them."

"They have all been afraid of our pack for years, and with all the raids we have done here to find traitors, most of the villagers are mistrusting of our kind."

"Our pack or the old Pack Lumen?" This was just wrong. People shouldn't be afraid of us. That wasn't any way to govern. Fear is what creates distrust and ultimately breeds hatred.

"Both," Brevan confirmed.

"We need to fix all of their mistrust," I informed him in earnest.

"Agreed, but right now, we have other pressing matters." Brevan's mind was on the task at hand, and rightfully so.

We turned onto a country dirt road, which led to a farmhouse sitting upon a small hill. To the left of the house was a rickety old barn with wood worn to the point it'd turned gray. The fields were newly harvested, and the trees created a natural property line. All in all, it was a private and secluded location away from the main village—a perfect place for our rendezvous with the others in our party.

The four of us entered the barn and dismounted the horses. Nova and Astraea were there awaiting our arrival. I was reasonably confident Nova had run all the way there with her vampyr speed. Still, Astraea was with her, and I was curious as to how she arrived. There were only the three horses we traveled in on.

Nova approached the four of us. "Are we ready to do this? We really need to get moving."

I could see and almost sense her anxiety. "I'm ready when everyone else is," I confirmed.

"We will stick to the trail until we reach the fork. Remember, from there, we must approach as quietly as possible. I have no doubt the woods will be teeming with Alfar and wolves," Astraea expressed her concern.

"Yeah, so no sneezing, coughing, laughing, speaking, or expelling of gas." Sloane's snarky remark deserved a backhanded smack, and I was all too happy to deliver. Sloane rubbed at his chest, feigning injury. I just rolled my eyes at him. We could joke later. At that moment in time, we needed to focus.

We split into our groups, and I nodded to Astraea. Together we cast the concealment spell, and both groups vanished. As Astraea led her group and Nova was leading ours, the going was slow and cautious. With any luck, we'd arrive at the temple maze entrance just as our ruse was about to play out.

After we left the farming village of Messis behind, we hit the trail, and our speed increased. Nova was swift on her feet and pulled our group along. I kept a keen eye on our surroundings, frequently searching into the trees and shrubs for the Alfar. Part of me was sure Brevan was listening for wolves.

The path was covered with pine needles and leaf litter, which made creeping difficult. My more considerable concern was snapping a twig. Every suspense movie out there always showed the clumsy sidekick making a noise and suddenly, the ensuing fight would begin. My hope was to avoid the cliché and make it to the entrance unnoticed.

When we reached the fork in the path, Nova steered our group straight forward, leaving the trail altogether. The forest floor was even trickier to navigate while the hairs on the back of my neck started to stand on end. If I didn't know any better, I'd say we were being watched.

Finally, we reached the tree line, and the path to the temple opening came into focus. I always thought it was slightly odd how the trees just stopped, and the mountain came into view. The temple of The Dragon and The Phoenix Mystic was held, not only within one of the Sleeping Mountains, but past a maze that constituted its own pitfall.

Nova paused momentarily, squeezed my hand, and moved us

onward. There was no time for reassuring or comforting words. It was time for us to put an end to all of this. I experienced a brief moment where my thoughts drifted to Mathias and Aisling. Again, I wished them luck and refocused my mind on our present situation.

We made it approximately fifty paces from the entrance when Nova stopped our party. Six Alfar guards and two cloaked figures approached from the left. We could tell the cloaked figures were both women by their body shape even though the cloaks did much to mask them. The smaller cloaked figure possessed a high-pitched lyrical voice, and the taller cloaked figure was being pulled along by restraints which bound her hands together. "Stay here and guard the entrance," The smaller of the cloaked women commanded two of the guards. They took up positions one on either side of the entrance. The remaining members of their party passed through the opening. It looked as though we weren't the only ones headed for the temple tonight. *Damn!* That just eliminated our hopes of getting there first and made sure it was absolutely out of the realm of possibility.

Brevan, who'd been behind me the entire time, tugged at my arm. "Drop the concealment." He released my hand, and as he came into view, he unleashed his sword. I guess we were going to have to fight our way in!

MATHIAS

DECOY

I felt uneasy about separating our family. It was already proven we were stronger together. However, a solid plan was made, and we needed to see it through. The only comfort I held was in the form of my dream. It had been a long time since I managed to have one so vividly. The last time was when my parents went on their last peace mission. I begged them not to go, but not even they would disobey a direct order from our Alpha.

I met up with our troops, who were assembled. Aisling was already there and stood next to Edon. It was strange to see him leading everyone again. Aisling was too young to remember him as Alpha, but I was not. As I approached the pair of them, I flipped up my hood.

I nodded to Edon, who gave me the same in return. Edon stepped forward and turned to face everyone. He spoke in a loud, clear voice, "On this night, we put an end to the fighting between our two sides, one way or another. It is not just about living in peace but stopping the tyranny which lies to the north. For far too long, we have turned a blind eye to what went on. NO MORE! Tonight, we stand united. Tonight, we are the unstoppable force. TONIGHT, VICTORY!"

The crowd of guards cheered. Everyone was high on energy from the supermoon, and tensions being what they were, after Edon's speech, pumped them up even more so. We were heading into dangerous waters with the Lycanthropes, who were now super-charged thanks to the moons cycle. I knew Brevan would want me to trust in the plan, but I shared a look with Aisling, who shared one back. I could see she was thinking along the same lines I was. We were balancing on the precipice of an abyss. One wrong move and in we would fall.

As our group moved out, Aisling and I further concealed who we were with our face coverings. The Vampyr and Dokkalfar planned to meet us there. No one could know that this was a giant decoy, or it would put innocent lives at stake. Edon led everyone through our pack lands and up to the bridge, just on the other side of Messis. We did not need to sneak through because we wanted the attention drawn to us.

The entire group marched over the bridge and formed a wall along the side of the Sleeping Mountain Pass. We did not need to wait long for Oren to show up, who was leading his coven as well as Nova's. With him came Amelia's friends Andrew and Jacqueline. They both possessed looks which would make an ordinary man's blood run cold. I suspected that should fighting break out, they held no intention of leaving as Amelia instructed.

Shortly after the arrival of the Vampyr contingent, Cedrik and the Dokkalfar guards arrived. It looked as though he brought with him his entire house. Not a word was spoken as half of them scattered amongst the rocks and trees, brandishing their bows. The other half mixed in with the rest of us.

Both Oren and Cedrick took flanking positions on either side of Edon while Aisling and I stood in front of them. The funny thing about prophetic dreams was the future was always in motion. Nothing was certain or written in stone. I supposed it was why I understood those prophecies. They were only a guide for what could happen, not what would happen. Some events were inevitable, such as, the supermoon and falling stars. What was not inevitable was a person's actions. Freewill dictated that.

I was only left to my musings for a short while, when off in the distance, approaching us was not only the Alfar but the wolves as well, led by none other than Lycandra. I sensed Edon stiffen, and Jacqueline sucked in some air when they noticed the captives. I glanced over and noticed Andrew had immediately clasped a hand on Jacqueline's wrist.

"Jackie, girl, calm down," I heard him speak softly to her. I suspected I knew why. One of the captives must have been family of some kind. In total, I counted six, four of whom I recognized as four of the six girls who were taken from the packhouse. They appeared as though they were going to give birth at any moment.

When the opposite side reached their position, Lycandra stepped forward. "Send forth the lost children, or these hostages will meet their demise!" her voice echoed through the pass clear as a bell.

Edon strode between both Aisling and me. "Lycandra, you hold no power here. Surrender now and live!"

Even from our distance, the expression upon Lycandra's face was one of utter shock and disbelief. "What trickery is this? Edon is dead!"

"No, Lycandra, I am very much alive," Edon declared.

With panic written all over her face, Lycandra quickly grabbed one of the hostages by the hair. It was a woman roughly Edon's age looks-wise, and Jackie stiffened. "Mom," she whispered.

"I will begin killing them, starting with this wretched one if they do not start moving, right now. I can see them from here," Lycandra hissed out.

Aisling and I moved forward, and each placed a hand on Edon's shoulders. Not a word was spoken as we moved past him and walked side by side towards Lycandra and her forces. "Start releasing the hostages, Lycandra. They are coming to you as you requested."

Lycandra let go of the woman while the hostages began walking forward. As they did, Lycandra's front line of men dropped to a crouched position, and her archers brought up their bows. Their aim was not at us but rather the hostages.

Each step felt as though I was walking through the thickest mud imaginable. Never before had I walked into the heart of a battle without a weapon in my hand, let alone with my sister by my side. I attempted to keep my heart calm and my breathing regular. The closer we got, I remembered to drop my gaze, so my eyes would not be noticed. We could not give any of our plan away too soon, or all would be lost.

As we reached the midpoint with the hostages, I refocused my attention. Lycandra's hostages were possibly ten paces in front of us when the first arrow was shot from above. The Alfar, wolves, and Lycandra's attention was drawn up and away from us.

General Pax's men swooped down from above, while Aisling and I moved towards the scared hostages. "Do not be afraid. We are all getting out of here," I assured them.

Lycandra let loose a blood-curdling scream, "Shoot them down!" One by one, the Gargoyles grabbed hold of a hostage and flew off again. I threw back my hood, brandished my sword, and took a fighting stance. When I glanced over at Aisling, she had done the same. The last two Gargoyles swooped down and grabbed Aisling first, then myself. We managed to pull off this part of Amelia's plan perfectly.

From this distance, I saw the face of true evil. Lycandra held nothing back from hereon. "KILL THEM ALL!" That was when the actual battle began, and both sides ran towards one another.

AMELIA (AMI) JANE GRAY

THE TEMPLE

Brevan made short work of the guards placed at the entrance. He moved like lightning and cut the head off of one of the guards before the other could even draw his sword. Sloane followed Brevan's lead and set the other guard on fire. I dropped the concealment spell, as did Astraea. So much for stealth mode.

Emmer took up a guard position just inside the opening of the cavern. Astraea and Nova once again took the lead, with Sloane, Brevan, and myself following closely behind them. The deeper we walked into the cave, the more I understood why it was called a maze. Sloane held a fireball in his hand as a sort of torch to light our way. At one point, we exited a tunnel into an open cave hall, and in the center appeared an oubliette. This naturally rounded formation of the maze held it's own danger with the entrance to the oubliette in the center of the room, partially hidden in the darkness. Sloane threw the fireball down into it, and we watched as it disappeared into the blackness which soon engulfed it.

"You must watch your step from here on out. There are many such dangers as these along the way," Astraea warned, and I absolutely chose to heed her words.

227

Sloane lit up another fireball, and we continued forward through the maze. The air grew stale and damp. The walls of the labyrinth were covered in slime and cobwebs. Some of them were enormous, and by enormous, I meant they were more expansive than an H1 Hummer. All I hoped for was that we wouldn't come across the spider who made them.

I possessed two deeply rooted phobias: which were someone coming up behind me, and the other was spiders. My arachnophobia took root when I was sixteen. Jimmy Dohrmann not only brought his pet tarantula to school but then placed it on my head during English class as a practical joke. I screamed so loudly the teacher thought I was being murdered. Of course, Jimmy wound up with a week's worth of detention, and I was sent home in tears. Needless to say, I never got over the feeling of when something was crawling down the back of my head, past my neck, and onto my back.

I shook off that feeling as our party moved onward. When we reached the last corner before the door of the temple, voices floated our way. Astraea brought our line to a stop and motioned for me to move forward.

When I reached her side, she and I pulled in tightly to the wall. The unrestrained hooded figure spoke again. "Position yourselves outside this door and along the hall." The guards did as they were instructed as the figure continued, "Come along, key. It is time for you to pay for your keep." She pulled out a dagger and cut the prisoner's bindings. "Open the door," the figure ordered.

"Cosima, I will never obey your commands. I would rather die!" The other hooded figure flipped back her hood to reveal my twin, but not my twin. It was my mother. She seemed pale and gaunt even in this light, which wasn't much. There was some graying at her temples, but she held her head high in defiance.

Cosima dropped back her hood and stuck the dagger to my mother's throat. "I would be more than happy to make those arrangements for you."

Without any forethought or warning, I drew my swords and stepped out from around the corner. "Let! Her! Go!" I demanded.

Sloane and Brevan stepped up to my side, both with swords drawn and at the ready, while Astraea and Nova vanished into the shadows. Cosima glared at the three of us with an evil grin and laughed.

"I should have known Lycandra would foul up her end of things." She held my mother closer. "See there, Melisandre, your babies have returned home," Cosima began. "They do so look like you and your mate. I wonder if they will fall upon his same fate. What do you think?" The pained expression in my mother's eyes said it all. She feared for our safety even still.

My mother grabbed hold of the dagger being held at her throat and sliced her palm with her left hand. She placed her hand upon the door and spoke, "Fuil mo chuid fola. Leis an íobairt seo d'iarr mé cead isteach."

"Mom, NO!" I yelled, but it was too late.

Cosima cackled, "Nice to see you can be reasoned with. GUARDS! KILL THEM ALL!"

As the guards stalked forward, Cosima dragged my mother through the door, and I watched as it slammed closed behind them. There was no sneak attack upon these Alfar guards. They were fully armed and ready for us.

Brevan, Sloane, and I stood, so our backs were towards one another. We needed to remember the Alfar blades were dangerous not just because of who wielded them but also because they were dipped in poison more often than not. The only ace's we held up our sleeves were Astraea and Nova. Neither of them were combat trained, or at least it was what I assumed.

As three of the guards attacked, the fourth was stalking closer towards us. Suddenly, Nova popped out of the shadows and leapt onto the back of the fourth. She sank her fangs into his neck and rode him like a bucking bronco. The tightly confined space of the hallway made fighting the Alfar difficult. At one point, Sloane yelled, "SWITCH," and he, along with Brevan, pivoted to change opponents.

Finally, after I'd gotten the upper hand on mine, I dropped down and sliced his Achilles tendon on one heel. I followed through with that as I skewered him right up through his groin. When I ripped my sword from his midsection, the guard fell backwards against the wall and slid down. Sloane gutted his opponent, and Brevan, I was finding out, was fond of decapitation. Nova managed to drain hers dry.

I slowly approached Nova and noticed she didn't kill hers without taking on her own wounds. The guard managed to spear her in the side with his sword. "Nova, stay still." I bent down, and my healing ability kicked in, but she halted me before I could even begin.

"There is no point. The poison has gone too far. Even ingesting his blood, it is only a matter of time." Nova hobbled over to the door. Taking her hand away from the wound, she placed it on the door. "Fuil mo chuid fola. Leis an íobairt seo d'iarr mé cead isteach," she weakly uttered the words to open it and slid down the wall. Nova resolutely peered up at us. "Stop her."

Astraea knelt down to Nova's side. "I will stay with her. This is your destiny now."

Brevan nodded, and I stood back up. "Astraea, if we fail, the task falls on you to stop her," Brevan stated.

"Brevan, if you three fail, there will be no one who will be able to stop her. Go, quickly before the door closes," Astraea directed. We stepped back and ran through the door.

We were out of the frying pan and into the fire. As we entered the full view of the temple, I noticed our mother was unceremoniously deposited unconscious in front of a stone altar. There was a hole in the ceiling in which the super moon shone through, and Cosima was standing at the altar with a glass container filled with what I could only assume was blood.

She didn't speak in an ancient tongue and what followed stunned me. "With the sacrifice of the innocents. With the blood of the Alpha. I call forth the ancient power." Cosima smashed the glass container upon the altar, and the ground beneath our feet shook.

"Cosima, stop! You do not know what you are doing," Brevan growled.

"I know better than anyone what I am doing. With the Dragon and the Phoenix's ancient powers, I will finally bring order to the entire land. All of you pathetic creatures will fall at my feet. My power will be unstoppable."

Two holes began to appear in the altar, and I could hear the sound of another stone moving upwards. Brevan kept speaking to her as though she were a wild animal, "Cosima, it is a power which has not been awakened for thousands of years. It is what keeps our land concealed from the outside world. No one person can control it. You must understand this."

Cosima followed Brevan's movements as he made his way around the temple. Slowly and quietly, I crept up towards the altar. When I was close enough to reach out and grab hold of my mother's ankle, I dragged her away from the crazy Alfar Queen. I managed to get her far enough away and shot some healing energy into her. I suspected the dagger Cosima used wasn't poisonous, just in case she needed my mother for something else.

When she began to stir, I stopped the healing. I needed to make sure I maintained as much strength as possible. As I peered up, I saw two crystals rising out of the altar. One of the crystals was amber-colored, and the other was blue. The blue one began to whisper in voices to me, and somehow, I knew it was the Dragon Crystal.

Brevan advanced quickly with his sword drawn while Cosima pulled one of her own. When their swords clashed, the sound echoed throughout the entire temple. Cosima matched Brevan move for move. It wasn't that she was more skilled than him, but she was more agile and faster. The two of them quickly became a tremendous blur of movement.

"Sloane, while she is distracted, we need to grab those crystals."

"Ami, I'm not sure. The amber one gives me the willies."

"Sloane, we don't have a choice."

"Alright, we'll do it together."

The debate was over. Sloane and I swiftly ran towards the altar. Simultaneously, we both called out, "NOW," and we each grabbed our crystals. With the crystal in my right hand and Sloane to my left, we both took a step backwards. Once we were both under the moonlight, Sloane and I instinctively reached for each other's hands.

When we made the connection as he held my hand, I felt an overwhelming rush of power. Suddenly, I found myself floating. I was there, but I was no longer in the driver's seat. As it became dark all around me, all I could hear was Brevan screaming out my name.

LORD BREVAN

THE ANCIENTS

Cosima was a foe not to be underestimated. I needed to keep her distracted long enough to give Amelia time to move her mother out of the way. The sheer fact her mother was still alive was nothing short of a miracle. How she managed to survive all this time was simply amazing. Although, with my knowledge of her daughter, it should not have surprised me in the slightest.

The Queen matched me move for move. I needed to keep my focus upon my opponent, but perhaps, I should have diverted my attention towards my mate. Suddenly, I heard "NOW," and Sloane, along with Amelia, both launched forward. Each one of them grabbed an ancient crystal and stepped back from the altar.

Cosima froze and watched in horror as Sloane and Amelia stood under the moonlight of the super moon. Their eyes glazed over, and the crystals began to glow. The power that was leaking out from the crystals quickly enveloped the pair of them. I seized at the opportunity of Cosima's distraction to knock her backwards and into the wall. I ran as fast as I could to my mate, but an invisible power would not allow me to fully reach her. "AMELIA," I yelled out to her, but she did not respond.

When their eyes came back into focus, they were not my mate's

233

eyes. Both Sloane and Amelia's eyes were black as pitch, and as they began to speak, they spoke with voices that were not their own. It was like multiple beings were communicating through them.

In unison, they proclaimed, "We are the past, present, and future. We are the dark; we are the light. Our power is eternal and ever-present. How dare you come here and defile our sanctuary!" They both glared towards Cosima and me.

I did the only thing I could think of. I slid down to one knee. "I pledge myself in all humility towards your divinity. My humble existence is yours. My sword is your weapon; my life is at your will. I pledge to you with my blood. My word is my bond." I sliced my palm with my blade and stayed on one knee as my blood dripped to the floor of the temple.

Cosima rose from the floor and slowly moved before Sloane and Amelia. I dared not glance upwards as she spoke. "You do not need to worry about me. I am your friend. Come with me, and we shall return order to your land. You can trust me."

Sloane erupted, "How dare you try to enchant us! You disrespect the power that stands before you. You are an unworthy creature."

I turned my head and watched as Cosima slithered backwards, just before the fire that exploded from Sloane completely encompassed the Queen and obliterated her into ash. The situation went from bad to worse and could still become catastrophic.

Sloane and Amelia spoke in tandem again, "You have pledged yourself to us in earnest. Therefore, you shall be spared. However, the battle such as the one waging itself, just on the other side of our sanctuary, is in clear violation of our mercy. Come, let us eradicate the problem." In a whirling vortex of magic, the three of us were scooped up and flown out of the temple.

When we landed, I scanned around to survey the scene before me. Sloane, Amelia, and I were deposited smack dab in the middle of a battlefield. In another wave of magic, everyone was blown apart from one another. The ancient powers who possessed Sloane and Amelia roared in anger.

"IS THIS IS HOW YOU THANK US FOR OUR MERCY? YOU HAVE BEEN WARNED!"

My instincts screamed at me. I stood and turned in the direction of my home. I pushed out my Alpha power, "EVERYONE LOWER YOUR WEAPONS AND DROP TO YOUR KNEES, NOW!" Every wolf in Pack Lingwir stopped fighting with my single command, dropped their weapons, and knelt down. I spun around and stared into my mother's face, who pushed herself away from my father. Her face was a mask of horror.

"Lycandra, you would be wise to heed my words," I warned in vain.

"Get up, you fools, and destroy them!" she ordered.

The Alfar guards and her wolves stalked towards us. When they realized not one of us was going to move, they charged, which was their mistake. Sloane and Amelia, with a snap of their fingers, froze them in place. As the two of them began to step towards the Alfar side, General Pax landed in front of Amelia.

"I do not know who you are, but you are not the owner of those vessels." Pax's observation stopped the destructive ancient powers dead in their tracks.

Sloane and Amelia peered at Pax with curiosity, every movement in sync with one another. "You are wrong," they informed him together.

"I am General Pax. Protector of the city of Tenebris."

Sloane and Amelia glanced at one another, then to Pax. "You are wrong. You are not how you should be. Give us your hand." Pax extended his hand towards Sloane and Amelia, who each took it in turn.

While this small distraction was happening, I motioned for our people to make their way back towards our side of the pass. The slight pause would not last for long, and the further back I could get my people, the better. Through the multitude of Tenebris fighters, a figure appeared. Mathias was attempting to make his way up to where I stood with our mate.

The ancient voices came from Amelia, "You made an error in judgement with your arrogance but have since learned from it. Your form, however, is still wrong. Your memories are still altered." She turned to face the Alfar and Lumen wolves. The next words she spoke were for all to hear. "Our magic is older than the stars." She placed her hand on Pax's shoulder before she continued. "Blessings turned into curses shall be undone. The past restored." Magic began to flow from her hand into Pax, and every single Gargoyle on the field glowed with the power from the ancients. "Wrongs shall be righted, and rewards shall be given to the faithful." Sloane and Amelia held the crystals up towards the sky. When the magic blasted out of them, the night was lit up with the colors of the rainbow. "The truth of this night has been revealed in the true heart of the one who stands before us." She pointed to Pax then turned to the Alfar and the Lumen wolves, including my mother. "You dare attempt to steal what is not yours. Your love of power is your downfall." Without another word, Sloane and Amelia turned them to stone.

Mathias took a step forward and reached out for Amelia, "Please, Amelia, stop."

Amelia grabbed his hand in what looked to be a vice grip. "How dare you touch us!"

"Amelia, I know you are in there. Please stop. It is over," Mathias begged through gritted teeth, and she shook her head.

I passionately gazed at her and drew up all the love I held for my wondrous mate. In one short stride, I stood directly in front of her. I lifted my hand to her shoulder. "My little wolf, I trust you. Come back to us." Amelia released Mathias and took hold of my hand. No longer did I wonder if it was a vice grip because I felt the power in it. I stood frozen without flinching. I kept pushing the love I felt for my amazing woman through our bond. She shook her head again, and Aisling soon managed to make her way up to where we were.

"Sloane, honey, can you hear me? Please come back," Aisling pleaded with tears in her eyes.

Slowly, recognition came over Amelia's face. "You love this vessel?" It was still the ancient who spoke.

"With everything that I am. She carries within her our future," I confirmed.

The ancient released my hand and lowered hers to her womb. When she peered back up at me, she spoke, "Perhaps, there is still hope for all of you yet."

In a flash of brilliance and power, we were all knocked off our feet. Gradually, my eyesight focused on Sloane and Amelia, who were still standing. They were soberly eying one another. "Ami, no one should possess such a power ever again," Sloane firmly noted.

"Sloane, you'll get no argument from me," Amelia countered.

The two of them tossed the crystals into the air, and at their peak, they both blasted the crystals into dust. The force from the explosion shoved them to the ground, and I watched as Amelia's head landed on a rock. It had rendered her unconscious.

A tall man with dark hair, pale blue eyes, broad shoulders, and white iridescent wings landed next to Amelia before I could get my ass up off the ground. He felt familiar, but I had never seen the likes of him before. Something was telling me to trust him, but he was also standing next to my unconscious mate. I growled, then rolled to a crouched position instead of rising, and was ready to shift in a flash.

"Calm yourself, M'lord. It is I, Pax, or more correctly, Paxanos." When he addressed me, it was not with the same gravelly tone I knew. It was soothing and calm. "The magic of the ancients restored me along with my men who were here with us all. I am guessing it affected all of the Gargoyles." He knelt down and gently touched Amelia. "She will wake in a moment. There is no permanent damage."

"Pax, old friend, what are you?"

"Lord Brevan, it is a long story, one I plan to fully tell you, but for now, all you need to know is the Gargoyles are no more. We now are what we were always meant to be." Pax stood tall. "We are members of the Two Hundred. Guardians of the island and protectors of the people. We are not the first of our kind, and we will not be the last." He gave me a quick nod and flew up into the sky.

Amelia began to rouse, Mathias and I quickly moved to her side. Aisling was immediately at Sloane's side in the next moment. "My little wolf, are you alright?"

"Please, the two of you, do me one favor?" she muttered as she rubbed at her head.

"What is it, my love?" Mathias inquired.

"Never ever let me explode a magical crystal again."

"My little wolf, you have a deal." I pulled her up off the ground and into my arms. She held on tight for a moment, not saying a word.

"Brevan, I love you!"

"I love you too," I answered her in return before handing her over to her other mate.

"My Amelia, you were really scary," Mathias relayed to her, and she laughed.

"Just remember my wrath when you try to steal my cake."

I could not help but laugh at their banter. It began to hit me. Not only did we all manage to survive, but I saw my future as one which was bright and filled with life, love, and happiness. We were a family and a strong one. All thanks to a stranger named Amelia Jane Gray, who landed in my life and turned my world upside down.

EPILOGUE

Amelia (Ami) Jane Gray
Four Years Later

$\mathcal{L}$ ife on the island was forever altered, to say the least. It turned out our interactions with the ancient powers not only ended the fighting between the north and the south, but it served as a reminder to never mess with forces you don't understand. Sleeping Mountain Pass was renamed *Living Statue Pass* due to the state of the wolves and Alfar, who remained frozen in stone.

Sloane and I received something akin to a magical download from our time being melded with the ancients. He and I both knew and understood spells and magic neither of us knew prior. We agreed we would put together our own spell-book with 'warning labels' attached to each spell between the two of us. Some of the things we knew shouldn't be used unless under extreme duress.

The change to the Gargoyles was one of the most extreme changes to the island. They were physically and mentally altered. Physically their stony and dark skin was replaced by golden-tanned skin and

239

beautiful soft feathery wings. Pax stopped by many times and, during one occasion, explained all of the Gargoyle's memories were restored as well as being gifted with knowledge none of them held previously. Some of what he told me, in particular, was unbelievable, even to my ears. He wound up with his own predictions of a time when the outside world would come to know the island's residents. He also knew the island would serve as a sort of sanctuary in a time when it was much needed.

Queen Lyra and her people were no longer strictly held to the ocean that surrounded the island. Their city and the people in it were also altered. Their entire civilization was raised from the sea's depths and would always be a gleaming white jewel off the coast of Tenebris. Queen Lyra's people could now walk on land, or should they be in the water, swim as they used to. The entire thing reminded me of the legends of the Lost City of Atlantis, although, Lyra confirmed this was not the case for her people.

To my pleasant surprise, Paxanos and Lyra were making their relationship known to others. While they both were at the packhouse one day, I summoned up the courage to ask them when it all began for them. Pax told me one day soon, when they both had more time, he would sit down and tell me about how the pair of them met. With their relationship finally out in the open, the members of the Two Hundred moved their home to Queen Lyra's island. It was nothing for them to fly into Tenebris as they served as guardians of the island. It only made sense for them to live there, especially with their upcoming marriage.

Edon began courting Prudence after a year. He informed everyone, "She needed the proper amount of time to grieve the loss of her husband." To my surprise, Marta commented on how alike Prudence and Lylaine were. Not just in looks but also in demeanor. They were set to become bonded mates within the next month after a very extended courtship.

Prudence was keen to start a school for the children on the island. When she approached the council with the idea, she received backing from every council member. Jackie was proud of how her mother adapted to island life. She finally relented about her mother and Edon when she saw how happy Edon made her mom. It wasn't easy for Jackie to jump into the role of coven leader, but with Declan's help, they managed to make the transition.

Jackie and Declan agreed they would share the coven leadership responsibilities. Mostly because Jackie was a council member and felt as though she had her hands full with those duties. The two of them were making the gossip rounds with their unique leadership style, but I never heard one complaint. They were turning out to be as loved as Nova.

The loss of Nova was felt by everyone. The city of Tenebris was shut down in mourning for a full month. Even though she lost her position on the council, Nova was still a well-loved leader amongst the people. Her funeral pyre was held in the city center and could be seen for miles.

My days in the training room were numerous. The Shadow Legion grew from the sixteen original members to thirty. With the increased numbers, I needed to promote from within, which meant picking a few leaders amongst the women. My top three choices were Aisling, Sadine, and Helaine. All three women held natural leadership qualities that I admired, along with the rest of the legion ladies. When I wasn't training or dealing with council matters, I spent my time writing. It was my goal to leave a legacy of the island events and history that weren't completely mind-numbing. Hopefully, one day they would provide an interesting tale for our heirs.

Mom and Gran were reunited in what I could only call a tear-filled reunion. Neemah was so grateful for the return of Melisandre. It turned out the women of our family were made of iron. While Alexander and Marissa were always the parents who raised me, getting to know Melisandre was a blessing I felt I never really deserved. Sloane and I made it a priority to get together with the two of them for supper at least once a week for 'family dinner.' Sometimes our mates would join us, and usually, I wound up bringing the triplets with me. Of course, mass confusion happened when Sloane and I didn't compare notes, and he would bring his two babies, while I brought my three. Family dinner always turned into pandemonium with five children and all of the adults. We always wound up laughing at the ridiculousness which ensued.

The triplets were born early. Five months after the Sleeping Mountain Pass events, we were graced with Risa, Alex, and Newt, all three of whom kept us on our toes. An hour after they were born, they shifted into wolves, which made it interesting trying to round them up as they wiggled through the apartment on their bellies. Although, I admit they were cute little balls of fluff as wolves. Brevan was able to use his Alpha abilities to get them to shift back. Little Risa was the smallest of the three, and she was also the one with the most enormous attitude. My guys would always tease me because she was just like a little mini-me. Thank goodness for Marta. The choice to make her our nanny was the best idea ever. She was so attentive to the babies. I couldn't ask for a better person ever.

However, it was not the only thing that happened the night of their births. Alex and Newt exhibited signs of being healers when what I called the bellybutton bump fell off wholly healed. It wasn't the only shocker we wound up with. Little Risa and her spunky attitude burst into blue flames when she wasn't fed immediately. I rolled my eyes and shrugged my shoulders when Mathias handed our daughter over to me for her feeding. Somehow, I guessed she got her daddy Brevan's looks. She was born with a full head of the same color hair as Brevan and black wolf hair. Silently, I wondered which of the two of them would wind up being the Alpha. I just simply enjoyed the time with them while they were still small.

Emmer, Aoife, the twins, and Laura were some of our favorite extended family. Laura decided she wanted to be the big sister to all the babies, stating in her way, aka hands on hips and a deadly serious expression on her face, "They need me to show them what to do." After Sloane's two were born, she huffed out, "Now, I really have too much to do." Her child-like seriousness caused me to internally laugh at her plight.

Milton and Laudy moved into the city of Tenebris. Their new business, a simple sidewalk café, took off and became a staple for us to visit on shopping trips into the market. Even though they'd adapted to life on the island, Laudy would occasionally come up with a 'daily special' that would remind us all of our lives before our arrival on the island. Her home cooking and unique flare brought in the local customers which they were more than happy to feed and get to know. Drew was so ecstatic when they opened their business, he used them to cater his latest fashion show. It ended up being a huge success.

Four years had gone by, and I decided to write this extensive history. I can confirm my babies were the one thing I knew without a doubt I'd done right. Alex and Newt wound up extremely protective over their sister, even if they teased her more often than not. Risa completely wrapped both of her fathers right around her little finger. Brevan and Mathias turned out to be fantastic with all three of them. Newt absolutely was the spitting image of Mathias, while Alex and Risa's looks were all Brevan except for his eyes and her nose. I made the decision to hold off on my latest plans until the kids were old enough to appreciate it. This winter solstice would be the first time we'd be celebrating Christmas on the Island. I explained the concept to Brevan, Mathias, Melisandre, Edon, Neemah, and Marta, who all seemed to be on board with it.

I supposed what I really wanted to impress upon anyone who reads our story, was they needed to be aware it was a recorded history. So, no one would ever forget past events, and also would always remember a family was at its strongest when they love and trust one another.

These are my historical memories, along with inserts from those involved. Amelia Jane Gray, Dragon Mystic and Leader of the Shadow Legion.

THE END

Acknowledgement:

This series wouldn't have been possible without two very special ladies. Thank you, Karen and Tracey, for all of your help and advice throughout this endeavor. You crazy girls kept me sane! Love you both.

Book License Notes:

You may not use, reproduce or transmit in any manner, any part of this book without written permission, except in the case of brief quotations used in critical articles and reviews, or in accordance with federal Fair Use laws. All rights are reserved.

This book is licensed for your personal enjoyment only; it may not be resold or given away to other people. If you would like to share this book with another person, please purchase an additional copy for each recipient. If you're reading this book and did not purchase it, or it was not purchased for your use only, please return to your book retailer and purchase your own copy. Thank you for respecting the hard work of this author, editor and cover artist.

Disclaimer:

This is a work of fiction. Names, characters, places and incidents are products of the author's imagination, or the author has used them fictitiously.

www.ingramcontent.com/pod-product-compliance
Lightning Source LLC
Chambersburg PA
CBHW070744180626
46818CB00007B/2975